IN THE COUNTRY
OF THE GREAT KING

ALSO BY ARDYTHE ASHLEY

Practice to Deceive (as Bess Arden)
The Christ of the Butterflies

In the

COUNTRY

of the

GREAT KING

ARDYTHE ASHLEY

AVAILABLE PRESS

BALLANTINE BOOKS • NEW YORK

An Available Press Book
Published by Ballantine Books

Grateful acknowledgment is made to the following for permission to
reprint previously published material:

Harvard University Press: Two poems by Emily Dickinson from *The Poems
of Emily Dickinson,* edited by Thomas H. Johnson, The Belknap Press of
Harvard University Press, Cambridge, Mass. Copyright © 1951, 1955,
1979, 1983 by the President and Fellows of Harvard College. Reprinted
by permission of the publishers and the Trustees of Amherst College.

Macmillan Publishing Company: Excerpts from "Her Anxiety" and "To the
Rose Upon the Rood of Time" from *The Poems of W. B. Yeats: A New
Edition,* edited by Richard J. Finneran. Copyright © 1933 by Macmillan
Publishing Company. Renewed 1961 by Bertha Georgie Yeats.
Reprinted by permission of Macmillan Publishing Company.

Viking Penguin: "Résumé" from *The Portable Dorothy Parker,* by Dorothy
Parker, introduction by Brendan Gill. Copyright © 1926, 1928,
renewed 1954, © 1956 by Dorothy Parker. Reprinted by permission of
Viking Penguin, a division of Penguin Books USA Inc.

Library of Congress Catalog Card Number: 92-90407

ISBN: 345-37993-4

Cover design by Ruth Ross
Cover art: "Angel of the Annunciation" by Guercino
from the collection of the Windsor Castle Royal Library.
© 1992 Her Majesty Queen Elizabeth II.
Text design by Debbie Glasserman

Manufactured in the United States of America
First Edition: April 1993
10 9 8 7 6 5 4 3 2 1

To my friend, Michael Bergmann
. . . who is not in it.

Part One

The

DAWN WALKERS

*Let what you love be what you do. There are one
hundred ways to kneel and kiss the earth.*

—RUMI

There isn't enough sex in it, thought Arista Bellefleurs, slapping the manuscript down onto the polished expanse of her cherrywood writing table in dismay. It was a fine table. It had been hand-joined, and rather too intricately carved about the legs, in Ohio, before the turn of the century, by her great-grandfather, Shadrach Brainard. Now it stood as the high altar in her comfortable, slightly worn, otherwise modern Manhattan apartment. Arista rested her cheek on the slick wooden surface next to the unfinished novel and wondered what she would do with the rest of her life now that she couldn't write anymore.

Arista descended from long-lived people. Most of her forebears, including Great-Grandfather Shadrach, had survived into their nineties. Arista was forty-five. She sighed. The idea of living another forty-five years was exhausting; imagining, as she was, all the suffering she would necessarily witness and experience, some of which she would doubtless inflict herself, inadvertently, of course. She thought of herself as an essentially kind, but flawed person. She had battled in life, and where the scars had formed, she was insensitive. Now she was facing the accelerating decline into old age. It wouldn't be graceful, she thought.

The subject that had most interested Arista throughout her life was sex, and there would be less and less eroticism, she knew, as the years advanced. She had hoped, at the very least, to continue writing about it. But she had been struggling now for over a year, unable to whip her current novel into any kind of passion. Worse, it was threatening to become a novel about a novelist. She loathed novels about novelists, which she judged, harshly, to be failures of sublimation.

She sat up and leafed through the pages helplessly. The book hadn't started out autobiographically. It had begun with a modern American Indian woman, a painter. Arista had intended to send out a sparse, intense novel about the souls of artists in a soulless culture: writers to be sure, but painters and poets and dancers and actors, and even a mime, like Katelyn had been in her youth—all the delirious, dysfunctional people who inhabited Arista's world. But the book had boomeranged back into her lap, where it now lay, limp, formless, refusing to pull itself into a seductive shape.

To her relief the doorbell rang. She admitted her friend Katelyn without ceremony. As prearranged, she handed the manuscript to Katelyn, who took it with undisguised pleasure.

"You've never let me read a work-in-progress before."

"I'm desperate."

"Thanks for asking me."

"Katelyn, I've lost it."

"Next thing you'll say is, 'Maybe I never had it.' "

"Christ."

"Didn't you say it was about religion?"

"No. About people, searching. Some people find religion."

"Umm."

"Umm, what?"

"Is this about that minister you had a crush on?"

"I don't know what it's about."

"Then, as I promised, I will read it and let you know."

"Thanks. I'll make you some tea."

"Arista, are you in it?"

"What choice have I got?"

Katelyn Wells smiled contentedly. She sank down comfortably into her accustomed place on the sofa, stretching out her long, still-graceful legs, and prepared to read. She liked Arista's novels. She often found bits and pieces of herself strewn among the characters. This time, Arista had warned her, she had been swallowed down and coughed up whole. She squinted at the title page, sighed, rummaged through her handbag, and put on her recently acquired, but often resisted, reading glasses. At least Serena had said she looked handsome in them. Arista hadn't remarked.

Arista Bellefleurs, having given her characters over to her friend for the day, began to putter uselessly about in the tiny kitchen. She had been hopeless as a housewife. She put on the kettle and then decided to chop some garlic for a spaghetti sauce, one of the few kitchen tasks she enjoyed. The smell of garlic on her hands reminded her of sex in Italy.

• • •

At the same time, in another world, Maggie Silvernails took hold of her hip-length hair with her strong left hand; with her right she gripped the heavy brush and began to brush rhythmically down, down, down. After three hundred strokes she began to twine and turn the thick, black strands up, up, up, into a coiling nest of braids, which she secured with a dozen glittering hairpins. She finished the arrangement with a flourish, stabbing the great twist in the back with two long, silver nails. Maggie was a beautiful woman, but there was neither a man nor a mirror for miles to tell her so.

She pulled on a pair of battered jeans and buttoned up a soft flannel shirt against the chill morning air. Clasping a cup of coffee, black and strong as grief, she stepped out onto the sloping front porch to assess the colors of the desert dawn—apple pink peeling into rose with a vein of blue purple at the horizon. There was a dusting of silver frost over the earth. Pleased, finding a place within herself corresponding to the morning's pallet, she swallowed down the remaining coffee, then leaving the cabin door ajar in case Fatpaws returned home, she grabbed her paints and water bottle from the back of the pickup truck and headed toward the sunrise. She would eat wild today, if she remembered to eat at all.

The desert surrounding her cabin was different in a hundred minute ways from the tribal lands half a state away to the west, though the desolation would look the same to white men's eyes. Maggie knew the differences—in sand and dirt, in the color of lizards' eyes, and in the length of cactus spines—the myriad differences that estranged her from this place. Yet she felt no desire to return to a life on the Zuni reservation, where, though she saw no one for weeks on end, everyone knew her business. Here, in this wilderness, there was only Maggie to study Maggie.

She had returned to her Zuni homeland many years before, leaving New York City abruptly and without a trace; but she had known that Luke would eventually come to the reservation to search her out, so she had disappeared again, disappeared deeper, this time into the desert, leaving deliberate traces that would read to any Indian that Maggie Silvernails wasn't dead, but wished to appear so to the white man's world. Had Luke been fooled? He was no Indian, but he was also no fool. Luke found it impossible to be unaware of the fact that his followers thought of him as a living saint. He was no saint, God knew. So did Luke.

He opened one eye to test the day. Sunlight had spilled onto the rumpled bed through the open window. He wallowed in its warmth for a while, aware that his old bones would have to wait out the crisp April day to find such comfort again.

A raucous blue jay commanded the attention of both his eyes as it lit upon the bird feeder outside his window, found exactly the kind of seed it most preferred, and let out an exuberant cry of delight. Tchaikovsky, the rooster in the barnyard, was periodically calling out the familiar notes of the 1812 Overture—Ta Ta Ta Ta Ta Ta Ta Ta Tum Tum—the last note in each repetition ending with a sour squawk. Sparrows, robins, and chickadees wove arias in the dawn.

"Hoot," hooted Luke, in what he considered to be a pretty good imitation of a large snowy owl. It gave the local birds a moment's pause—and one small hoot made getting up a little easier. He stretched luxuriously and sat up awkwardly, succeeding in pulling back the quilt and swinging his legs over the edge of the bed. His feet sank down into the thick carpet. It was not easy being old, he mused, but it was interesting. Except for some mild arthritis and a few extra pounds he was, at seventy, in relatively good health and reasonable masculine shape. But his energies gathered slowly in the mornings now.

It was Sunday. One of his gatherings was scheduled for

today. A dozen tense and troubled people would arrive in the late morning and form an anxious group at his feet. He was mildly embarrassed by the arrangement. But his stiffening back required a chair. The people who came inevitably declined the chairs and sat on the floor. People needed to look up. One by one, as the day progressed into evening, these shy communicants would move forward from their places in the circle and talk of their troubles. And then, sometime late tonight, relaxed and relieved, wheeling in change, and struggling with new hope, they would disperse, wondering how Luke Sevensons had touched the very place within their souls that needed to be touched, and had to be turned. It was his one gift. He could help people.

Except for Maggie Silvernails. "I am taking a day off from our love affair," Maggie had announced. But she didn't come back on the next day, or any day. He had waited many years. So had Jamie Callahan. Was she dead? Eventually Luke had ridden the long, slow train west to the reservation. There, Deerfinder had told him with steady eyes and inflectionless voice that she had wandered into the desert and gotten lost and died. Luke didn't believe that old coyote. In Luke's experience Maggie Silvernails never got lost. But now, after such an eternity of emptiness, he sometimes doubted his doubt. Perhaps she had, after all, come to dust, joined her breath with the wind and broken her body into motes. Perhaps there were sparkling particles of Maggie Silvernails dancing before him in this morning's stream of sunlight. That would be just like her, he decided, beckoning, teasing. Get up old man, she would say, and join this day. Ta Ta Ta Ta Ta Ta Ta Ta Tum Tum Squawk.

Winter and summer Luke slept in the nude. He liked the feel of the smooth sheets around him and the freedom to move, like in a good skinny-dip, without the constraint of human clothing. Mariah the cat usually slept with him, warm and sleek against his leg, but she had long since awakened and jumped out the window in search of dewy adventures.

Alone in the chill air, Luke reached for his sweatsuit and running shoes, and a moment later he was out on his morning walk. He barked sharply, bringing Raindrop and her puppies out of the barn in a joyful tumble. He greeted each dog with pats and nuzzles: Raindrop, Puddles, Splash, and Drip. Then he set out with the romping dogs to explore their farm.

He missed his young friend Buff Carrington. The dogs missed Greta Garbo. They had all gotten on well together, dogs and men, during the late-winter months, in spite of the thick snow that had surrounded them and the thick terror that Buff had brought congealed inside himself. Where was the terror now? Melted, spilled, evaporated? Dancing in the sunlight with Maggie Silvernails? Luke didn't know. A transformation had occurred, so Buff had announced, and then he had returned to New York with a calm heart, Greta Garbo leading the way. Luke would see them both, man and dog, on his next visit east. Or perhaps he wouldn't.

A blue jay darted through a stand of scrawny pines demanding his attention. Softly Luke intoned a singsong chant that he had learned from Maggie:

> "Come, you wing-eds
> Come, you wing-eds
> Tell me what I need to know
> Show me where I need to go
> Come, flying things . . ."

The jay cocked his head and, beady-eyed, considered the singing man; then, melting its sky-blue wings into the sky-blue sky, it flew a short distance south to the apple orchard, where Luke was glad to follow. The plump green buds were bursting with blossoms, and tips of tiny tender leaves had begun to appear. When he was deep in the grove and surrounded in scent, Luke stood motionless, letting the dogs and the breeze be his progress and the tree be his silence. He was green and white and coming once again into new life. He was surging through the grasses and the first fallen blossoms yelping with youth. He was flowing with invisible strength. His roots went deep. He held the blue jay on his budding branch. He snuffled at his own trunk and barked at his own bark. He absorbed sunlight.

"Come, flying things. . . ."

As the chant continued, his thoughts flew forward—to the day ahead, to the work, to the people who would come to work with him: local people, Ohio people, housewives, salesmen, teachers. Small, kind, desperate—those whom history would not record. Not like the tough, wily ones who had found him in New York City, the poets and the painters, the dreamers and the schemers who congregated in America's great *shakra*.

He would return to New York later this month, gather them about, and struggle with their metropolitan demons. Would he hole up alone at the Algonquin Hotel, communing with literary ghosts, or would he stay with Jamie Callahan, that old roan stallion, and tie one on? Arista Bellefleurs had offered Luke the use of her apartment, but he was nervous about staying in her home.

Arista reminded him of Maggie Silvernails. There was a deep knowing in Arista that she did not yet know. Her unborn wisdom pushed at her consciousness, forced her to constant questioning, sent her searching. It lodged behind her intelligent eyes—those two heavy brown stones that held the rest of her fragile body on the earth—waiting for its time.

Arista Bellefleurs stirred up wonderful ancient feelings in Luke, desires that, once indulged, might become painful longing, and Luke had longed long enough. He was unsure if her invitation had included any such indulgences. He was too old to be thought of as a sexual being by most people. But perhaps Arista had seen through the wrinkled ruse of age to the youthful man who flared within.

She was a woman yet asleep to herself, but perceptive of others. She had taken hard bites out of life and life had bitten her back. She lacked spirituality, considered herself a realist, an atheist with a propensity for the dramatic and a love of the ironic, but sitting quietly in the midst of the Old Gray Presbyterian congregation, she gave every appearance of a good Christian woman attentive to the reading of the Scripture. In truth, she was ruthlessly sizing up herself as she sized up the service.

> "This is my commandment, that ye love one another, as I have loved you. Greater love hath no man than this, that a man lay down his life for his friends."

Good, she thought, approving of the minister's decision to read from the King James Version. The seventeenth century had been a magnificent era for the English language. The text itself she found distressing, as usual, disconcerting. Did she have a friend for whom she would lay down her life, or one that would lay down a life for her? She thought not. Certainly not Clayton Grant! Not failing

Jerry Phails. Not Buff Carrington or Quentin Cox, though she loved them dearly. Katelyn Wells, her oldest friend in New York, was precious to her. But would she die for Katelyn? Not on her life!

It was Katelyn's fault that she was in this alien enclave. Arista shivered, chilled and damp from the short walk through quiet Greenwich Village on this drizzly April morning. The neighborhood had seemed like an abandoned stage set, left over as it was from the glittering gods of Saturday night. Or maybe it was Luke's fault that she was here. Luke Sevensons had set her searching for something. Unknown. She knew, of course, that it was her own damned fault. She had, long ago, learned to hold herself accountable for life. It was an annoying truth. It was as if her relentless, bedeviling curiosity returned her each Sunday, like a renewed library book, to this shadowy church full of well-scrubbed Protestant people, and their ancient ghosts, so long resisted.

She had been coming to the Sunday services, with increasing frequency, since last December, when, at her friend Katelyn's prompting, they had attended a Christmas Eve service—candles, carols—an alternative to the secular massacres taking place in department stores all across the city.

The suggestion had seemed harmless enough at the time. Arista had not attended church in over twenty years; oh, perhaps for a wedding or a funeral here and there, but not for real. The Christmas season was a lonely time for her. Most of her friends for whom she would not die were visiting their families. Arista had no family. Even Clayton had been out of town on a ski trip; dear deficient Clayton, who was almost handsome and moderately talented and very self-involved and very, very young. These days Arista purposely pursued romances that were, unbeknownst to her lovers, destined to brevity, thereby avoiding unpleasant shocks.

She and Katelyn had chosen a pew high in the gallery, where, during the organ prelude, they had alternated between companionable silence and whispered conversation. Katelyn, who had for so long been drawn up into herself, seemed miraculously happy and sociable that evening, and her cheerfulness had, in turn, warmed Arista, who had lately been feeling as cold and brittle as the December night.

She hoped that Katelyn was finally returning to life after the deadliness of her nervous breakdown, if it was a breakdown. In Arista's judgment it was Katelyn's heart, not her nerves, that had broken. And her mind was more than a little warped. She had been crying for the last five years. Any reminder of Nelson Little would set her off. And the city they had roamed together was land-mined with his memory. Buildings they had once entered together became shrines of remorse that had to be avoided at the cost of long, inconvenient detours. An accidentally overheard melody that had once accompanied their lovemaking could send her to bed for days. Once, choking with sobs over a bowl of fettuccine, she explained that Nelson had once enjoyed that particular sauce. Perhaps, Arista had dared to think, on this cold Christmas Eve half a decade away, the evil spell cast by Nelson Little on his way out the door was finally over. Then, in the midst of the singing, Katelyn had burst into tears.

"What is it, Katelyn?" she whispered. They *couldn't* have sung Christmas carols together, thought Arista. Nelson Little was a depressed and unharmonious Jew.

Katelyn tried to speak, but heaved and gasped instead. What was it? Arista wondered. Then she realized. They were singing "Oh *Little* Town of Bethlehem."

"Oh, for Christ's sake."

The Christmas service had progressed, Katelyn now sniffing and blowing in her accustomed way. Arista, after consoling her friend as best she could, found herself watching the religious rites somewhat like a traveler in a primitive, foreign country—fascinated but not awed, sometimes slightly amused as the preacher went on about Christ moving among us, or through us, or in us. Then to her surprise he said something that moved her. Something she would be embarrassed to repeat, and so she had, to this day, repressed it. Damn, she had said to herself as she responded to the sermon, as the tears welled up in her eyes. Not this, not now. But there had been a whisper.

The following Sunday, she was drawn back to the church—almost, it seemed, against her own will. The handsome minister spoke of Christ's quiet, mysterious shepherding of lost souls. A whisper was one thing, but the possibility that she was being herded, like some fat sheep, into faith horrified Arista. Sheep were stupid. She was not a herd animal. She didn't believe in souls. She was not yet ready to think of herself as lost. She did not wish to be found. She did not wish to be hooked, like a failing vaudeville comedienne, and dragged from the stage of secular life at the whim of a long-dead, gravely misunderstood rabbi. She had, after all, Clayton. Clayton, insubstantial as he was, represented her claim to a place in the rational, solid, sensual world. The *real* world.

Nevertheless the Reverend Christian Davies, with his shock of snow-white hair and his shocking faith in the goodness of God, was making a formidable claim on her attention. From childhood, she had been drawn to such men—to professors or activists or politicians—men who dared to stand up before other men and declare their beliefs. Men she could look up to. There were fewer and fewer such men as she got older and taller. But a preacher? A magician? Never! Well, not since her grandfather, who was, no doubt, the model on which all her other men were made. Grandpa Brainard, the Reverend Elam Brainard, had saved her from her father, the only saving she had ever wanted, or ever needed.

On the Sunday after Christmas she was back. She had taken Communion on New Year's Eve because she had wanted to see the preacher up close—wanted to see the lines around his eyes, hear his breathing—wished for some form of communion with Christian Davies. She had taken the soggy wafer, which was all that was offered. She had begun to want to know what this strange man would say about life and how he would say it.

Once, in her bathtub, she imagined that she was a believer, that she had bought the whole kit and caboodle: the angel, the virgin, the manger, three wise men, God walking the earth as a man—the whole nine yards—even resurrection; and though it was impossible for her to believe, she noticed a subtle change in her feelings as she entered into the fantasy of faith. She felt calmer, open, responsive, warmer. Her characteristic tenseness—a guardedness, a fear that her mind would be torn away from her—had, during the moments of her daydream, lessened. From time to time over the next few months she had tried the fabrication on, like a hat. Once she even looked into the mirror as she did so. Yes, her features softened, not in stupidity, but in relief. The imagination of faith gentled her. Belief was out of the question, of course. Reason simply had to prevail, even if, *especially* if, it was tougher.

The sermon had begun. Reverend Davies was telling his congregation about his childhood; about bluebells and little girls in Ireland. Arista arched an eyebrow. There were no bluebells in the fields of her youth. She remembered goldenrods and golden buttercups, black-eyed Susans with yellow-gold petals, daisies with yellow-gold centers and white petals to be torn off, one by one. He loves me, he loves me not. And wasn't there something about holding buttercups under your chin? She was called Abigail then.

She and Ted Hackett had made love for the first time among the wildflowers. She had liked it. Ted had been allergic to all the pollen and had sneezed repeatedly and his eyes had puffed up, so after that first fondling in the fields they had made love in the backseat of Ted's parents' car, like all the other teenagers in all the other backseats of all the other cars belonging to all the other parents. Arista had missed the feel of the earth at her back, the beating of birds' wings above them, and the sun-saturated air. She had been carefully conditioned by years of parsonage life to believe that sex was sinful, and she had tried and tried to feel guilty about it. But she couldn't. Sex, she discovered, was too *glorious* to be sin. In Ted's arms she began to resent religion with all its rules and restraints. She soon detested her grandfather's sermons, which had, until the loss of her virginity, intrigued her.

Ted had been more tentative about sex than she, a characteristic she would discover in many men over the years to come. Yet those first caresses had, in some gentle way, been more exciting than all the lovemaking that had followed. She could not forget him. He could not forget her. Could any man? Ted looked out across the lake where he had first made love to Abigail, who was now Arista, in the hot, dry, flower-filled fields that had long since been plowed up and flooded over and now rippled with sky-blue water.

Why was he thinking of her at all? It must be twenty years since she had left him and Boar's Wood, Ohio, for

New York City and yet she had appeared in the dawn as if she, and not a dream, had entered his bed.

"You'll be back in a month," he had said to her years ago, helping her up onto the train. She had smiled a pensive smile from the clouded train window, waved once, and was gone. She had written to him for a while, and in spite of her artful, vivid descriptions of galleries and coffee-houses and walk-up apartments, he couldn't imagine where in the world she was. He could only think of her here, in her hometown, in the high school they had attended together, in the strange parsonage where she had lived with all the old Bible thumpers, and in the fields. He remembered her most vividly in the fields. Later, in the dark backseats of automobiles, she had seemed hidden from him, though she was always quick to disrobe. Ted Hackett had not replied to her letters. He realized now how monstrously angry he had been with her for the abandonment. At the time he had thought his refusal to write was just a shrewd move; that she would come to miss him and would return to him. But she hadn't and she didn't. He had waited. Then he didn't. He had married Ivy Sue and been unusually happy—usually.

Ted returned to his gardening, but soon found himself staring again at the lake, trying to see back through time and down through depths to where he and Abigail-Arista had been young and tender lovers. The water was almost still, reflecting the sky, revealing nothing.

"How's it going?" shouted Ivy Sue from the deck.

"How about a weeping cherry right here?"

"Good idea."

The earth waited. Ted dug deeper. What, he wondered, had possessed Abigail to change her name? He liked Abigail. He liked calling her Abigail when everyone else had called her Abby. And how was it that his wife, even now, knew so much about the woman who had once been her high-school rival?

"I wonder what happened to Abigail Brainard," he had mused over their leisurely Sunday breakfast.

"She doesn't exist anymore," Ivy Sue had replied.

"What do you mean? She's not dead, is she?"

"Sort of. She changed her name to Arista Bellefleurs."

"Pretty."

"Pretty pretentious."

"I wonder why she changed it."

"She's a writer now."

"She always was, Ivy Sue."

"Well, that's what she calls herself now. And every year she either gets married or divorced or takes another lover."

"And how is it that you know these interesting tidbits?"

"Grapevine."

"Gossip."

"Are you looking for an argument, Ted?"

"No. But changing your name isn't the same as committing suicide."

After breakfast Ted Hackett lingered in the breakfast nook, watching as his wife took down the family portraits one at a time. They were all lovingly preserved in matching brass frames with nonglare glass. She sprayed Lemon Pledge on the paneling and polished the wall carefully; then she sprayed Windex on each of the pictures and polished the glass; then she rehung the pictures. There were all the Hacketts, hanging before him: young Ivy Sues and Teds, smiling through college graduation and courtship and marriage. There was Seth as a happy infant, and Holly, also an infant though less happy; the two kids, older, posed together, looking strained; the four of them together, arranged in a traditional family group looking out at life with nonglare eyes. He felt a moment's pride for his well-polished family. His exactly-as-he-had-been-raised-to-believe-a-family-*should*-be family.

Ted sighed. Except for Seth. Seth was exceptional. Music had bubbled up and spilled out of the boy since infancy. Seth had come into the world singing. A toy piano had given way to a real one by the time he was three. There had followed a succession of horns and stringed instruments, all of which hurried into melody at his touch. His final choice, a flute, now sent up strains of Mozart from the music room in the basement as it did during most hours of the weekend.

"You know, you didn't do a very good job with the soundproofing in the cellar, Ted," Ivy Sue complained. "Holly has taken to wearing earplugs when she's not wearing her Walkman. And I may invest in a pair myself."

"I'll get some more acoustical tiles and put them up next weekend," he promised, knowing he wouldn't, for in truth, he loved to hear the kid play. He wished he could communicate better with Seth, but the music made a distance between them. Ted couldn't read, let alone play, a note himself. He could not carry a tune and had difficulty remembering one. He had no knowledge of the grand and complex world that his son inhabited, no language in which to speak to him. Seth, for his part, had shown no interest in business or sports or hobbies or television, the natural items of discourse between father and son, so they seldom spoke to each other except out of necessity and then, awkwardly—about Seth's schoolwork, which presented no problems, or to arrange the day's mundane activities. He hoped that Seth wasn't gay.

Ivy Sue got out the vacuum cleaner. The Saint of Ceaseless Sanitation. Ted suddenly felt the need to move.

"Where are you going, Ted?"

"I thought I would dig out the dead evergreen in the backyard."

"Good idea."

It didn't seem like an idea to Ted. It felt like an escape, though he didn't know the name of his enclosure. He was glad now to be at work in the earth. The roots of the tree went deep and the ground was hard. He remembered that as an adolescent, hired about the neighborhood to do yard work, he had planned to be a gardener. Now he noticed he had worked up a sweat in spite of the chilly morning air, and his breath came heavy. He was out of shape. Too much success had weakened him. What would Arista think of him now? What would she say if she came home for a visit?

He rested on the shovel again and cataloged his kingdom. She would see a convenient, conventional ranch-style house, a white gravel driveway looping toward the double garage holding matching Mercedeses, acres of well-kept lawn, hedges, hillocks covered in domesticated flowers; a dock covered in AstroTurf jutted out from the edge of the lawn into the private lake; a small Sailfish was tethered to the dock; snowmobiles were parked in the town garage awaiting the white, cold pleasures of winter. These were not the accomplishments of a gardener. His successful real-estate business was elaborating into a regional chain. He should be content. She should be impressed.

"You live your life like a laundry list, Ted," Abigail-Arista had once said to him. He had been very angry. She had been very angry. He couldn't remember why.

He stepped hard onto the shovel. Damn it. This was no list. This was the best place to live in Boar's Wood, Ohio—and he was glad he had stayed. His life made a recognizable kind of sense. The television sets in the corners of all the major rooms reflected his life like mirrors.

"You wear the golden handcuffs like a whore wears a rhinestone bracelet," she had taunted him in a dream. A nightmare, for Arista could get angry, but she wasn't vicious. They were different sorts of people. That was all. He just wasn't like Arista. He didn't court fear. And she, underneath her quiet resolution, had been frightened to leave their hometown. She wouldn't admit it, but he had sensed it, and those city letters full of the picturesque and the optimistic, had beat, beneath the upbeat, with a pulse of fear.

Before she had left town, her great-uncle Meshach had given her a gun, a small two-shot derringer with a mother-of-pearl handle; and he had taught her how to shoot it. She became skilled at hitting the empty Coke bottles lined up on the fence out behind the shed, enjoying the explosions as they shattered into aqua shards of light. The derringer wouldn't kill a rapist, Uncle Meshach had explained, but it would slow the bastard down. A woman had a right to defend herself. Arista wondered what had become of the little gun. Had she hidden it in some forgotten cranny or tossed it away into the trash? In those first weeks after her arrival in New York the gun had been a comfort to her. Arista recalled its reassuring weight in the palm of her hand as she crept down the darkened hall of the Ashcraft Hotel on her way to the bathroom in the dark middle of a hot Manhattan night.

The hotel, her first residence, was located just off Times Square and was cheap—full of weak, old people and tough, old whores. She had been scared to death, but determined to live here, in spite of her fears, in spite of the terrible aching loneliness, even longing, for home, and Ted, and the safe familiar lanes of Boar's Wood. Yet she knew she had to be in New York. She had imagined, with the romantic truth of youth, that this city held her destiny, that she must experience and suffer and persevere in this place, and then write and write and write. Ted had no experience with inspiration.

It was right that he had stayed behind. He would not have been happy. They would not have been happy. Of course, *she* had not been happy. Writers are not happy people, she reminded herself. Narrative, like silk, is spun by the worm of pain. There were other examples besides herself. Her friend Katelyn was another proof of Arista's theory. Through all the long years that Katelyn Wells had been miserable over Nelson Little, Katelyn's poems had improved, as if she had scratched out her lines with blood and a used razor blade.

· · ·

The new minister startled Arista back into the present moment with a burst of William Butler Yeats, the randy, rascally Irishman who was as good as they got:

> *"Red Rose, proud Rose, Sad Rose of all my days!*
> *Come near me, while I sing the ancient ways. . . ."*

All the men she had ever loved, loved Yeats.

She realized that while her thoughts had been wandering she had been staring blankly at the man in the pulpit, and as a result her eyes were playing tricks with the light. The Reverend Christian Davies, in the center of her vision, was clear to her—glowing, haloed—while the periphery of her vision had become misty and dim. Her eyes watered and her face warmed. He truly was a handsome devil. And he knew it, by the look of it. Strong, even features, prematurely white hair edged in black, black robes edged in white. Coincidence? She thought not. There was a theatrical surge to his speech. He had carefully kept his

Irish brogue. There was a glint of gold on the third finger of his left hand.

Arista Bellefleurs at forty-five years of age, with her cynicism honed by the slow surcease of her biological clock, two marriages, a half-dozen love affairs, and one middle-aged passion, all failed, all behind her, was finding her way to yet another man. If Christ was indeed moving within her, she thought, Christ had a genuinely strange sense of humor, causing her to fall in love again and again like the devout, demented schoolgirl she had once been.

When Katelyn found out about this particular crush, she would laugh and shake her head disapprovingly at Arista. They were not, either of them, lucky in love.

He's killed himself, Katelyn was thinking. He's not *actual* anymore. It's not just that he's hidden. He's *dead*. Am I responsible? I cannot be without guilt. Katelyn had reached out and taken hold of Nelson Little's limp left hand and felt nothing. Nothing at all.

She had, throughout her life, felt responsible for the failures of her men; thinking if only she had loved them more or understood them better, they would have flourished. She imagined that loving men was her vocation, one in which she constantly fell short. Arista had often chided her about this belief and the waves of disappointment that followed inevitably in its wake. "You can't make up a man like you can make up a poem," she declared. "They don't scan." Still, nothing in Katelyn's history had prepared her for the shock of Nelson's deflation.

In truth, the love affair had killed them both. Katelyn dragged her mind back over her own dead time, the first three years after she had broken off with him—no, she had not been dead, though she had wished she would die. The memories had congealed into one mental picture. She saw herself lying in her own bed, gripping the bars of the headboard behind her, her knees drawn up in agony, as if giving birth to the emptiness that would be the rest of her life. She had tried to put the broken pieces of her world back into some semblance of order but there were no pieces. There was no husband now, or child, or dog. Victor had taken Great Daniel, their toy poodle, away with him. And Amas, her teenage son, had walked out of her life.

Katelyn discovered that without Nelson, without her family, she could not go on, in spite of women's liberation, in spite of therapy, in spite of the concern and support of her friends. Alone, she had teetered around without direction, finally paralyzed. A nervous breakdown, it was called. It was then, in that time, when she could no longer move at all, that the words had begun to come. She began to scratch out jagged verse across the empty plains of middle life, wishing, hoping, longing, willing, wanting, praying, and bargaining with God for Nelson to come back.

Only the poetry came. Luke Sevensons had encouraged her to write, and she, at long last, had fallen upon her work like a lover. She wrote endlessly about her sadness, for no one, she discovered, wanted to listen to her talk for very long. The poems, they read. Critical success, like critical mass, had been reached and her popularity exploded. Privately she felt her work was overworked. She could not write as simply, as directly, as Tennyson:

> My life is dreary,
> He cometh not, she said,
> She said, I am a weary, a weary,
> I would that I were dead.

She was but an elaboration on those four lines. Even after Lester arrived as a kind of consolation prize.

Lester would kill me, she thought, if he knew I was here, holding Nelson Little's hand, feeling only damp, unresponsive flesh. No. Lester wouldn't kill me. *Arista* would kill me. She dropped the hand.

"Do you remember the first time we made love, Nelson? It was in Quentin's other apartment."

"That was a long time ago."

"Only ten years."

"I don't like to think about it," Nelson said. "I don't like to think at all."

"But you're a genius," protested Katelyn, appalled.

"Not anymore. I probably never was. The book I wrote was second-rate."

"You were wrestling with a difficult subject," she argued, defending him against himself. "Your turns of thought were sublime." In truth, his damnable book, a convoluted criticism of Edgar Allan Poe, had defeated her. "You were brilliant." She said this on faith.

"Brains aren't everything."

"I idolized you, Nelson. Not without reason."

He sighed.

"You still teach, don't you?"

"I still teach."

"There. You see. You must think in order to teach."

"But I don't have to like it."

Surely this must be a pose, she thought. Nelson, who once thought to distinguish himself, now sought to extinguish himself. He was punishing her, trying to demonstrate the extent of his own devastation. Or else he was trying to drive her away again. It was Katelyn who had broken the smooth, unbelievable years of their silence. It had taken all of her nerve.

"What *do* you like then?"

"Allan, my new baby. But that may not last either. Affections change. Who can tell?"

Now she knew she was being punished.

They were sitting together in unknown space. Katelyn's friend Quentin was away on vacation for two weeks, and he had asked her to come by to water the plants during his absence. Quentin had moved into this new apartment only a week before he left it. The empty unfamiliarity had driven him away. Now it provided Katelyn and Nelson with private, neutral ground on which to meet. Nelson, in response to Katelyn's telephone call, had agreed to come without recognizable reluctance or enthusiasm. At five in the morning. He said it was his only free time. Not really free, for he would be sacrificing his morning jog, but his absence at that hour would not raise his wife's suspicions. Katelyn had, of course, agreed.

She had been shocked at the sight of him as, out of breath from the five flights of stairs, he had entered the apartment looking older and shorter and smaller and fatter. He was grayer, too, not just his hair, but his whole being, as if he had been covered with a fine layer of dust or ashes. His face, once handsome with happiness, was expressionless and dull. They had been talking, mostly not talking, for the hour between dawn and early morning, both of them so immobilized by the encounter that they had failed to turn on a lamp, and now sat side by side on Quentin's low-slung leather couch in the dim, watery light, wishing for a return to the cover of darkness.

They had been tentative when they first made love ten years ago, she mused. Ferocious, when they last had sex five years ago. She had made love to no one else during their decade. He had made two babies with his wife.

The advent of Nelson's first son, Edgar, had caused the breach between them. Now there was another son. News to Katelyn. She had, of course, known that Nelson would hurt her. Nelson always hurt her. She had thought she could handle the pain, that she was ready, that he couldn't hurt her *that* much anymore. But, as usual, he had penetrated her defenses, and the announcement of little Allan's existence punched her in the belly of her feelings with the force of a cannonball.

She drew breath and fired back. "I'm getting married."

"Oh, really?" He was a picture of indifference. "Why?"

She had been prepared for who, not why. "Love, I suppose."

"Ah. Yes. Love. One does suppose."

"And Lester wants to be married before we . . . well . . . before we have sex."

"How very modern," Nelson said, and made a hateful sound somewhere between a snort and a guffaw.

Unbeknownst to Katelyn the phantasm inside her psyche that called itself Nelson Little had begun to die.

There was a sudden loud knock on the door, startling them both. Then the harsh sound of the doorbell.

"Who could that be?"

"Quentin, let me in. It's Buff," came the angry answer through the door.

"Is it locked?" asked Nelson.

"Of course it's locked. But I'll have to let him in. It's Buff."

"Who's Buff?"

"Quentin's lover. He's been missing for months. Quentin finally gave up and moved out of their old place in despair."

"I didn't come here to get involved in a gay soap opera."

"Neither did I, Nelson."

Katelyn got up awkwardly, bumping into Nelson's outstretched legs. In an unwelcome flash of feeling she remembered their legs entwined under warm, heavy blankets in the snowy dawn of a long-ago winter. He had been so alive then. She flicked on the track lighting. One badly positioned bulb sent a savage shaft of light directly onto Nelson's face. He flinched, then glared.

"Don't let him in. He might recognize me."

"No, he won't. He's blind."

She pulled open the front door and Buff lurched into the room, threw his arms around Katelyn, stumbled backward in surprised horror, and almost fell over a large German shepherd who was struggling forward and backward through the doorway, as confused as he.

"Who are you?"

"Buff, it's okay. It's me, Katelyn."

"Katelyn! How good. But where's Quentin? He's not sick, is he?"

"No. He's in Italy."

"Oh, hell! The minute I turn my back he flies off to screw beautiful Mediterranean boys." He moved awkwardly past her into the apartment. "Oh, how am I to cope? Everything is new here. I don't know where anything is." And he slumped abruptly down onto the floor near Nelson's feet and began to weep. The dog lodged his nose in Nelson's lap.

"Get away!" cried Nelson, pushing himself away down the couch. He was afraid of large animals.

"Who's that?" wailed Buff.

"The dog won't hurt you, luv," Katelyn assured Nelson. "He's a Seeing Eye."

"Who is here?" insisted Buff.

"A friend of mine."

"It's about time, Katelyn. Your nunlike habits haven't been at all healthy. Quentin and I have been worried sick about you."

"Buff!"

"Sorry." He began to wipe his face on his sleeves.

"And where have *you* been all these months? Talk about worry."

"Ohio." He was crawling toward Nelson, who was struggling to extricate himself from the couch and the dog.

"I have to go now, Katelyn," declared Nelson. "I'll be late for my first class, as it is. I'll leave the two of you to catch up on old times."

"Please, don't go," pleaded Katelyn. She felt that nothing had been accomplished by the meeting.

"Oh, dear, I've upset everyone as usual," cried Buff. "Come to me, Greta." And he clutched at the dog, catching up one of Nelson's legs, as well as the dog, into his arms. Nelson shook himself free, none too gently, and made for the door.

"Another time, Katelyn."

She slammed the door shut and barred the way with her body. "No!"

"Be sane, Katelyn!"

"No! I'm tired of being sane. I've been sane and sensible for five years. I've never troubled you, never asked for your help, never blamed, never intruded."

"This is not the time for a confrontation." He shot a meaningful glance in the direction of the blind man and the dog.

But Katelyn felt a tightly cinched belt inside her psyche come suddenly unbuckled. She was undone. Her voice became low and full of menace. "I can't believe you took what we had and made babies in your wife with it."

"Not now!"

"Then and now."

Nelson, furious, seemed to be deciding whether or not

to shove Katelyn aside. He thought better of it and stepped back, his face darkening with his anger. "And just what is it that you imagine we had?" Buff and Greta Garbo remained huddled together on the floor, all ears and eyes.

"Love. More than love. Passion. All that people search for and almost never find. We had it. We had it all, and you jerked it all away."

"Love isn't everything."

"It should be!" she protested. "Look what we have become without it, without each other."

"And just what do you imagine we've become?"

"Old. Old and scarred and scared and sad."

"Everyone gets old. I'm not scarred, and I'm not scared or sad. My life is quiet and normal now, and I'm happy."

"You're not happy."

"But I am, Katelyn. You don't want to see my happiness. It interferes with all your puffed-up pretensions, all your romantic notions of me as an unsung genius, of yourself as my savior. Look closer, Katelyn, and you will see a contented man, a family man, a man who grows tomatoes in his window boxes, a homebody, a nobody whose wife has tolerated him—just as he is—for twenty-five years. It's time to let your idealizations go. It's time to let your memories fade. It's time to go save someone else."

"You are gloating . . . on your failure . . . on mine . . . on our failure . . . you wanted us to fail . . . you enjoy watching me writhe, watching you fail."

"You're talking like you've gone crazy."

"You're the one who is pridefully growing fucking tomatoes! Is that sane?"

"It's just life, Katelyn." The anger had left his features, and he looked, suddenly, tired. He looked, and she could see it now, as if he didn't care whether he grew tomatoes or children or malignant tumors.

"You destroyed my life!"

He took a deep breath, and like a teacher whose patience is tried, but intact, he informed her: "You did that all by yourself. You decided to leave your husband all on your own. You didn't even ask my permission."

"Why, you pompous ass! He was *my* husband. *I* was the one who had to live with him. Victor deserved to be left."

"I'm not so sure about that."

"Divorce was my decision to make."

"Then having made your bed alone, you can lie in it alone."

"I loved you. I still love you."

"Let it go."

"I can't."

"You must."

"I won't."

"And just what kind of marriage are you proposing to have, my dear Katelyn, for surely you have done all the proposing, to your new, dear . . . what is his name?. . . Lester, if you're still whistling our old tune?"

"Lester understands."

"Well, good for Lester. Does he know you arranged to meet me today?"

"No."

He smirked, the smirk changing abruptly to a grimace. "Ouch! Hell! Get him off me." Terror had taken hold of his features as Greta Garbo had taken hold of his ankle.

"Greta, no!" Katelyn bent down and tried to loosen the dog's jaws. "Let go." The dog released Nelson reluctantly, and backed off sulkily. Nelson took advantage of his sudden freedom to lunge for the door. He pulled it open and she could hear his footsteps, ever faster, as he made his descent. Katelyn stayed on the floor with Greta and Buff.

"What kind of a man *is* that, Katelyn?" asked Buff. "See-ing Eye dogs don't bite."

"That was Nelson."

"Ah. The legendary Nelson. How can you love *him*?"

"You don't get to choose who you love."

"He doesn't know how lucky he is. Another minute and I would have bitten him myself." He patted the dog. "Now, who's Lester?"

"You'll like him. I'm going to marry him."

"So I heard. But who is he? Someone you met while I was away? Are you crying?"

"Yes. There. I'm stopping. Maybe I'll write to Nelson."

"A poison-pen letter?"

"I need to make a statement."

"How about a letter bomb?"

"Buff, be serious."

"Face it, Katelyn, Nelson is a germ."

"Lester is an angel."

"That doesn't tell me a whole helluva lot."

"I met him at Luke Sevensons's last gathering in New York, two months ago."

"Funny. Luke didn't mention him to me."

"You've seen Luke?"

"I've been with Luke, on his farm in Ohio."

"All these months?"

"Yes. Except when he was off somewhere working. I needed Luke, and he just opened his door to me. 'Mi casa es su casa,' he said. I had to face something, Katelyn. Something very big and at first very terrible. I have AIDS."

"God, no, Buff." She began to cry again.

"It's all right. I'm all right." He found her hand and held it. "I know I caved in a bit when I first arrived here and re-alized that Quentin wasn't home. I was so eager to see him and to know that he's . . . healthy. It was the sudden disappointment. But, really, I'm all right. For now."

And the sureness of his voice, the strength of his grip told her that he was. Was she? she wondered. The thought of losing Buff, though not in the same league with losing Nelson, was appalling. She had worried during the months of Buff's absence, but had harbored the consoling notion that he had eloped with someone, or gone away for reasons best known to himself, and that he would return to them all someday. As he had done. She observed him closely now, looking for signs of his illness. He looked a little thinner, and, as if it were possible, a little kinder.

All those months with Luke Sevensons! It was an enormous thought. The most time she had ever spent with Luke was a weekend, at a two-day gathering. There had been several such weekends in the past few years. Each had held a blessing. The last gathering had held Lester. Katelyn hadn't expected to meet anyone to love in the groups that collected around Luke's ankles; she hadn't expected to meet anyone to love ever again anywhere, and the groups drew a pretty borderline bunch. She and Arista had gone to Luke to work on their work—to move a little further, with his guidance, along their respective paths of poetry and prose. When Luke spoke to Katelyn, she answered in new voices.

The last time Luke came to New York City he had worked in the paint-bedazzled loft that served as the home and studio of a friend of his, the artist Jamie Callahan. Callahan was away for the weekend, disappointing Arista, who had hoped to meet him.

Katelyn and Arista had entered the studio together. Arista had seen Lester first and had nudged Katelyn. He was young and handsome. Lester had seen Katelyn first. He had looked directly into her eyes, then bowed his head

as if in homage. With his head still lowered, he had extended his right hand to Katelyn and she had moved hyp-
notically to take hold of it. No words were spoken or
needed. Katelyn and Lester had then looked toward Luke
and it felt, in those first silent moments, as if Luke had
joined them—though Luke was unaware of his participa-
tion in the posting of the banns, for Luke had seen Arista
first and had felt a flush of warmth suffusing his chest.
With his eyes he had returned the warmth to Arista, then
to Katelyn and Lester, and then to all the others.

That gathering had been special, one that had nurtured
Luke with its heat and light and movement. The present
group was arranged before him in a semicircle on floor
cushions in among the potted plants of his airy porch at
the back of the farmhouse. The wide plank floorboards
had, the night before, been scrubbed clean by Methuselah.
The screens, recently reinstalled after the hard winter, admitted the breezes and bird song but kept all the tiny flying things outside, where they collected to watch the
work. This was a small gathering, mostly townspeople that
Luke had known for years.

There was one new presence. Seth. An old soul in a
youthful body by the look of him. Seth. A musician—
young enough in this life and gifted enough from the past
to soar. Luke could sense the boy's music nearby, soft and
sad and full of grace. At the beginning of the meeting
Luke, as was his way, had asked each person in turn what
it was they desired from the day's work. Seth had asked for
the courage to run away from home. But he was only a
boy, thought Luke! A thin, worried-looking boy with pale,
midwestern features, armed with a flute. Where would he
go? Luke felt like a worried grandfather for a moment as
he pondered the youngster. He remembered a Presbyterian
minister he had met not long ago on a train to New York

City. That man, with more wisdom than one would expect for one of his calling, had told Luke what he knew about young people: "What they think they want they never want. What they want is not ever what they think."

When it was Seth's turn to work he placed himself, as the others had done, near Luke's feet, and sat with his legs folded, the flute across his knees, his eyes closed, listening to Luke's hypnotic voice. He was already in the lightest of trances. Luke Sevensons was reciting a poem that had arrived for the boy.

"The music of the reed is fire, not air ...
Such longing.
If I were also touching the lips of someone who spoke my language,
I would tell all that could be told."

"A Sufi poet wrote that, Seth. A man named Jelaluddin Rumi, caliph of the Mavlevis, the whirling dervishes. You know about the whirling dervishes?" The boy nodded. "Yes. You would know of the dervishes. They are part of your world. They dance ecstatically to the music of the reed flute. Can you imagine the dervishes? See them in the eye of your mind, whirling there. Just watch them turn in their soaring black robes while I speak to you. They are whirling in order to know God—just as the Shakers shook and the Indians dance, just as the Gregorians chant and the Jews pray and sway at the wailing wall. Now these lines I spoke to you are from the *Mathnawi*, a poem by Rumi that runs for fifty-one thousand verses, an ocean of wisdom." Luke could see Seth's eyelids quivering; eyelid catalepsy, it was called. The trance was now deep enough to begin. "Now tell me, Seth, why do you want to leave your home?"

"It's an empty place."

"Now, just behind your eyes, I can see that tears begin to form. If your tears could talk to you, what would they say?"

And the boy's cavernous loneliness, edged with the sharp, rebellious pain of adolescence, engulfed them. He spoke of the lives of his family: of his mother, Ivy Sue, and her endless war on dust; of his father, Ted, and his continual acquisition for the sake of acquisition; of his sister, Holly, who was desperate for what she called popularity. He didn't understand the importance of these desires. And his family did not understand that he did not understand. "They don't care about the things I care for. They don't read books. There is no poetry in their lives. No music."

"Surely your music is in their lives."

"Mozart's."

"And Tchaikovsky?"

"Yes. And the other great composers."

"But not your own?"

"I have no music."

"Ah. Will you play me one note on your flute? Not two. Only one."

In spite of the trance Seth appeared slightly puzzled, but he dutifully raised the flute and sounded one clear note.

Luke nodded. "Was that Mozart's note?"

"No. I mean it could be. It could be Mozart's or anyone's. It's just a note."

"Just a note. Could I hear it again?"

Again the boy complied.

"This is a very lovely note. If this note could be anyone's, then it could be yours."

"No." Again the boy began to weep.

Luke did not wait for the tears to subside. He spoke

with authority, almost with anger, though his natural gentleness robbed the anger of its ability to hurt.

"Play me another note." Seth played again. This note a little higher, a little sweeter than the first. "Put the first lonely note with the second, Seth. Put the notes together for company. The emptiness you feel in your home is the space around you where your music should be. The vacuum is not caused by mother or father or sister, but by you, Seth. You are afraid to make your own music because you are afraid that it will not be as glorious as the music of a Mozart or a Bach or a Beethoven or a Tchaikovsky. You are afraid that the great composers, those who went before you, and those who are your real family, will not understand you, or approve of the music you make."

He could sense the boy's tension increasing. "Now, see them here in the room with us, Seth. Can you see these great men in your mind's eye?" Seth nodded slightly. "I want you to speak to them. You may do this silently or aloud, but speak to them. Ask your questions. They are here to help you." He could see that Seth was in the awesome presence of his mentors. "Now you must listen to them. They are older and wiser than you. They have lived and died for a long time. They will tell you what you must do. Talk to them, listen to them."

Deep inside his trance, Seth spoke with a silent voice.

I never imagined I could talk to you.

Mozart chortled. There was no other word for it. Bach glared, first at Mozart, then at Seth.

It was, surprisingly, Chopin who replied: THAT IS BECAUSE YOU ARE A PRODUCT OF OUR IMAGINATION. WE CREATED YOU.

You created me? Why?

WE LIKE TO HAVE OUR MUSIC APPRECI-
ATED. AND SOMEONE HAS TO CARRY ON,
YOU KNOW. IT'S TIME FOR YOU TO STOP
COMPLAINING AND MAKE WHAT WILL BE
YOUR MUSIC.

What if it isn't any good?

YOU KNOW GOOD MUSIC WHEN YOU
HEAR IT! COMPOSE UNTIL YOU HEAR
SOMETHING THAT SOUNDS GOOD.

But I'm not like you. I'm just ordinary.

Mozart snorted and cut in impatiently: OH,
DON'T BE SUCH A BOOBY, SETH. ORDINARY
PEOPLE DON'T HAVE EXPERIENCES LIKE
THIS.

This is nuts.

Unmoving, Luke watched Seth and waited patiently. His
back was hurting a little. He spent some time with the
pain, getting to know its sharpness, glad when it changed
to a numbing warmth. The boy was quiet for the length of
a sonata. Then, slowly, he lifted his flute and began to play
the plaintive music that Luke had sensed was in the nearby
air, caught it on the wing with his silver flute. Sound sent
by the gods for the delight of the gods.

It was in such moments that Luke most loved his work.
Maggie Silvernails had loved him because he loved his
work, as she loved hers. The work was always the same: to
capture the messages. This morning's messages were carried by soaring black birds wheeling against a yellow-white
sky; by a dusty red mesa clotted with restless desert

grasses, by a desert wind humming tunelessly in her ears, by brown, fat Fatpaws, doggedly sleeping beside her while the yellow-white-red-green-brown pigments made their oily way along the bristles and down, down, down onto the canvas.

Man coming.

Maggie felt his footsteps long before he came into view. There was nothing in the earth's subtle reverberations to frighten her, but she wondered who was approaching now, treading on her shadow. She turned and waited with her eyes as the distant figure emerged from the horizon, wavy in the heated air, walking steadily in her direction.

Fatpaws woke up and barked sharply, stopping at her hand signal, then sat beside her waiting with his nose—alert and eager. The man's stride was familiar. A big man. Not Indian. Not Luke. Callahan! He saw her, and began to trot, his arms outstretched. Joyfully she raced to meet him, but Fatpaws got there first, and so he embraced them both with his mighty Irish arms, and they laughed and cried and barked and slapped each other's shoulders and stomped the ground and then rolled in the hot sand with the dog until they could laugh no more, and lay spread-eagled, side by side on their backs, exhausted from the twenty years they had been apart.

"Maggie Silvernails, your beautiful hair is still as black as a crow's wing."

"Jamie Callahan, you have turned as gray as the muzzle of an old dog."

"Deerfinder told me that you were dead."

"Why didn't you believe him?"

"Henry Chang sent me."

"That old Buddha! He still breathes?"

"He still does my shirts. He'll have a helluva job with this one when I get back." Callahan sat up and began to slap at the dust covering his clothing. Maggie stayed where she was, flat on the ground, letting the hot sand push up against her back muscles, letting the sun cover her face.

"What exactly did Henry Chang say?"

"Well, I went in to retrieve my shirts last Monday morning as usual, and as he passed them over the counter he said, 'Twenty years of sadness is enough sadness, Carrahan. Time fries. Go find Maggie Sirverrails and smire again.' "

She laughed, thinking of the short, shriveled Chinaman with his steamy clean face and his head full of wonderful, Eastern, yellow wisdom that was inevitably, exactly, woefully wrong for the rational, Western, white mind. He had sent Callahan here to her. Was that wrong? Time would tell. Henry Chang had seemed a hundred years old when she knew him in Greenwich Village two decades before. Perhaps he was immortal.

"And what exactly did my friend Deerfinder say?"

"He put on his solemn face, his reservation face, and said that Maggie Silvernails lived now only in the grandchildren of vultures and her stone-white bones glowed in the light of the desert moon."

"Yuk! Must be the result of that unfortunate poetry class he took at The New School."

"Well, I just didn't believe that old Henry Chang would send me all the way out here on an adventure ending in vultures, so after I got Deerfinder drunk on some very fine Irish whisky and he still stuck to his dead-Maggie story, I was stumped." She could see his affection for Deerfinder glinting in his narrowed eyes. "Why is it I believe that red fox even now? When Deerfinder lies, he sounds decidedly more trustworthy than when he's telling the truth. Anyhow, I was stumped and I decided to get drunk myself. I woke up remembering about how you inherited a shanty somewhere east of Eagle Nest."

"Who told you about my cabin? Nobody knows."

"You did," Jamie shot back. "One day when you were sad and full of grass-fire smoke. You said your father's mother's brother, who was a contrary, had died all alone in a cabin east of Eagle Nest, and that you had found him and buried him upside down and that made the place yours."

"You believe any old Injun blarney you hear?"

"Not Deerfinder's."

"So you sobered up and asked all around Eagle Nest for a crazy old Indian woman with paint on her face and you found me."

"I followed your paintings. They're all over this corner of the state."

"A girl's got to live."

"They're marvelous, Maggie. Better than before." He nodded toward her current painting. "That one already shows courage and you've only just begun."

"Good."

"Hey, Maggie." He leaned over her and looked down close into her eyes. His shadow was cool across her face. "Would you like to make love?"

"Oh, Callahan. I would like to make a powerful lot of love."

"Then let's go find a bathtub and a bed."

They helped each other up, as old people do, though they felt childlike in spirit when they touched. They walked quietly, hand in hand, in the direction of the cabin. Callahan carried her gear. Fatpaws ran ahead, his excited dog-brain spilling over with visions of a rabbity lunch.

The shack was soon in sight. Maggie could see Callahan's belongings piled up, weighing down the porch.

It looked as if he was planning to stay for a while. Fatpaws gave the luggage only a cursory sniff as he ran into the cabin and emerged with a soup bone to gnaw on under a creosote bush. The two humans who loved each other stopped for a moment, each considering what they were about to do.

"He's still alive, Maggie."

"I know."

"He still works."

"Is there a woman?"

"Only Maudie. He calls her Methuselah now, and claims she is older than Henry Chang's grandmother. No romantic interests. He gets an occasional crush on someone in one of his groups, but it never comes to anything."

"He still heals."

"As he still breathes. I don't think Luke Sevensons could *do* anything else."

She smiled, recalling with pleasure quite a lot of other things he could do. "Do you remember when I gave him that Indian name? Sevensons. Suits him better than his Swede name."

"Swenson, wasn't it? Oh, that was a time, Maggie. We three." She was silent watching the dog gnaw. He continued: "I've never blamed you for leaving us, Maggie. But I've missed you like hell and hell again."

"Don't need to miss me now." He took her in his arms then, and the goodness of it stunned him.

• • •

Jamie Callahan had always made a point to make love as often as possible, mostly with the young art students he met in the Village cafés. He deemed it good for his art and good for his health. He liked making love, but not falling in love or being in love, particularly in the unripe forms that were generally offered up to him. But Maggie Silvernails proved an exception without rules. During their bath she had undone her braids, and later, as they moved in the bed, her hair had covered them like a billowing wave. Now it lay like a spray of dark sea foam across the pillow where she slept. He looked at her brown, taut body, bending slightly toward him as she slept, so little changed from the days he had positioned it, gazed upon it, and made it the subject of his art. He had always judged his series of Maggie paintings as the best of the lot.

Seized suddenly by a need greater than sex, he sprang from the bed and rummaged about the cabin, finding the assortment of paint tubes that would make up his palette, grabbing a brush of likely form, and reaching for a canvas already stretched and prepared from Maggie's unused stack. Happily he went to work, finding her again in the most significant way he knew.

As he brushed her dreaming image onto the canvas he pondered her life. Twenty years had passed, Maggie said, since she had last been in the arms of a man. That man had been Callahan. Or, maybe, Luke. That, Maggie hadn't said. He wondered what she had found—out here in the wilderness—what inner thing had sustained her through the dehydration of her love life? The Great Spirit? What a terrible waste. Or so it seemed to Jamie Callahan. He knew there were young people today, young people with a little life left in them, who would revere Maggie's choice, who would badger her for Red Indian wisdom if they could. They meditated and sat *zazen* and talked to rocks and chanted. They were searching for a meaning to their lives, a meaning that came to Callahan as easily as getting up in the morning. If the young people discovered Luke, he worked with them, trying to keep the flame burning in their culture-dampened souls. Had he and Luke and Maggie ever been as spiritually forlorn as the current rendition of American youth? He thought not. They had had art. They had had life.

He remembered their life in the Village with a purple nostalgia—all of them brash—talking and writing and sculpting and painting and panting after one another with enormous appetite. Disturbed by life. But not lost. Later, much later, they had gone astray. He and Maggie and Luke had held together in their torturous triangular box for twenty years. Then they had been apart for twenty.

". . . All true love must die," Yeats had written. How did it go next?

> All true love must die,
> Alter at the best.
> Into some lesser thing. Prove that I lie.

He looked up from the painting and stared at Maggie. He deftly added a soft shade of brown to a nipple that was becoming too pink. He loved her as much in this moment as he ever had done. There had been proof in the bed. There was proof in the painting. His eyes played over her body as the poet's voice played on in his mind.

> Such body lovers have,
> Such exacting breath,
> That they touch or sigh.
> Every touch they give,
> Love is nearer death.
> Prove that I lie.

He had wasted twenty years of his life!
He must not think of this. He corrected the line of her

thigh. Opening her a little more. Oh, they would all die soon enough. He, and those who had been his companions in life. The friends of his youth. The bearers of his middle age. He knew that now. But not then. Then death had been a vaporous, transparent idea. They had all been too, too solid flesh back in those early days—immortal, living in an enchanted village.

Of the others he knew that Marxie, after a checkered love life, had become an alcoholic and killed himself, and Denise had died of lung cancer. Such a high price those two had paid, for they had all smoked cigarettes and knocked back whiskey until they reeled. There had been drugs, too—but not many, and not for long. Drugs, they had discovered, interfered with their work. They had all worked like donkeys.

How had they fared for all their work? Eve had married Callahan, which had had about the same effect on her poetry as leukemia; her verse had become paler and weaker, trailing off into meaninglessness until she fled in despair, leaving the ground clear for Maggie Silvernails. Deerfinder had always been and would always be an unknown quantity, living out his life in the shadow of Maggie. George Eliot Isaman wrote banal books and only dreamed of depth. Oakley Klapper had become famous and had stayed famous, though, in Jamie's opinion, his abstract paintings resembled nothing so much as mud puddles at their best and piles of pigeon droppings at their worst. Callahan himself was what was known as well-known, but foundering, unable to swim against the tide of modernism that had swept through their lives like sewer water. Gone, all of them, the comrades and heroes of his past, altered into lesser things.

In the early days Maggie Silvernails had been mother to them all. Luke Sevensons had vied with Callahan for the role of father figure and won an incomplete victory. Enigmatic Luke, who was not a painter or a poet or an anything definable—just Luke who helped. On his last visit east, just a few weeks ago, he and Callahan had talked about the current crop of Village artists like two old women comparing cabbages. Luke had shown Callahan a book of poetry written by a woman named Arista Bellefleurs. The book had been dedicated to Luke and said:

> "To my brother and teacher, Luke Sevensons, who as Shakespeare so beautifully wrote, 'finds tongues in trees, books in the running brooks, sermons in stone, and good in all things.' "

"You in love with this woman, Luke?"

"No. But she reminds me a little of Maggie." Their eyes and voices had lowered then, for they seldom spoke of Maggie.

"I'd like to meet her, your Arista Bellefleurs."

"She's searching, Jamie."

"Aren't we all?"

"Not everyone. Some people are too busy talking about money and food," Luke had answered, and then looked at him with those glittering, laughing lake-blue eyes that always made Callahan feel safe and loved and glad to be alive. Except on the rare occasions when Luke got angry. Then the pools of sparkling blue changed, turned navy, almost black. Ink spots.

Callahan had painted Luke's eyes many times, but never captured their message. The message was something to do with love or with God, he thought. But Jamie Callahan was a lapsed Catholic and held no defined belief in God. He loved life and he painted and that was enough for him.

Well . . . that and Maggie. Why couldn't he capture Luke's eyes? he wondered.

He knew that a person's eyes were always the most elusive feature to paint, but if you could nail them, the rest of the portrait came of itself, even self-portraits. His own eyes often eluded him, full as they were of amber Irish whisky and green Irish blarney. But sometimes the mirror reflected eyes brimming with Irish imagery—Celtic, magical, lyrical—that splashed onto his canvases and into his memories. His work had the power to kindle the imagination of others, and Maggie, while pretending to sleep, watched him work through her thick, black eyelashes, thinking she had been fortunate to love Jamie Callahan . . . and Luke . . . and Deerfinder, too, in an entirely different way.

Only a woman who can live without men can truly love them, Maggie reflected. She lay quietly for a while, imagining a spectrum of futures now that Jamie had rolled back into her life and into her bed and into her body. Had he ever really been away? Would he want to stay with her now? How curious and difficult it would be to live with another human after the decades of solitude, and yet how welcome was the vision. Or, perhaps she would return with him to Greenwich Village and resume her old life. Without Luke? Impossible. With Luke? Impossible. They had fancied themselves special—the three of them—above ordinary forms and conventions. And perhaps they had been. But not now. The desert had burned away all of her pretensions. She had stayed on and on here, far from the two men she loved, for whenever she had taken her question into herself, communed with her soul, followed her spirit deep enough to the place where it was no longer just her soul, the answer was always the same:

DON'T CHOOSE.

So she could not return to either of them. The cost had been unimaginable.

"How is Elinor?"

"You're awake, beautiful old woman."

"Watching you paint, serious old man. When you finish immortalizing your illusions, would you paint me up an early breakfast?" He nodded. "Your Elinor must be thirty-five or six by now. She was a glorious child, your daughter."

Our daughter, he thought as he put down his brush and began to poke about the kitchen, putting together a pickup meal.

Callahan had no answer to Maggie's question. He didn't know how Elinor was. He remembered her pale, little face all alight as she sat for hours on the studio floor while they worked; he recalled her delight in their paintings that had been the storybooks of her childhood. He remembered her adolescence; gawky with green feelings, she had ripened into a graceful golden young woman. How was she now, his grown-up Elinor? It was well past midnight here in New Mexico, so it would be just past dawn in Ireland. She was probably up already. There in the North. How could that bastard Brian have taken her to Belfast of all the places on God's green earth? No one moved *to* Belfast. Not from America! Not with his bright and beautiful Manhattan-bred daughter. Elinor had run off from him just as Eve, her real mother, had run off before her; as Maggie, her adoptive mother, had done, too. Why did all his women flee from him? He loved them with the deepest shades of crimson and the most royal shades of blue. Yet they escaped from the canvas of his life, jumping off into unknown spaces, looking for all the other colors of love.

Callahan knew he should have flown to Belfast and visited Elinor years ago, if only to see his grandchildren. There was one now, little Paul, who he would never see. It wasn't for lack of money, he thought grumpily as he rummaged around slicing bread and frying beans. But he was too mad and too black stubborn to set his foot across a threshold belonging to Brian O'Neill. Fortunately there were eggs. As she dropped a dozen of them, one by one, into the large cast-iron frying pan, the twelve unbroken yokes, sizzling in rich summer-yellow butter, stared at her like the six pairs of wide eyes that belonged to her living children.

Elinor Callahan O'Neill felt melancholy this morning, for Bren, the last of her little ones, was going to nursery school for the first time today, on his way into the world. Ah. What a world. There would actually be some quiet in the house for the first time in . . . how many years? Since Paul's first cry eighteen years ago. Paul. How she missed him. Dead these three long years.

"Hallo! Everybody up! Breakfast now." She gave out a cry for the living.

And in they straggled. Bridget first, of course, fresh in from the outdoors, as if she had been up for hours. She was the most cheerful of Elinor's children and the most awkward for loving—all angles and edges when you tried to hold her. Almost grown now. Colin and Grady arrived next. Born only nine months apart, they were often mistaken for twins. They did everything differently, but were always together, usually with an argument rumbling along between them, but never an outright fight. Doreen slipped in, still asleep, by all appearances. Megan, all in a whirl, ran for Elinor's skirts, turned her mother around, asked for help with her braids, and once done up, joined the others at the table, asking about their sleep and their dreams. And then wee Bren, looking sheepish and shy, leaned around the kitchen door. The children fell silent and gave him a long, collective look. Elinor had carefully cut down a school uniform that had once belonged to Paul. It fit Bren well enough. Bren marched bravely into their midst.

"Today's it, Bren."

"Off to Mrs. McMurphy's prison for little boys."

"You look grand, Bren."

"Dressed to kill."

"Enough," interrupted Elinor, slapping down eggs and fried bread. "Let the boy have his breakfast in peace."

"Last meal for the condemned man."

"Stop it, Colin, Grady. What's come over you? You both like school, and you know it. Don't torment the lad." She looked at Bren. He seemed to be holding up well under the barrage. She was being overly protective of him again. It was hard not to be smothery. He was small for his age and as charming as a cherub. But being at the end of a line of O'Neills would have toughened him up even without the tragedies. Those he seemed to have put away on a very high shelf, determined not to deal with them until he had grown up tall enough to see them eye to eye. Wise as well as smart, her Bren. He could hold his own among his siblings by the force of his fierce intelligence alone. At five he could read the Bible and do multiplications through tens. Let Mrs. McMurphy try this O'Neill out for size. She smiled at the mischief of it, for she hadn't warned the teacher that a wee wizard was coming her way today.

The children seemed to inhale their food, so she added a bowl of boiled potatoes and a jug of cream to the table. She often served ordinary food at unusual times to make their plain fare more interesting. The milkman had got through the barricades without incident this morning, so there was plenty of cream to go around. She took a moment to be glad for the good fortune of it.

Doreen seemed to be sleeping again, though her plate had been scraped clean between catnaps.

"Why is that child so tired?" Elinor asked herself aloud.

Megan, the little mother, answered: "She reads."

"You all read. You're not tired."

"She reads most of the night."

"Since when?"

"Since she fell in love with Sean McKinney."

Doreen jerked awake as the name of her beloved was spoken. "I haven't a care for Sean McKinney," she protested, making a grab for one of Megan's braids.

"You do, you know," piped in Colin, "and he fancies you, too."

"He's the smartest boy in the class, and you read all the time now so you can make a show for him," added Grady.

"What are you reading?" queried Elinor.

"Just my lessons."

"Well, it's all right then, isn't it? If love is to make a scholar of you. My electric will go up, but so will your marks." In truth she hadn't paid the electric bill in months. It was part of the protest, and the Protestant electric-company men were too scared to come into the Catholic Clonnard district to read the meters anymore. Poor men, she mused, and was glad that her neighbors couldn't read her thoughts. She had never been able to hate Protestants properly, even after they murdered her boy Paul. And, in truth, the culprits could have been her own people. No one laid claim to the bomb that had gone wrong and blown up the two boys the day of the guru. That entertainment had been meant for adults.

"Mum, can we have some jam?"

"Too late for jam."

The children scuttled for their anoraks and school bags. Doreen primped at the hall mirror. Bridget appeared restless with the morning routine and drifted off down the front walk. Bren lingered at the table for a moment and Elinor flashed him an encouraging smile. He smiled back his tender little smile, then went to get his satchel. The school bag was new for him, with a pencil box inside, and she was glad she had managed to find the money to buy it, a child's paraphernalia, to mark the specialness of this occasion. Bren, of all her children, had the capacity to make the beginnings of a better life for himself out of the poor stuff of Mrs. McMurphy's lessons and the disaster of his environment. She listened to the local radio report as she donned her worn cloth coat. Belfast was cold and hushed this morning. Spring seemed reluctant to arrive.

As the family grouped on the front steps she gazed, as she always did, across the narrow street to the Ryans' house, now an empty shell. The Ryans' boy, Kevin, the only son of the family, had been killed alongside Paul, and the force of the explosion had reached across the city, destroying the whole of his family with its might. The night following the boys' violent death, Kevin's father had stolen a car and driven it into the army barricades on the Dublin Road. He had been shot to death for his trouble. Kevin's mother had died of heartbreak within a fortnight, and her aged mother had taken the remaining children away in the night. Elinor knew not where. God knew what future they had. Her own family, fractured as it was, still had a chance. The looted house watched her with its empty, accusing windows. If only she had said, "No, Paul, you cannot go." If only Mrs. Ryan had said, "No, Kevin, you cannot go." She shuddered.

Her children had begun making their way down the steps and across the tiny stretch of tufted grass that passed for a yard when she saw Mr. Carris, the postman, coming along the street with his mailbag. Glad to be distracted from the direction of her thoughts, she waved a friendly greeting.

"I've a letter here for your bonnie girl Bridget," called Mr. Carris loud enough for all the neighbors to hear. "From the United States of America, as usual." Bridget turned red, but Elinor could see the happiness in her eyes.

Elinor took the letter and handed it over to Bridget. "It's a fair wonder that your Seth has time to do anything else for all the letters he writes you."

A wave of homesickness rolled over Elinor—for America, for America's ease and America's bounty. Seth Hackett lived in a small town with the unfortunate name of Boar's Wood, somewhere in Ohio. He had been selected at random through an international service as Paul's pen pal.

After the tragedy Elinor took on the task of writing to Seth in the middle of that first sad summer, describing the day when Paul had gone downtown with his friend Kevin to watch a guru from India stand on his head. It was to be a protest for peace. The unlikely event had drawn a large crowd, and so the two lads had climbed onto the roof of a parked car—a hearse—the only kind of automobile that was then allowed into the center of the beleaguered city. As the Maharishi Ranchi Gee, a brown man in saffron robes, prepared to perform his mindful absurdity in opposition to Belfast's mindless obscenity, the hearse had blown up and killed both children instantly. The guru and several other spectators had died later in hospital. After sending her explanatory letter, Elinor had not expected to hear from Seth Hackett again, but he had written on lined musical composition paper, first to her and Brian—a letter of surprising maturity expressing his condolences—and then to Bridget. Paul, it seemed, had written to Seth at length about his pretty sister. Bridget had responded and their correspondence flourished.

Elinor hoped a meeting could be arranged between the two youngsters sometime in the future, and Brian, after a perusal of the early letters, had approved. How fitting it would be if Bridget were to go back to her mother's country from her mother's father's country. Elinor's mother, Eve, was probably in America, too, though her whereabouts had almost always been unknown to Elinor. Eve had left Jamie Callahan when Elinor was only two years old, leaving not a memory behind. Elinor had learned what she knew of mothering from Maggie Silvernails (who hadn't done badly, considering Maggie had no children of her own), and from her own bone-deep longings for nurturance. She remembered a verse scrawled in one of her mother's abandoned diaries:

> Your children are not your children
> They are the sons and daughters of Life's longing for itself.
> They come through you but not from you
> And though they are with you yet they belong not to you.

Elinor decided that her mother had taken those Kahlil Gibran homilies a little too seriously. Elinor could not imagine a life that did not belong to her children. Her world was so stuffed full of them. How could a mother choose to leave a child? How could Eve have left her? Elinor had stared and stared at the photographs of herself as a baby, as a toddler, as a little girl. She had been a pretty infant. She had looked brightly into the camera and smiled and smiled. But still her mother had gotten up one day and packed a bag and left her—pretty, smiling, wee thing though she was; left her for someone or something never defined, never explained. At moments of great happiness—the day when she had married

Brian, when the babies came—Elinor wished her mysterious, missing mother well, wanting her happiness to flow outward and seep across space into Eve's life and make that life, wherever it was, joyful. But in the dark times—kneeling at Paul's barren little grave, remembering the rifle shots that came later—she blamed her mother, hated her, knew her to be responsible for all that was evil and wrong in her life . . . in New York, in Belfast, in the whole of creation. In the bad times her absent mother became the font of all illness, all pain, all death and destruction. A Grand-Medea-Mother. Eve Callahan had O'Neill blood on her hands. In those terrible moments of rage and grief Elinor wished her mother misery, wished upon her all the despair of all the mothers of all the dead children in all the world. Elinor stopped for a moment, trying to free herself from the ropes of pain and hate that had suddenly entwined her. She never knew when such moments would come.

She decided she would step into St. Mary's after she walked the children to school. Raised religionless, she had discovered, in late adolescence, a desire for devotion: first to Brian, then to his church, and then to his children. Jamie Callahan, that beat-up old beatnik of a father, would never understand! The decision to visit the tranquil parish church should have calmed her down, she knew, but she was still feeling jagged. She took a deep breath, trying to smooth her emotions and clear her thoughts. The devil was at her this morning, and the devil, as usual, was only the wrenching past. She forced her attention to the present, to the rompings and ramblings of her brood, as she chucked them along toward the school yard that was enclosed by sandbags and barbed-wire fences, then past the concrete guardhouse, its window slits bristling with machine-gun barrels, and, at last, into the entranceway of the bleak, brick schoolhouse, which, irrationally, felt safe in its solidity. Bren, along with the others, was quickly pulled along by the tide of heedless, head-long children. He turned to her for one brief moment to wave goodbye. Reminding her of Paul.

What had life come to in this godforsaken city? Why didn't the rest of the world notice what went on here? Why wasn't something done? The insanity in Northern Ireland had become predictable, acceptable. She knew she was at fault as well as the next person. She fought for normalcy—for breakfast at the right time, for well-cooked eggs, for new pencil boxes—when she should be burning her hair and throwing her children from the rooftops in protest. The struggle for habit and stability and continuity forced you to look away from the guns and the barricades and the bombs. The endless, orderly funerals followed es-tablished custom and turned your mind from the rape of death. The rest of the world, bent on its own need for reg-ularity and sanity, revolved its face away from Belfast. Away from Beirut. Away from Biafra. And, of course, the fear kept you quiet, too.

Alone now, Elinor grimly entered the sanctuary of St. Mary's Church, aware that the morning's anger still had hold of her. The interior of the granite sanctuary glittered busily with the light of offertory candles. The smell of melting candlewax suffused the empty air. She walked past the altar of the Blessed Virgin and the agonized Crucifix-ion, heading directly to the high altar. In the plain lan-guage of her American childhood, she needed to talk to the boss. Kneeling, she tried to pray, but no prayer came. Only a silent cry:

Why did you kill my son?

I NEEDED TO THINK ABOUT MY GRAND-MOTHER.

Startled, Elinor wheeled around looking for the source of the blasphemous voice. No one. Had her grief and anger driven her mad? It was possible. She felt inexplicably drawn into the auditory hallucination.

What did you mean? About your grandmother?

SHE WAS A WOMAN WITH MANY CHILDREN, ONE OF WHOM DIED. NOT HER ELDEST. SHE SAID NO ONE COULD UNDERSTAND HER PAIN, THE LOSS OF A CHILD, EXCEPT SOMEONE WHO HAD SUFFERED IT THEMSELVES. I WANTED TO TRY TO UNDERSTAND IT, UNDERSTAND HER . . . BECAUSE I LOVED HER, I SUPPOSE. AND BECAUSE I MISS HER.

But it was my son who died, not yours.

ARE YOU SURE?

Elinor felt both confused and contrite. She thought for a moment. Was this the voice of God or the voice of insanity? Could God have a grandmother?

YES.

Was your grandmother a goddess?

I ALWAYS THOUGHT SO.

And her son died?

YES.

I'm sorry.

THANK YOU.

*Did taking my son help you? Did you come to under-
stand your grandmother better . . . feel closer to her . . .
through me?*

I DON'T THINK SO.

Elinor was suddenly filled with rage.

Then give him back! Goddamn it! Give him back to me.

BE PATIENT, ELINOR. YOU HAVE ETER-
NITY. ONLY GODS DIE FOR GOOD.

She felt the rage leave her then, making room
for a limp surrender. There were only questions
now.

*Then why, after you took my son, did you then take my
husband?*

AH. THAT IS ANOTHER STORY.

The church was silent again. She knew it would remain
so. Elinor stood up shakily and made her way up the aisle.
She felt hot with fever, eager to return to her quiet home
and her lonely bed. She thought she must be very ill. She
was about to pray, out of habit, pray that the illness would
not be serious. Then she stopped. She knew she would
never pray again. If she wasn't better by tomorrow, she
would go around to the doctor. She could not afford to be
seriously ill. She had children to care for. She was seized
by a sudden spasm of homesickness, increasing her distress. She missed her father. Perhaps it was time to tell
Callahan that Brian was dead. Perhaps it was time to give
up and sell up and go home. Would it be a betrayal to arrive on Jamie Callahan's doorstep with Brian O'Neill's children? To turn Brian's brood of tough little Irishmen into

soft, lost American kids holding Walkmans to their ears? They would be richer, of course, and so better fed. But would they be safer? She feared the streets of New York City. Maybe somewhere else, another part of the country, would be safer. In her reeling mind, she heard the sad voice from the church explaining the death of her eldest son. There is no safety, thought Elinor. There is no safety anywhere. There is only whim.

She stood before her house, seeing it as it had appeared to her since Brian's death, not as a home, not as a refuge, not as a fortress, but as a fragile shell, worn, battered, dilapidated, given to leaks and mice, standing uncertainly between her shrunken family and the enormous and violent outside world. It could be entered at will.

She went inside wearily and made herself a cup of tea. She knew she must try to think. She could not give way, this way, to delusion and depression and despair. God's grandmother was right. No one who had not themselves lost a child could understand this grief. She had lost two children. Unable as she was to raise them, she had never stopped loving them and never stopped missing them, both, but especially her daughter Elinor, with her gold-red hair.

Killing herself would not be a sin, Eve Callahan decided, though the practitioners of her ancient, suffocating religion would insist on its sinfulness. When exactly would her jump become a sin? she wondered. In the moment of her intention to die? If that was the case, she was already damned. Or sometime during the deed? Halfway down? Falling was an ancient sin. When she hit the pavement? When she died? When would she die exactly? At what moment did death begin?

Eve had decided that her fall must look like an accident. She knew too well that the practitioners of the modern religions—science and technology, the twin buttocks currently sitting on the human spirit—would soon have their way with her, carefully carving and cataloging her remains. She was certain there would be no traces of drugs or alcohol in the tissues. Let them cut and spin and study. She had been sober for days. They would find no evidence of her despair. Her suicide was to be a private act, owned only by Eve. She knew there were always people eager to lay claim to a suicide, people who would feel guilty and people who would say she did it to spite them. Some would shake their heads and some would pray. She wished she didn't care what people would think about her death. Of course, if she didn't care what people thought, she probably wouldn't be committing suicide.

She wanted to die painlessly. She had always been a physical coward. She hoped for a moment of pure transition—from this life to the next—to light or to darkness, or to whatever came. She was, ironically, optimistic about death, certain that it had to be better than life. She remembered a poem. Dorothy Parker, wasn't it? She searched through her library, still packed in boxes from her recent move, every volume a first edition, and found the small book, and then the poem itself. "Résumé," it was called:

> Razors pain you;
> Rivers are damp;
> Acids stain you;
> And drugs cause cramp.
> Guns aren't lawful;
> Nooses give;
> Gas smells awful;
> You might as well live.

Dorothy Parker was dead.

Eve leaned her forehead against the window and
looked down the twenty floors through the gray grit of
dawn. Monday. The worst day of the week. The streets
would soon be full of automatons marching off to their
deadly day. Corporate corpses who would go through
the motions of living in little booths and boxes, breathing the recycled dust that passed for air in their glass-
enclosed buildings. Prisons. Their jobs meant nothing
and their lives meant nothing. They would come home
to families that didn't relate, or to loneliness that didn't
relent. She knew about loneliness. Alone, there was no
one to blame but yourself for what you did and how you
felt. Eve had, for years, felt pushed and pulled by unseen
forces that randomly sent her soaring into esctasy or,
more often, crashing into depression. The diagnosis was
manic depression. But diagnosis, even prescription,
didn't tell you how to live, didn't explain the reason for
all the dreary business of being and becoming. She had
once hoped to forge a meaningful life in a declining
world. She had ended meanly, declining the world.

She had long supposed that her one opportunity for sat-
isfaction had rested with her children, first Elinor by
Callahan, then Jerry by God-knew-who—dead Dan Phails,
she presumed, and had so labeled him. But she had abandoned them both, her daughter and then her son, when
they had turned from mindless infants into thinking, grasp-
ing little humans. The relentless responsibilities of motherhood had overwhelmed her, had made her feel inadequate,
incompetent. They demanded so much, children, so much
more than she had to give. They did not recognize *her*
needs at all—her depressions, her insecurities. They expected her to be competent, consistent, fearless, simply
because she was their mother. Who did they think she

was? God? They didn't know her at all, and she had convinced herself they would be better off if they didn't.

It was all so long ago, those tries at normalcy, ending in flight; the flights ending in despair. She had never been able to give a single person who asked her what it was they wanted. She could give and give to those who did not ask. She considered this perverse. She could not even give herself what little she asked for herself—a moment's peace, a little happiness. She had tried. Religion, art, philosophy, meditation, marriage, motherhood, poetry, sex, drugs, and rock 'n' roll. Nothing worked. Or to be more precise, everything worked for a while. Everything began in promise and ended in hopelessness. Every daydream decays. But this was the last morning that Eve Callahan would get up from her sagging bed and put on the cactus shirt of life. Now, in the end, it was the exhaustion that prevailed, not the pain. She was just too tired to face any more future.

She slipped her wedding ring off her finger for the first time in forty years. It came off too easily, for she had grown gaunt in these last weeks, since her return to the Village. She dropped it out the window, watching the glint of gold as it fell, almost slowly. While it was still in midair, about halfway to the street, a blue jay swooped from a nearby ledge, caught it up in its beak, and carried it off. Somewhere nearby in a dense evergreen his waiting mate would ruffle her feathers and cry out happily at such a shining gift. Then she would tuck it carefully into their nest next to two tiny speckled eggs. She smiled. She hoped that God, in all His infinite uncertainty, would notice her smile in the face of a planned, determined death.

She reached into a silver dish for a chocolate and, disliking the coconut filling, dropped the bitten candy out the window, too. Unrescued, it fell all the way to the sidewalk, smacking against the cover of cement and asphalt that covered the earth. Underneath the sidewalk there was ground, earth that had, for thousands of years, held living creatures—moles and slugs and earthworms down among the roots of grasses and trees. Dinosaurs had tramped upon its mosses and deer had run along its paths. Man had gotten mud on his shoes, and so he had sealed up the offending earth in a coffin of stone. Nothing lived below the pavement now.

Eve went to the utility closet and removed a plastic bottle of Windex and a cleaning rag. She opened the window and sat on the ledge, her feet firmly on the richly designed Persian carpet inside the apartment, her torso high in the cold air. She liked it here. She imagined the drop. This would work. The conflict resolved, she sprayed and wiped the windowpanes. Then she leaned away to survey her work. She almost fell. Unbidden, a quotation from Franz Kafka popped into her mind. So it was to be Kafka, not Dorothy Parker, who would have the last word.

From a certain point onward there is no point in turning back. That is the point that must be reached.

No more bending and turning. No more ups and downs. Why should Kafka have the last word? She wondered. Shouldn't she have her own last words, even if no one would ever hear them? Eve had, long ago, written poetry. Poetry had been her childhood discovery and refuge, her continuing education, her connection to the past and to the good. It had saved her life more than once. It was natural to want to contribute to the ongoing verse. One simple, lovely, perfect poem, rich in ideas that would involve the heart and mind of others. Trouble was, she had never had an original idea in her life. All of her ideas came from books, from other people's novels, from other people's poems. Even her thoughts about unoriginality were unoriginal. Terence had said it simply enough:

Nothing has yet been said that has not been said before.

And he had said it two thousand years ago! Perhaps she should call in Luke for a quickie consultation. That man got everyone else moving. She had never let him near her. Never let him know her. He had been helpful anyhow. Just being around Luke Sevensons was soothing. It was years since she'd been soothed. No. She wouldn't call on Luke. He knew too much of her humiliations. And he loved that Indian bitch. He'd probably talk her out of jumping, and then he'd go on being peaceful while she went on being miserable. No, Eve decided stubbornly, she would perch here all alone until she thought of her own bloody last words.

The window was now very clean. Nevertheless she would sit and she would wipe until an idea came to her. Maybe she would never die. She would become a strange fixture, here on the fringe of the Village where the tall buildings began, stuck on the window ledge, waiting and wiping into eternity. She looked through the glass at the cartons holding her treasured library. Her grandchildren, whom she had never seen, would have them. Neatly wrapped. The best of gifts, from their unknown grandmother. Her last words came at last.

"Words last," she said.

The pleasure of the origination flooded her being. So this was why people lived for their art! It wasn't selfishness; it wasn't narcissism; it was rightness. It was a kind of . . .

well . . . joy. This moment was, she thought, something she could write a poem about.

Should she live? She lost her balance. She watched as her still-lovely ankles and small feet came up, up, up and then cleared the window as the back of her thighs slid effortlessly into space. The world turned head over heels and sent wind rushing by her ears. Her new challis skirt, with its collage of brilliant colors, billowed out for a moment, then dropped around her head, blocking her vision as the sounds of the city street came up to meet her—the honk of a car, the warning cries of pedestrians. All was crazily askew. In the same instant there was a subtle change in air pressure, causing Henry Chang to look up just in time to see the finale of Eve Callahan's spectacular fall, giving him only a split second to prepare himself for the horrific explosion as she hit the pavement at his feet, splattering him from head to toe with tiny spots of blood. He stood now, shaking his head over Eve who lay still and broken against the unrelenting reality that had killed her, and while Christian Davies (who had jumped away fearfully at what he imagined to be a big bag of groceries hitting the pavement a few steps behind him) felt the splash of warm liquid on the back of his pants, and wheeled around to see a shattered woman where he had expected broken pickle jars and smashed vegetables. The woman's head resembled a burst watermelon. A Windex bottle careened along the sidewalk and into the gutter. Christian's heart clutched painfully. Sharing his distress was a wizened Chinese man in red polka-dot clothing shaking his head over the body.

Christian thought he might be ill, then collecting himself, and acting from a practiced sense of responsibility, he began to direct the crowd that was gathering near the fallen form. Someone ran to telephone for the police. He knelt and took the wrist of the dead woman. As expected, there was no pulse so he began to pray. In the fold at the back of his knees he could feel the warm stickiness of blood soaking through his trousers.

This was the Reverend Christian Davies's second prayer of the morning. The first had been a prayer of thanksgiving. He had thanked God for the challenge of his work; for his delivery six months ago from the calm, suburban church on the outskirts of Seattle to the hubbub of Manhattan, so much better suited to his temperament; for God's help with the rather ferocious but rather good sermon he had delivered yesterday to his tense, now expectant congregation; for the warm expressions of approval he had received following the service; and for the beginning of a new day. This second prayer, at the end of a life, was a prayer of intercession. Christian prayed for the soul of the unknown woman, killed in a terrible accident. He knew such prayers well, for he still mourned and prayed for Grace after all these years. He wondered who this woman was and who would mourn for her. He returned the lifeless hand to the pavement and covered what was left of her face with a rag he found lying nearby.

He could hear the approach of sirens and the disturbing remarks of the onlookers who continued to gather in a circle around them. Christian looked up into their faces—some horrified, some sad, some indifferent, all morbidly curious.

The small Chinese man, eyes unreadable, stepped forward, knelt next to Christian, and spoke to him. He recognized the polka dots now as rapidly drying bloodstains that bookended his own.

"I know this woman."

"I'm sorry. It's a terrible tragedy. She must have fallen while she was cleaning the windows."

"No, I think Eve Carrahan, she jump. She saw old Jamie

Carrahan on street, first time, rong time. She vely upset. She say she been clazy woman since she reave Carrahan twenty years ago. Hurt all time. He not take her back. I say, Eve, you pay attention to old Henly Chang. I say, here is wisdom of Seng Ts'an: 'Stop talking, stop thinking, and there is nothing you will not undelstand.' Now Eve Carrahan not talking, she not thinking, but I think she still not undelstand." He shook his head again, but his expression remained impassive.

Christian thought the man might be mad.

A police car pulled up, and he stood up as two uniformed men got out. Henry Chang spoke again, this time under his breath. "We say to cops, Eve have accident, no?" Before Christian could protest, the Chinaman was bowing to the approaching officers, one fat, one thin. "Hi, Salgeant Dooney."

"Hello, Henry," greeted the heavyweight cop who was wearing a standard blue uniform. He turned to his dapper, black-suited companion. "Let me introduce my new partner, Detective Finger. This is Henry Chang. Henry runs the laundry just down the block. Knows everybody and everything in this neighborhood." Henry Chang bowed again. Sergeant Dooney, who had with one quick glance determined that the woman was dead, now looked up the side of the apartment building.

"Eve Carrahan sripped out the window."

The officer looked skeptical, but Henry had scooted to the gutter and returned with the Windex bottle, which he held triumphantly aloft.

"She vely sanitaly woman, Dooney."

"Well, maybe so, Henry . . . but . . ."

Christian stepped forward and was about to speak, but Henry cut him off.

"She Cathoric woman, Dooney."

There was a pause while they all considered the implications of this remark. The policeman nodded. "I see. Okay. Detective Finger will go upstairs and snoop around a bit. Just to be sure she wasn't pushed or anything. I'll ask these people here if they saw anything suspicious. If there's no evidence of hanky-panky, nothing to the contrary, then she fell. You call Father Mothersole."

"I go get," said the Chinaman, and hurried off.

"Perhaps I can be of some service, Sergeant Dooney," said Christian. "I'm the pastor at Old Gray Presbyterian. My name is Christian Davies."

"Did you see her fall, Reverend?"

"No. I was just passing. She fell right behind me. Right ahead of the Chinaman. No warning at all. It sounded like a bomb going off."

"You were lucky. One less step and you'd be needing yourself to speak at your funeral."

Shock, so far, had kept the knowledge of his own close call from Christian's consciousness, but with the policeman's words reality caught up with him and he felt his knees go weak. He knelt.

"If you don't mind staying with the body till the priest gets here . . . you okay, Reverend?"

"Yes, yes, of course."

Christian watched the black-and-blue police team go about their duties with nonchalance. This was New York City. Something was wrong here.

Yea, though I walk through the valley of the shadow of death I will fear no evil for thou art with me. . . .

Buff, his arm thrown over the peacefully sleeping canine, cried softly and tried to remember the ancient psalm for the comfort of it. He had not slept well in this new place.

Yesterday Katelyn had taken him around the apartment, larger and newer than the one from which he had fled, the one that Quentin had recently abandoned. Buff had counted and memorized the steps from room to room and found his clothing carefully hung in the spare closet. In the kitchen he had been touched to find that Quentin had placed all the utensils and condiments in the same order that Buff had learned in the old place—a clear sign that Quentin still hoped for Buff's return. Katelyn, of course, had assured him of Quentin's love and loyalty, but the careful arrangement of their day-to-day items was an unseen, deeply felt message between the two men.

Katelyn had gone out shopping for Buff and brought in fresh fruit and vegetables and dog food for Greta and milk from the nearby Korean grocery, and she had stayed with him into the afternoon, talking and raging and crying about Nelson and AIDS and her son, Amas.

"He was last seen in Milwaukee, Buff. He's rumored to be married and he has a child. I don't even know if it's a boy or a girl."

"Our Katelyn—a grandmother."

"He still won't talk to me. What did I do that was so wrong? I tried to raise him with feelings. What do we mothers do to our sons? He's like Victor, even at his best, and like Nelson at his worst."

Amas Wells had left home when his mother had left his father, Buff knew, and he was secretly fascinated with the boy and with his quest. Amas had been eighteen at the time, and when he left his broken home, he had no idea where he was going, so he started walking north, and then west, following the perimeter of his country. What had begun as running away from home in a blinding rage had in time become a way of life.

The walking of man and all animals is a falling forward.

He, like Emerson, had discovered that he loved walking.
The simple, repetitive movement of one foot following the
other—now sad, now joyous, now tired, now strong—had
become his ritual, his sacred dance, his meditation. Five
years had passed in the practice of his strange religion.
The only distraction to his peace of mind was the ever-
present trash. To throw trash onto the roadside seemed to
Amas the equivalent of defacing a painting or smashing a
sculpture. Most Americans heaved out their beer cans and
cigarette packages without a thought, creating a garbage
heap to live and travel through. He had tried carrying garbage bags for a while, filling them as he went, but there
was too much trash for a man to clear even his own path.
Now, as he walked, he pondered the refuse. What sort of
people did he live among?

Amas had arrived in Milwaukee, Wisconsin, and as he
strolled along a stretch of quiet riverbank, he decided it
wasn't a half-bad city. There was a lot of land given over
to parks and the cold, blue lake licked all along the edge
of the cream-colored shore. He thought he might stay
here for a while with his infant son and his wife,
Illuminada, though not for long. The road lay seductively
before them.

He had met Illuminada while he was trudging through
Hammond, Indiana, in the rain. She had offered him a lift
in a beat-up Pontiac, and when he explained that he only
traveled on foot, she drove slowly along beside him, jok-
ing and talking, until they began to fall in love. He had
had a series of flirtations along the roadside with young,
metal-enclosed, rubber-wheeled women who were attracted to the handsome and weathered stranger. He had

lost his virginity in a Chevrolet near Bangor, Maine, and had, most recently, been gymnastically entertained by two cheerleaders inside a hot, red Toyota near Ashtabula, Ohio. Illuminada had driven back to her home at the end of their talk and he assumed he would see no more of her. But the next day, and a few miles along the road, she was back behind the wheel, offering him orange juice and conversation.

YOU ARE NOW LEAVING HAMMOND, INDIANA, said the metal sign, mottled with the BBs of local marksmen. Illuminada had parked her car behind the sign, slammed the door with a sense of finality, and joined Amas on foot. She had packed a backpack. He liked that: the mixture of spontaneity and careful planning. She held up well until the seventh month of her pregnancy and then insisted on resting until their son, Walker, arrived, feetfirst into the journey that would be his life.

Amas wondered what Walker Wells would make of his parents' gypsy life-style. He would begin by accepting it, of course, knowing no other; but in a few years he would begin to wonder at the unmoving houses filled with their fixed residents. By adolescence he would rebel and fall in love and, holding firmly to the hand of some stationary local woman, he would watch his parents wander off into the distance. Then he would put down deep roots where he stood—into the red clay of Louisiana or the sandy soil of Florida's Gulf Coast—and he would never budge again. "Old Walker Wells," the locals would say. "Don't know where he came from, but he never sets foot outside the county."

Amas chuckled at his fantasy. Children were seldom like their parents, he had noticed. Practically every pastor had a poet for a son, every poet a businessman, every businessman a musician, and so on and so on until the earth was properly peopled with all variety of rebel and its population was again restored to the right number of pastors. He, for instance, though encouraged in the arts by both his parents, couldn't paint a picture or dance the two-step. He could not stand to hear a line of poetry, which he associated with every manner of suffering and sadness. His mother's verse had lacerated his adolescence, and he was grateful now just to be out of earshot. Would they ever reconcile? Mom and Dad? He and Mom? He had vowed not to return to New York City until he had walked through his disappointment and come out the other side of his anger. That time had not yet come, though the birth of Walker made him wonder what all the unhappiness was for. Katelyn, he knew, would love her grandchild. Doubtless Walker would love Katelyn. It was not to be. Not yet. Maybe by North Dakota.

. . .

"You have a grandson, Katelyn."

"A boy? How do you know, Buff?"

"Luke told me."

"Is Luke omnipotent?"

"He's been in touch with Amas, or rather Amas has been in touch with Luke, since Cleveland."

Buff shrugged, watching Katelyn turn even this reassuring news into sadness. He loved Katelyn in all her melancholy moods, of which she had more than anyone else, but he was exhausted when she finally left him alone in the new apartment. Later his dreams had been filled with foreboding as he wandered in a landscape of cold, sharp shapes, pressed against them with ungloved hands.

He could tell by the sounds of the city that it was now dawn, and he was scared and he was lonely and he was feeling a little ill. He wanted Quentin.

Telephone calls had gone out, of course, and Quentin

had been located in Rome. He was returning from Italy to-day, arriving tonight. Whenever Buff thought of their re-union, he cried, for it would be a mixed blessing, a joyful, terrible occasion. Buff would have to tell his lover the dev-astating news that they had not escaped the curse of their kind—the debilitating, life-destroying illness that had cut a swath through the life they had once known, felled their friends one by one, and left them living in a limbo of fear, now realized.

He had lost his mind when he first heard the diagnosis, for he loved life and he loved Buff and he was a doomed man now. He had boarded the returning Alitalia flight without a flicker of regret, though he had only arrived in Rome the day before yesterday. For the last six months Quentin had lived in perpetual fear that he would never see Buff again. What a thrilling mix of elation and anger and relief and longing had surged within him when he had heard Katelyn's voice calling across the seas, "Buff and Greta are home, Quentin. Come back, come back." She went on to say that Buff had been living with Luke Sevensons. How absurd that they hadn't told him! Surely Luke wasn't gay. No. That wasn't possible. Quentin was certain that Luke was as straight as an arrow. What had possessed Buff to go into hiding?

Quentin had suffered profoundly from his lover's sud-den, unexplained disappearance the previous autumn. He had worried about an accident. Buff's blindness led to a world of dark imaginings. Then, as the days passed with-out news, he thought that Buff might have committed suicide, though there was little in Buff's day-to-day cheer-fulness to support the idea. As the months went by with no word and no body, he had finally entertained the no-tion that Buff had eloped with another lover. But why had they kept him in the dark? The cruelty of it! He would find out soon enough. He knew, in spite of the agony that he had endured, that he had already forgiven Buff. This was a time when they must both rush to forgive. Tonight he would hold Buff in his arms. Then, of course, he must break his sickening news.

Last December Quentin Cox had fought his way through the first feverish bout of pneumonia. No one knew that he had AIDS, except Henry Chang, who had brought him newspapers and wizened, useless advice while he was in the hospital. Everyone else had assumed he was out of town for the Christmas holidays. At present he was in relatively good health, but he knew another bout of sickness could strike at any moment. Together he and Buff would have to face the terrifying double tragedy of this disease—that Buff would get sick, too. Which of them had contracted the virus first? he wondered. Although they had been a couple for . . . what was it . . . twenty years now . . . they had each had occasional escapades outside their union, he more than Buff, of course. It was harder for a blind man to cruise.

Just last night he had enjoyed the comfort of a lonesome, young Italian who professed to be a Muslim and called himself Mullahboy. Quentin had no interest in sex anymore. Safe sex, they called it. Plastic sex, it felt like. But he liked to hold and be held. Buff would be pissed when he found out about Mullahboy. They were usually discreet with one another about such matters, revealing their erotic exploits only in moments of pique that added a high drama to their infrequent arguments. But Mullahboy sat beside Quentin now, evidencing a substantial amount of nervousness about the impending flight.

Mullahboy had insisted that Allah in his infinite wisdom had called him to New York City to nurse Quentin during his last illness—and Quentin's lover, too, if and when Buff got sick. Otherwise, explained Mullahboy in outrageous English, he would be forced to stay in Rome and shoot the pope—his other Allah-appointed mission. It had seemed to Quentin the lesser of two evils to bring the boy along in the hope that he would straighten himself out. He had bought the airline tickets with a guess that Mullahboy would disappear before the baggage arrived at JFK, or possibly *with* the baggage at JFK, never to be seen again. That was okay. Quentin had found that along with sex, he had lost interest in clothes, in personal items, in all manner of *things*.

He still worried about money. Would there be enough between them to see them out? Fortunately he and Buff were both well insured. He hoped for a little humanity on the part of doctors and hospitals. They would need it. God, which of them would die first? He hoped it would be Buff. Then Quentin, if he wasn't too ill, could nurse him through; not leave him to die alone in darkness. Who would look after Greta Garbo?

"The plane ees to go up now? Capish? Mamma mia, Santa Lucia."

"*Si*, Mullahboy. It's all right. Just a big noise." And he would have taken the boy's hand, but a stewardess was nearby, making her last seat-belt check, so he gave him a playful, masculine punch on the shoulder instead. God-damn it, he thought, making a vow that in the next life he would kiss any angel he saw, right on the chops, regardless of sex. Did angels have sex? he wondered.

As the plane taxied down the runway Quentin encouraged his mind to conjure up happier times: when he had starred on Broadway, when he had run the New York City Marathon, when he was strong and well. He was glad the stewardess had passed out of view, for Mullahboy had gripped his hand in horror as the plane began to move. Quentin wondered how Mullahboy, fresh and foreign, saw him. Quentin was a good-looking man, he knew, always thin, now thinner, with light blond hair graying gently over a broad forehead and smiling eyes. He had a strong jawline. Women thought him handsome and, when they found out he was gay, sighed deeply and arranged to become his friend.

He had many true friends, even now, after so many deaths. How would they take the news? Arista Bellefleurs and Clayton Grant and Katelyn Wells and Katelyn's son, Amas, and Jerry Phails, who still talked about singing again, and Florian Agincourt, an astronomer who had discovered a new comet and was waiting to hear if it would carry his name, and George Eliot Isaman, forever at work on the first line of his classic, epic novel, and Buff—dear, unsighted, insightful Buff.

A friend should bear his friend's infirmities.

He sighed. Quentin had played a mean Brutus, a respectable Hamlet, and a dynamite Iago. He had been good enough to overcome the prejudice against gay men harbored by most directors, and had often landed the plummier Shakespearean roles. He sighed. He would never play Macbeth now, let alone King Lear.

Well, he and Buff had borne each other's infirmities for over two decades. Now they had his AIDS and, possibly, Mullahboy to bear. Would Buff be changed? He couldn't have lived with Luke Sevensons all that time and not be changed. Perhaps they should arrange to die together, like Romeo and Juliet, but without the mistakes. Or maybe, God willing, though he didn't believe in God, there would be a cure. He hugged Greta Garbo close to him like hope itself and drifted back to sleep for a few minutes, awaking with a start from a morning dream in which he could see.

During the past six months Luke had taught him to see. Only in his *mind's* eye, for his two real eyes had been destroyed by an overdose of oxygen in the incubator on the day of his birth. This was Buff's first sighted dream—a tall tree, with perfectly fan-shaped branches. The leaves of the tree were what Buff imagined green might be, but in their centers they were red. The entire tree was glowing in the light of a golden sun. Burning without being consumed. How did he know what light was? Buff awoke in a sweat, wondered if he was dead, realized he was alive. Greta Garbo stirred and yawned and stretched beside him. Time to get up.

He made his way to the window to take the benefit of the early-morning breeze. Looking down, he noticed a small cluster of people standing around what appeared to be a woman lying in a peculiar position like a discarded doll or piece of fallen statuary. Was she ill? There was something familiar about her. He recognized Father Mothersole from Our Lady hurrying toward the crowd. Henry Chang was with him. The priest knelt down next to an already kneeling figure and they appeared to exchange a few words.

Clayton Grant brushed the drying clay from his hands and leaned farther out the window for a better view. A police car had drawn up over the curb. It was then that Clayton realized that the woman on the sidewalk had fallen or jumped. He looked upward at the apartment building across the way until he saw the wide-open windows near the twentieth floor. My God, he realized, it was his new-found friend, Eve Callahan! And she was surely dead.

Or so she thought, for she had sailed right through the sidewalk, leaving her body on the cement like discarded clothing, and she had found herself falling, falling through the earth, like a diver through deep water, until she realized she could float back up to the surface, where events were in full swing, and so she did.

She sparkled in the dawn air just over her corpse. People seemed to be making quite a fuss: Father Mothersole, the police, strangers, Henry Chang, and some sort of Protestant clergyman who was down on his knees. What was his name? It came to her. Christian Davies.

But she found she wasn't much interested, so she floated farther up and recognized Clayton Grant glaring down from his studio across the street, and on the floor below him a blind man with a dog was taking no notice of the spectacle she had made of herself. So this was what came next. It hadn't hurt at all.

Amazing, she thought, which was an extremely pleasurable experience, involving her whole self in an act of self-creation, for she was pure psyche now. She flew about for a while. No wings. Bit of a disappointment, that. She brushed thoughts with those of the clergymen huddled below. Why, they were prayers for her! How nice. She noticed Clayton forming a bad idea for a sculpture based on the position of her body. She had sensed the possibility that Clayton was talented when they had met for the first time, such a short time ago, but she couldn't have imagined she would become his model. The blind fellow was worried. Oh. He was dying. She wafted closer, hoping to reassure him with her own experience, and saw him relax a little as what he took to be a mystical idea entered his consciousness. This was wonderful. She didn't hurt anywhere. She wasn't anxious or angry or pained or depressed or helpless or hopeless or sorrowful or confused or homesick or disgusted or repelled or regretful or fearful or any of the repertoire of emotions that had made up her life.

Still, somehow, she was Eve, she thought. Again the shiver of ecstasy. All feeling, no form. All *good* feelings:

pleasure, excitement, curiosity, love, joy, happiness, confidence, hope, relaxation, humor, well-being, bliss. What had she ever done to deserve this? Wasn't she supposed to burn in hell or something?

"No. That's a dumb idea." It was a nearby idea speaking.

"Who are you?" she asked before she realized that she knew.

"Grace Davies."

"The preacher down there—he belongs to you?"

"So far. He clings to my memory like a sloth to a tree branch. I've been trying to free him up for years. I've even found a companion for him. Arista Bellefleurs. Did you know her?"

"No. But I think Clayton mentioned her once. I was only back in the Village briefly before I fell."

"Want to visit her? She's an interesting being. A writer."

"Do we have time?"

"What a strange question."

"Well, I assume that all this is some kind of hallucination while my brain cells are dying."

"If that's what you want it to be." She had the sense that Grace had shrugged, though there was nothing of her to shrug. "Why not assume something a little more life affirming?"

"Where exactly are we?"

"Still in the Country of the Great King. Different perspective."

"The Country of the Great King?"

"Yes. The designated dimension for everything that's ever been created. Like us, or the world we were just watching. If you look over there"—she indicated a direction between left and right, one that Eve had never noticed before—"you can see Hamlet, and Winnie the Pooh, and Raskolnikov. They're a great bunch. Music is right

here, of course. What do you like?" Before Eve could answer, a *Brandenburg Concerto* (her favorite) flooded the air.
"Paintings and sculpture stay where they've been put unless
they've been destroyed. Then they're here." She indicated
another new direction. "There's Michelangelo's *Pietà*, *before*
the lunatic hit it with the cudgel. Michelangelo has positioned it himself."

Eve felt pleasantly discombobulated, like a tourist arriving in Venice for the first time. "Who's the Great King?"

"Oh, you know, God."

"God?"

"YES?" A very powerful presence was suddenly all
around her, and benignly attentive. She felt a surge of
love, overwhelming in its intensity.

"I don't think I'm ready for this yet." The presence vanished. Grace hovered close by, amused.

"He's like all talented artists. He takes some getting used
to. By the way, Eve, everyone in the Country of the Great
King has a vocation. I'm sorry you couldn't see yours from
the surface of the earth. We're parts of a magnificent work-
in-progress and we're all called upon to perfect it. It's easier
to glimpse the overall idea from this angle, though God
only knows the grand scheme in its entirety. He's working
in mixed mediums: time, space, movement, materiality,
spirituality, light and darkness, life and death, good and
evil, all at one go. At present He's doing a lot of experi-
menting with changed perspectives. Fortunately His mate-
rials are in infinite supply, and He can afford them. You'll
be able to accomplish much more of your own work as an
angel. Of course, you don't have to remain in this form.
You can transform at will."

"To what?"

"Well, sometimes I become water and I rain for a while
where it's most needed, that sort of thing. Or you can

move on to another life, or sleep for a few centuries, or disperse into light. But if you stay with us, in this era, I promise you there's plenty to do. Everyone down there needs a visitation now and then. Especially as most of the educated people have become atheists."

"Won't *they* be surprised when they die and see this place?"

"No. They'll never see it. People go where they expect to go. You thought whatever-came-next would be better than life, so you're here. Atheists don't go anywhere."

"Where do the agnostics go?"

"Your guess is as good as mine."

Eve was glad that God had noticed her smile. "I think I'm ready to visit Arista Bellefleurs now," she transmitted to Grace.

"Can I come, too, Grandma?"

"Who is that?"

"I'm Paul. Paul O'Neill, your grandson. I'm so glad to have some family nearby. Dad won't leave Belfast. We'll have such fun."

"A grandson? Here? Elinor's son, it must be. Oh, I have never been so happy. Of course you can come. What do we do?"

"I'll show you." And humming like happy children, they swept off to work a few wonders.

"Here we are," said Grace.

"Here I am," said Arista, and then woke up. She let the silver light of dawn peek through her eyelids. The sound of the dream song continued to run through her mind, a hokey-worded, beautiful-sounding hymn from yesterday's service.

> God, that madest earth and heaven, darkness and light,
> Who the day for toil hast given, for rest, the night,

May thine angel guards defend us, slumbers sweet
Thy mercy send us;
Holy dreams and hopes attend us, all through the night.

Surely *madest* wasn't a real word. As a writer, she found it hard to tolerate the lyrics, but the ancient Welsh melody was seductive. The rest of the dream was fading fast, but there had been angels in it again, and she knew that Christian Davies had been central as well. She felt wonderful. She loved falling in love. When poetry failed, when a good modern novel could not be found, and a good classic novel could not be faced, Arista's life felt empty. Unless she was in love. She depended on love. One love could enhance another. A new love could help her through the loss of old love. There were always the losses.

Throughout her adult life Arista had searched for a man who was her equal. Sex was better among equals. Sometimes, rarely, she found one. They were lately, it seemed, inevitably, married; which, when she cared to think about it, made them unequal, for these men assumed a portion of their wholeness, of their complexity, of their strength and solidity, from their wives. Their unbalanced affairs always ended in dissatisfaction, and Arista sustained the losses. She had been accused of only being attracted to unavailable men. It was an absurdly simpleminded accusation. Availability was not the issue. She responded to men who made her feel more alive.

There would be time enough to be dead, she thought. Twice, in her youth, she had located unmarried specimens. So she had married them. The ideas of marriage— monogamy, privacy, fidelity, even social acceptance—had once been exciting. Twice, been exciting. The actuality of each event had been stultifying. Jason she seldom remembered. Marxie she preferred not to remember. Those two catastrophes were losses of a different order.

Now she was being pulled toward loss again. She didn't know how she would lose Christian Davies, given that she had not as yet gained him, but lose him she would. It was written.

Yesterday morning, after the service, Arista had jostled her way into the reception at the church house, sipping at warm, watery coffee, aware that the process gave her a pinched Presbyterian look around the mouth. Surprisingly, she found herself too shy to speak to the man who was the center of everyone's attention. She knew instantly that she did not belong to this flock, to these odd birds—the tall darting deacons, the pot-bellied elders, the bald-headed ushers—wearing their Sunday plumage and beaky smiles as they cooed and flapped around the Reverend Christian Davies. Could this man with all his poetry belong among them? Arista was in the habit of garnering her share of attention, but among the fine feathered fowls of Old Gray Presbyterian she had played the peahen, and had not come to Christian's notice. His ability to induce in her such uncharacteristic shyness increased the appetite of her interest.

Today, pleasantly preoccupied with the current menu, she wandered around the Village, ending up at the Caffe degli Artisti, where she had some real coffee, thick and strong. And then sat, wondering what possessed a man to become a preacher. Some weakness in his reason? Some strength in his soul? Weren't souls just a construction, like a poem, made up out of the collected memories of one's self? Later in the day she would have some real wine. The Presbyterians, like the Methodists, drank grape juice at Holy Communion, which Arista found bloodless, sacrilegious even. If you're going to do it, she thought, do it.

Christ showed no fear of fermentation. She wondered
what Christian Davies drank in private. She wondered if
he could talk about anything except religion. Surely he
must. He had quoted Yeats. She wondered what he did
when he was on vacation. And she wondered what he was
like in bed. She wondered if he was corruptible, and then,
if she was salvageable.

Clayton Grant found her at the table, as he often did in
the late mornings, and an afternoon of lovemaking
loomed. To the surprise of them both, she declined. He
tried to hide his disappointment by telling her of his newest idea for a sculpture—bronze, he thought—a woman
fallen from a building with three men bending over her
body, too late to be of any help. That sounded about right
to Arista.

"Grim, Clayton."

"I saw the scene this morning."

"A fallen woman? The Village is full of them."

"No, really fallen. But I think she was a suicide."

"Oh."

"I knew her . . . a little. I liked her . . . a lot. Her name
was Eve Callahan."

"What was she like?"

"She was a woman who led with her mouth and jaw,"
he replied. Arista was always amused by his sculptor's descriptions. He continued: "Her mouth was always held
slightly open so she could begin speaking without changing her expression, the voice, hoarse and deep, coming from the back of her throat. It could give you quite a
start. Her eyes were hidden behind thick glasses, making
sight a secondary sense. That gave her a tentative, doglike
walk, as if she was sniffing her way through life, but by
her expression she didn't like what she was smelling. She
had interesting architecture, solid, yet curved from the

waist up as though she was protecting her middle parts from assault. Good legs. And she was a tough, old survivor. She had just moved back to the Village from San Francisco in search of an old lover or an old husband or something."

"You're not old. How did she find you?"

"Henry Chang thought I would be good for her."

"That perennial pimp! Doesn't he know you're taken?"

"Not this afternoon, it seems," he said wistfully.

She took his strong, stone-hardened hand, noticed the clay beneath his fingernails, the mark of his artistry, the closest of all the arts to the earth. "Forgive me. I'm just in a black mood." She wondered how Christian's white hands would feel. She noticed how old her own hands had become.

"Do you ever feel really bad? I mean, would you ever consider killing yourself?"

"Disinclined, Clay. Not suicidal."

"No. Seriously. I can't imagine wanting to kill myself."

"You are overly fond of yourself, my dear. Most people feel despairing enough sooner or later to think about suicide. I have. More than once."

"Surely not. There is always something to live for, though we can't always see what it is."

"Not if there isn't a mirror handy, sometimes if there is."

"Seriously—"

"I am serious, Clayton. You're too young and too straightforward to know about despair."

"But surely there is always something to love or something to do."

Sometimes his youth taxed Arista's spirit. "If you are truly in despair, Clayton, loving and doing are little else than two versions of predictable hell."

A disheveled-looking man, dubbed Headstone Brown

by the Village denizens, walked solemnly into the café, stopped, looked at Arista with curiosity, and abruptly sat down on the floor in a posture of absolute dejection.

"What's the matter, Headstone?"

Headstone, who only spoke in epitaphs, told her. "He saw American television of a morning, and died a careless viewer's death."

Headstone Brown plucked a flower from the bud vase on Arista's table and, holding it upright on his chest, lay flat and quiet until the manager came by.

"What do you think did this to him today?"

"My bet would be *Guiding Light.*"

The manager roused Headstone with difficulty and moved him on. Arista slipped him a five-dollar bill as he left the café.

"Do you think you should encourage him?" asked Clayton.

"He should have been a court jester," she replied. "He was born after his time."

"Well, the Muses *will* gather," exclaimed a deeper, rougher, masculine voice. They looked up into the swarthy, smiling face of George Eliot Isaman. "Here we all are: the sculptor and the scribes. All we need is a painter. Or perhaps a musician. Let's look serious and dissipated and see who we attract."

"George! Where have you been?" Arista was delighted at the interruption; Clayton, mildly disgruntled.

"Digging in the ditches of pedestrian prose. Welding and riveting my sentence structures. Screwing together and nailing down the most trenchant of paragraphs, one by weary one. And, *voilà,* as a result of this ceaseless, sweating labor, I've completed my next tome for the common man."

"Entitled?"

"*Murder on Fourteenth Street*. It just sends shivers up your spine, doesn't it?"

"You've got to be kidding."

"Would I lie? I have to do something to support myself while I write my masterpiece. It's better than waiting on tables."

"Is it?"

"No, Actually." Arista was certainly in high color today, he noted. The flush in her cheeks added to her beauty. Something was up with her. And Clayton looked down-in-the-mouth as usual. Had Arista found another man? Or finally recognized his own virtues? George knew that Arista was fond of him, but never considered him for romance. Clayton didn't care for him, but he didn't know why. "Did you hear that Buff Carrington is back in town?" he asked. "As it turns out, he wasn't dead after all. He was only doing time with Luke Sevensons, putting his spiritual house in order."

"Does Quentin know?" This, surprisingly, from Clayton.

"Quentin is flying back from Rome today. Katelyn Wells told me. I found her walking about the streets, weeping as usual."

"I thought she was drier since she decided to marry the illustrious Lester."

"Doesn't appear so." The men of their group often discussed Katelyn's melancholy. She supposed Katelyn made them feel ineffectual. Their talk made Arista feel uneasy. She wondered what they said about her when her back was to them.

"Surely Nelson Little hasn't hurt her *again?*"

"Yeah. Apparently she arranged a secret meeting with him, and his sadism had aged over the last five years like strong cheese." George shrugged sadly. "She carries a tune a long time, our Katelyn."

"A *tune?* It's a goddamn requiem Mass."

"I think she's in a competition with the Statue of Liberty for how long one woman can carry a torch." He ordered some wine and Clayton began to make leaving motions.

"Don't go, Clay. We haven't attracted our painter yet."

"I've begun a new project. I need to spend some time alone making the preliminary sketches." Clayton wasn't sure why he didn't like George. Perhaps it was the affected name, or the perfect fit of his clothing. Clayton always dressed for work: overalls, jeans, T-shirts. His young, fit body wore them well, and they announced his artistic seriousness to the older and larger world. George's clothes were too neat, too expensive, too tailored for seriousness. If he was going to look like a businessman, he should work for IBM, thought Clayton uncharitably. "I have to get back to the studio."

"He's taken a dead woman as his model."

"Then why hurry? Surely she'll keep fresh in this snappy weather. Anyone I know?"

"Eve Callahan."

George looked stricken. "Oh, my God. She was a pal from the early days. I had heard that she was back in our territory after years in San Francisco. What will this do to Jamie?"

"Who's Jamie?"

"He's just the sort of painter we're looking for to complete our charmed circle: realistic, imaginative, narrative, and damned good."

"Jamie Callahan? I love his work," mused Arista. "I'd like to meet him."

"His ex-wife just killed herself, Arista. Surely that should be some kind of warning to you."

"Nobody knows for sure if she killed herself." Clayton found himself defending his new, dead friend. "She may have fallen."

"Henry Chang would know."

"He's closed today."

"I wonder what that old egg roll does when he closes."

"He writes to his grandmother."

"Is she immortal? Henry Chang is eighty if he's a day."

George shrugged. "He says she's a very humble old woman living in Shanghai, who, in her youth, radically changed the course of human history by dropping a teapot."

"How?"

"He doesn't say."

Clayton had grown more and more restless as the conversation rambled. Early on, the mention of Quentin Cox and his imminent return had bothered him. He had been trying to deny the disquiet ever since. Quentin had recently moved into the loft just below his studio, and to Clayton's consternation he had begun to have dreams about Quentin. Erotic dreams. And as he had never thought of himself as gay, nor ever had a homosexual experience (the idea of which in waking life he found repulsive), the dreams were extremely disturbing. He had, after all, Arista, his beautiful and accomplished mistress, as his claim to a place in the normal, heterosexual, sensual world. The straight world. He surreptitiously enjoyed an occasional, delicious tryst with one of his young models. Women. The dreams must be symbolic, he reassured himself, of anger or hunger or change. The 1990s was not the decade to discover he was living inside a closet; it was not the right time for sexual experimentation. A guy could get himself killed.

The image of Eve Callahan's broken body came back to him. He must make something of it, something of beauty, or those lifeless limbs, all at the wrong angles, would haunt him. He wished Arista would come home

with him and make love. He had been in love with Arista
for several years. He thought a love affair with her might
increase his ability to write a great—really great—novel.
But it seemed a forlorn hope. In the meantime he
cranked out the same dismal paperback junk. He couldn't
go deep enough into the mire that was his mind. He had
tried everything for inspiration: music, drugs, sex. Last
month in desperation he had opened the Bible, closed
his eyes, and stabbed his finger blindly into the holy
text, deciding to take whatever passage he hit upon as a
sign. It read:

Judas went forth and hanged himself.

Bowed, but unbroken, George had tried again. Another
page, another stab. It read:

Go thee forth and do likewise.

It appeared that God, like Arista, was not to be his
muse.

He had taken as his pen name—for the classic he knew
was somewhere inside him—George Eliot Isaman. Trashy
books like *Murder on Fourteenth Street* he wrote under his real
name, George Ernest Cheetwell, a name he regarded as fit
for an insurance salesman in Grimes, Kentucky, whence he
had sprung.

Arista Bellefleurs, he knew, was a pen name, too, but he
didn't know her real name. She was a woman of few, well-
chosen words, but many vivid emotions. He thought of
her as a treasure, who, like himself, had somehow surfaced
out of the furrowed Midwestern soil, but he didn't know
from where exactly. She didn't encourage inquiries. What
was she hiding? Or who was she hiding from? He felt she

disapproved of his hack writing. Actually *he* disapproved of it and figured that everyone else he respected would do so, too.

Quentin Cox, who would not even recognize his pen name, had come right out and said, "Cheetwell, you're ruining yourself, and if you don't stop dishing out the drivel, you'll never be able to write anything but." Leave it to a fairy to put it to you straight. Quentin had quoted Jesus at him for Christ's sake!

> If you bring forth what is within you, what is within you will heal you. If you do not bring forth what is within you, what you do not bring forth will destroy you.

In his innermost being George knew the Gnostic exhortation to be true.

Still, every time one of his new books arrived on the revolving racks of the Grimes Variety Mart, his mother wrote to say how proud she felt. There would be an announcement in the local papers. Grimes, Kentucky, would collectively scratch their minimal heads and wonder about the skinny Cheetwell kid who had been so out of step back in high school, and now wrote the kind of books that your ditzy aunt Mitzi read on the bus to Poughkeepsie. Royalty checks appeared in his mailbox regularly. From time to time there was excited talk of a movie offer, the money from which, if one ever went through, would certainly set him free to write his great book. So he kept on with what he was writing—writing what his publisher called *product*—knowing it wasn't any good. He was sure Arista Bellefleurs had never experienced this variety of despair, though she wrote sexual desperation quite wonderfully.

He had always wanted to write, but whenever he faced a typewriter, it seemed to challenge him, to wait with the question "Do you *really* have anything unique or important to convey? Anything more than can be said in a Sunday sermon? Do you even have enough stuff in you for a homily, week after relentless week?" Yes, that he could do.

But what Christian preached on Sunday mornings was only a footnote to the word of God. He knew his craft. He could construct a reasonably good sermon—an acceptable theme, a tie-in with the scripture lesson, a dash of humor, a punch at the end—with his eyes closed. But long ago he had begun to rely on, and be thankful for, grace. For usually the message was sent through him. He was renowned for his sermons. They were inspired.

For years he had lived in taut relationship to Sunday mornings, waiting for the words, wondering if they would arrive in time, working them into his mind when they did, spilling them out into the ears of his congregation with a joyful heart. It was his favorite twenty minutes, the center of his week. But lately a mild dissatisfaction had come over him. He wanted to write more than a sermon. He wanted to write something personal and profound. He wanted to write a book. A great book that would carry him into the generations to follow. A novel? An autobiography? A scholarly text on some facet of the Christian calling? He could not bring himself to begin. No words came to him.

He had mentioned his desire to write to an elderly gentleman with whom he had shared a train compartment on a long, slow journey from Erie, Pennsylvania, where he had gone as a visiting preacher. Christian never flew. The old man had boarded in Albany for the last leg of the trip into Grand Central Station. He had worn a turquoise charm on a golden chain around his neck, but otherwise

appeared quite ordinary. Somehow they had never ex-
changed names, but they had entered into one of those curiously intimate conversations that occur between strangers
traveling together on trains. The focus had been on Christian's life, for the man had taken an unusual interest in his
religious calling and in his personal problems. Most people
shied away from ministers, either in awe of their spiritual
strength (if they happened to be believers), or in pity for
their intellectual weakness (if they were not). This fellow
was different.

"It's a hard time for preachers, isn't it?" he had asked.

"In this country, yes," Christian concurred. "Ministers of
the Lord are not in fashion, except among the fundamentalists, and the fundamentalists are an ignorant lot. They
give us all a bad name. No, this is an era of gurus and psy-
chologists. Self-help books, support groups, too. Look at
this list from the Erie newspaper." He passed over the
newspaper.

"You'll have to read it to me," said the old man. "Since
my last cornea operation—it was not successful, the doctors tell me—I live in a rather beautiful but hazy world."

"Oh. Yes. Excuse me." The way the man spoke, with
quiet acceptance, precluded condolences. Christian took
the newspaper back and read aloud. "Now, here the list begins with the standard Alcoholics Anonymous meetings,
and their splinter group, Adult Children of Alcoholics—
you understand, I support these organizations?" The man
nodded. Christian continued: "Here is the rival to the last,
the Dysfunctional Families Support Group, then comes
Cancer Care, the MS support group, three for AIDS—
one for gay men, one straight group, and another for
people who know people with AIDS—then there's the
Colostomy-Iliostomy group, and the Wounded Child
Within group; here's one for parents who may batter their

children, and one for the children who get battered, then Gamblers Anonymous, Drugs Anonymous, Cocaine No More, a midnight meeting for insomniacs, Women Against Drunk Drivers, two meetings for trance channelers, one for crystal healers, then a multiple listing from The Lighthouse for all their activities—oh, here's a group meeting for people with cornea-transplant problems." The old man chuckled. "There's more, but certainly you have gotten the gist. The list goes on and on. I don't know what all this huddling together signifies, actually. But people need sustenance. They're looking, and seeking, and meeting to share their problems. That seems all well and good. But for a reason I don't understand, this list disturbs rather than comforts."

"I think these people are searching for wisdom."

"But are they looking in meaningful places, or only into each other's ignorance? What has happened to the pursuit of knowledge? To reverence for the wisdom of the past? For ancient truth? I worry. Especially about the young people. I was taught to listen to my elders, that the lessons of their life experience were gifts passed along to me. And I did. And they were. Even the little phrases, the sayings that people fell back on in times of conflict were wholesome: 'A stitch in time saves nine,' or 'Waste not want not,' or 'A penny saved is a penny earned,' 'It's better to have loved and lost than never to have loved at all.' Valuable, in their small way. But youngsters today are brought up on 'Once a week, Drāno in every drain,' and 'Coke is it.' Every television series tells them that life is exciting only in its moments of criminality or illness or accident, and so every news program is replete with rape and murder. No one tells them that the meaning of life—life's wonder and its glory—is found in the contemplation of it, in thought, in moments of compassion and tender love." He paused. "Why, I'm going on just like a preacher, aren't I?"

The old man smiled and, with a nod of his head, encouraged Christian to continue.

"What chance have these young people got? Why, I talked with a young man in my study the day before I left Seattle. That was my parish before I was called to Greenwich Village. The boy had no idea how to grow up. He wasn't bad or crazy. He was just lost among his peers. He had no grandparents living nearby to talk to him; his parents were caught up in their careers. The media—the substitute for culture these days—told him he should know everything already anyway. Yet he knew he knew nothing."

"What did you tell him?"

"Rule youth well, and age will rule itself."

"That's a Celtic proverb."

"Why, yes, it is. He didn't know what I meant, of course, so I went on a bit—just common sense—told him to keep the right and the good before him, study hard, read the classic texts, including the Bible, listen to the great music, stand before the fine paintings of the world. I counseled him to educate himself in civilization. I warned that his education would be difficult at first, that he wouldn't know how one thing fit together with another, but, in time, he would begin to know—and he would begin to know what he believed in and what he didn't; he would begin to know himself, to build a character."

"Was he surprised? I expect he expected you to go on about the commandments or about following Jesus."

"But that is what I *was* on about. I believe Christ was a cultured man. He knew his ancient texts; he recognized beauty; there is much poetry in his sayings, much wit in his parables. He loved the world and loved the good. As

Christ he could do no other. But as men we have a choice."

"Have you lived your own life in this manner?"

"Insofar as I have been able."

"Has it worked?"

"Worked? I believe it has. Enough to go on, to enjoy life, to do my work, which I love. But mine has been a quiet life. A private life. Not interesting—I mean, to others—nothing that could go into a book."

"Perhaps. But I, who am older than you by a score of years, have learned another truth: when a man of your age and intelligence cannot write, it is because he is hiding something from himself. Something he is afraid he will find if he begins to write. Could that be true for you?"

"It may be so, but—"

"But a man must face his fears. Why don't you tell me your story? If I am right, at least you will not be alone when the truth confronts you. And if I am wrong, if you have nothing of interest to say, I will fall asleep."

Christian smiled. "I'd like to try, but I feel a little self-conscious."

"Pretend that I am a congregation. Perhaps, at my age, I am a congregation."

"All right, I will." And Christian began to speak, tentative at first, then gaining the momentum of a good Irish sermon, his brogue flavoring his phrases. The eyes of his companion sparkled.

"Patience was my mother's name . . . and she was the soul of it; my father's name was Frank, and he always was, especially when the whiskey was in him; my name is Christian, and you will have to decide for yourself about that. I'm a preacher who lives in a lean time for preachers. But I can remember a different time . . . I can remember a

different place. . . . You probably think of Ireland as green,
but to me, to someone born and bred in the heart of Ireland, it is a land of blue and white and yellow gold, full of
bright promise, fringed in green, to be sure, soft and thick
underfoot; here and there in the trees and hedges the
seven greens of growing things spring out upon you. But
to me, mostly, it is blue sky and white clouds and golden
afternoons. Ah. I was always looking up, you see. And
though I've been told that Irish skies are often full of rain,
not a single drop splashes against the summertime of my
childhood; though a wet autumn day turns up now and
again and there you will find me, an undersized boy
pressed against the windowpane, holding in my hand a
cup of tea—strong Irish tea, black as a night with all the
stars poked out. It was, however, on a summer day in my
eighth year, in the town of Ballycore, a village so small
that the locals (who were always losing it in amongst the
hills) took to meeting in the forests to do their shopping
and gossiping, until they chanced upon the town again; it
was in such a strange and magical place that I first came to
know that I would be a preacher."

The clack of the wheels against the tracks provided a
steady counterpoint to the natural rhythms of Christian's
speech.

"It wasn't that I thought it out. I was far too young for
such an achievement. No. The experience was like walking
into a decision, not making one. A foreordination of what
I would someday become. On that summer's day I was out
in the fields. Just dandling about as small boys do, kicking
at stones and watching the grasshoppers, when I chanced
to look down the lane toward a stand of white birches and
I saw her there, a little girl, a stranger, a rarity in Ballycore.
Now, this little girl was beautiful as only little girls of five
or six can be; with the lightest skin and hair and eyes. She

glowed, or so it seemed to me. She wore a light blue dress and a white apron, as was the fashion in that long ago time in that faraway place, and her hair was burnished gold, and she held in her hands a bunch of bluebells. The bluebells matched her eyes. It is a simple composition, even now, in memory's eye: a little girl, with red-gold hair, wearing blue and white, standing in the dappled lane, in front of white birches; behind the birches a sky of deepest blue, bluebells in her hand, a ribbon in her hair, everything covered over and, at the same time, shot through with sunlight; the grasses, golden, too, with the approach of autumn in them.

"And the voice of my young boy's mind asked a question. My young boy's mind, which, until that exact enraptured moment, had taken every earthly thing as it came, greedily and for granted; the little boy's mind with a voice of its own that still I hear when I'm at evening prayers; the small boy's voice that, high and pure, sang solo from the choir at Christmastime, 'Once in Royal Day-ay-ay-vid's City,' and in the singing of it, made his mother proud; the child's voice asking a man's question, as great poets and theologians asked before me, as every person who is, for just one moment entirely happy, asks: Where does all the beauty come from? All of it—color and form, changing, glorious, harsh and tender, sorrowing and reveling, dark and glowing, ancient and newborn, sunlit and sodden, blue and white and gold, and gold again—where does all the beauty come from?

"Do you know? Do you care? I know only this: because beauty exists, I can leap, without a particle of ground beneath me, without the feather of a wing to support me, without looking back, without looking down, to God."

He stopped to catch his breath and the old man smiled at him. "This is a certainly a charming story. . . ."

"But . . . ?"

"But it does not answer our question."

"You mean, what I might be hiding from?"

"Yes."

"I don't know what it could be."

"Do you want to know?"

"Yes . . . I suppose I do."

"Then start again."

"Start over? With Ballycore and all that?"

"No." The man looked at him with deadly seriousness. "Start in the other place."

Christian slumped back against the cushioned seat. "Ah."

"When you're ready, I will listen."

It took all of Christian's courage, and some that he borrowed from the patient eyes of his newfound friend. He began again, and the words came, from the other place: "Of the one hundred and forty-four people who got on the plane with me in Chicago, Illinois, one hundred and twenty-seven of them were dead when I crawled out of the smoldering fuselage into a cornfield near Davenport, Iowa. I didn't know I had gotten off a plane, or that I was near Davenport. I just knew I was in a cornfield and that it was night, and there were flickers of firelight illuminating the cornstalks; cornstalks all around, flashing green gold out of a black background, and the air smelled of nameless burning things and newly opened ground. Then there were sirens and red, glaring lights and I could see the broken bodies all around me in amongst the cornstalks and the great white curve of the plane like the belly of Ahab's whale, half in and half out of the smoldering ground, smoke like ocean spray curling around it, and I began to know what had happened.

"I heard the bodies then, some moaning, some asking for help, weakly and patiently; and I gave what help I could until I was taken away. Do you know what help I could give? Almost none. With all my training and all my belief I was near to impotent in that tragic field. I prayed, of course, but the bodies, the people, didn't seem to care very much whether I did or not, and I didn't either. They were in too much pain. It's different, you know, to pray with a couple of hundred well-dressed, well-heeled parishioners on a sunny Sunday morning, full of promise, in a well-designed church with the choir above you; it's different from the time you pray holding a writhing, bloody man in a cornfield in the night when it is very cold and the smoking air carries the stench of diesel fuel and the sound of scything screams."

There it was. Half of it. Could he go on to tell the rest? Under the old man's gaze Christian felt his soul being quietly unpacked, unfolded, searched.

"Yes. You can continue."

"I was taken to a hospital, though I was unsure why. I didn't feel sick or injured, though by the look of me I should have been near death with the blood and mud all over me. Everyone was very kind and reassuring. One young nurse read my wallet and began to call me Father, and I hadn't the heart to correct her. Many young people today don't know the difference between the religions. It didn't matter. I was given a sedative, and pushed under and through a lot of machines, and given another sedative— and when I woke up the next day, feeling hung over and bruised and angry, I didn't know why at first, or about what, or at whom.

"And then I remembered Grace. Grace had been with me on the flight! Grace, my wife."

Christian's eyes were brimming with tears. A vital part of himself, he realized, had never gone on. In time he had appeared to recover from the shock and then from the grief, though his hair had turned a startling white. He had gone through the contortions of mourning and had accepted the condolences of friends and parishioners. He had often wondered why people, in the wake of tragedy, emerge with stronger, not weaker, faith in God. When he was in the depths of his pain, he, like everyone else, simply wanted the agony to stop. But as the pain pressed down through his consciousness, as it slowly began to recede, life, he noticed, went on. And it was in this procession of minutes that his faith was nourished; for in a thousand little ways he was brought back into life—a box of cookies here, a poem sent to him there. A puppy full of floppy love arrived in a basket at the door of the parsonage; dubbed Caleb, he was, even now, sleeping his furry old age away curled up in the warmest corner of Christian's kitchen. People could be so good.

He came to know that he had been spared for the work he was called to do among the people, good and bad. He was to bring the reality of God's grace into their lives, strong enough to stand against their sufferings; to help them to say, whatever befell them, that life on this earth was a gift and that it was good. He was strengthened by his work. How he loved his work! And he knew that in this one way he was like God. He had slowly regained a measure of equanimity, and as time progressed he had been called to Akron, and then to Seattle, then to New York; ever-bigger churches; ever-increasing multitudes given over to his vital ministry. He had preached and sung and shaken the hands of his followers in moments of congratulation, and he had held their hands in moments of sorrow, understanding so much. But the heart of his soul had remained in Iowa, searching, searching through the cornstalks of his memory for the remnants of what had been his life.

The old man asked a gentle question. "If your tears could talk, what would they say to you?"

"They would say, I never forgave myself."

"For what?"

"For forgetting her."

"Would remembering her have helped her?"

"No. She was killed instantly."

"Do you remember her now?"

"Yes. Of course, every day, every hour. I remember how loving she was, and how much I loved her."

"Then she must have forgiven you. She wouldn't visit your mind, you know, not so very often, if she were angry."

"Do you think so?"

"I think your regret is a sorrow to her."

"Oh, that would be terrible. I would not wish to give Grace any further sorrow."

"Then forgive yourself and be in harmony with her."

Christian closed his eyes, lost in memory, lost in thought.

By the time they reached Grand Central Station, a profound sense of peace had enveloped him. He got up reluctantly as the train pulled in, bending to shake hands with his now silent companion, who showed no sign that he would ever leave the train. As Christian reached the end of the aisle he turned in a gesture of farewell, and was startled to see that the elderly man had produced a gourd rattle from out of a yellow plastic bag. He shook the rattle at Christian and chanted a phrase, too softly to be heard. Something with wings. He wondered what it was.

Christian had decided he would begin writing at once. But it was the morning that Eve Callahan had fallen, in the shock wave of that awful event, that he actually began. The sound, or rather the feel of Eve Callahan's explosive flesh had blown him into his quiet study. He had swallowed a cup of weak church tea in one gulp and begun to write.

It was a few minutes later when he had noticed a smear of red on his shirt cuff and was suddenly overcome with revulsion. He stripped down to his underwear and slipped into a pulpit robe for decency. Opening a crack in the great double doors of his study, he handed his clothing out to Alice May Patoon, his startled secretary, with instructions to find a dry cleaner.

"I believe there's one nearby," he said. "On Bleecker Street—Henry Chang's? He has a speech impediment."

"I'm sure I don't know, Reverend Davies."

"I'm sure you'll find out," he encouraged her, and he smiled his smile—what he thought of as the Clincher Smile. He'd had it since childhood and the charm of it had never failed him. Alice May, who had served two of his predecessors through years of quiet ministry, was a formidable challenge. Here she was, an intelligent, genteel, and proper person, being handed, without explanation, a pack of bloody clothing from her almost undressed boss, who was only six months on the job. He kept smiling. He saw her melt.

"I'll see what I can do, Reverend Davies."

She didn't curtsy, of course. No one had curtsied in years. But she gave the impression that her knees bent and her head bowed without actually moving a muscle. The Clincher was a major blessing. He reread what he had written. They were the first musical notes he had ever dared to write down for himself. They danced on the page where he had carefully penned them onto the lines. He called the melody "The Dance of the Seven Suns."

He thought of Luke as he wrote, and of his dead pen pal, Paul, and also of Paul's little sister, Bridget, so far away in bloody, burned-out Belfast. He wished the music could reach them. It was a beautiful melody, thought Paul as he brought the notes to Seth, one by one, for careful arrangement. Yes. The quarter note should go there. He played through the notes again. They were not by Amadeus Mozart or Frédéric Chopin. They were by Seth Hackett. No, he decided, just Seth. Hackett belonged to his father, to the real-estate business, to the world of money and acquisitions. This music was by Seth. He played it again and heard an improvement waiting to be made; tried the change, first in performance, then on the page. He was as concentrated as he had ever been, and if he had taken the time to notice it, he was happy. In his own home. At sixteen. The melody went on and on, toward the dawn. Hearing the music, music that he did not recognize, he lay, sleepless, called out of his dream by the new melody.

In the dream Ted had been dancing with Abigail-Arista on the front porch of her grandparents' house down by the tracks. Her grandfather, the Methodist minister, kept trying to warn them against the evils of dancing, but whenever the old man opened his mouth to chastise them, a song flew out—a song praising sexuality, not God—then Ted and Abigail would laugh at the preacher's consternation and whirl away across the porch. He had waltzed into consciousness on the strains of Seth's music, and now lay missing the joy of the dream.

Ted glanced at his wife, Ivy Sue, sleeping peacefully beside him. Perfect, like a pressed flower between the matched pastel sheets. How did she manage to sleep without mussing her hair or makeup? Wasn't she supposed to be covered in face creams and pinned into ugliness for the night? Ivy Sue was more beautiful asleep than awake. She will make a ravishing corpse, he thought, and shivered, even though the room was always kept at an even seventy degrees. The music, he noted, had an Oriental sound to it ... Chinese ... or Japanese ... calling him eastward. If he traveled east, he would come to Abigail ... Arista ... in the towers of New York City, where she had been hidden from him for so long. If he went, she would let down her hair, and he would climb—up, up, up, into her tower room. He could tell Ivy Sue it was a business trip. It was business. His. And Arista's.

Seth's music had stopped abruptly. And he heard the boy make his way to bed. Agitated by the silence, he got up and put on his bathrobe quietly. He stepped out onto the deck and stood looking out across the lake. It was serene and liquid black, sprinkled with the reflection of the predawn stars. Ted knew he was bereft of poetry, and yet he needed to speak it. Nothing came. Then, looking upward, he recalled a verse from childhood. It returned to him, like light, across the years.

> *Twinkle, twinkle, little star,*
> *How I wonder what you are. . . .*

And he did wonder. He hadn't wondered as a boy.

For the first time in a million years, the music of poetry stirred within the soul of Ted Hackett. ". . . How I wonder what you are," he sang softly.

But there was no one to hear him.

Part Two

The

DAY DREAMERS

*You never enjoy the world aright till the sea
itself floweth in your veins, till you are clothed with
the heavens and crowned with the stars and perceive
yourself to be the sole heir of the whole world, and
more than so, because men are in it who are every one
sole heirs as well as you.*

—THOMAS TRAHERNE

"What were you thinking when you chose 'Twinkle, Twinkle Little Star'?" asked Katelyn, looking up from the manuscript for the first time.

Arista was glad for the break in the long (and, for her, tense) silence. She hesitated for a moment before she answered. The choice of Ted's poem had come easily. "Well, if a man has never responded to music or art or poetry, if his whole life has been making money, making a family, succeeding within middle-class norms, and he suddenly has a moment of wonder, well, he would have to fall back on a childhood poem, wouldn't he? There would be nothing else at his command."

"I can live with that." Katelyn nodded acceptingly. "You've revealed more of yourself in this book than ever before. You ought to show this to your shrink."

"I don't have a shrink anymore. He gave it up to become a potter."

"I guess you cured him."

Arista was still edgy. Katelyn's intent reading for most of

the morning had been a good sign, but she needed to hear more of the review.

"What else, Katelyn?"

"The characters are . . . real . . . uh . . . characters. I mean if you met one in life, you'd say, 'What a character.' I even think the Katelyn based on me is interesting, and I never thought I'd feel *that* . . . about then. You will change my name?"

"Of course. How about Deirdre? Or Dolores?"

"I don't cry like that anymore."

"But you did."

"Yeah." A pensive look reminiscent of the old sadness crossed Katelyn's features. "Those were alien times. I'm glad you've written about them. It makes me feel like they have been properly laid to rest."

"Do you ever miss him?" asked Arista. Gently, for Arista.

"No. Not for a long time."

"Do you ever miss men?"

"No. I love Serena. And sex with a woman is so different, so encompassing. For me it's a completion, a tender homecoming after a long journey in a hostile country, and the experience of it has absorbed everything, all my other desires. Life is . . . well . . . easier."

Inwardly Arista shuddered, understanding for the first time the masculine fear of absorption, she decided she would go out for a brisk walk while Katelyn finished reading the novel. She often walked and worried about Katelyn who no longer aimed at anything. Katelyn no longer mimed, nor did she write. She carefully cooked the dinner. She complacently cleaned the house. She was becoming a little tedious. Arista kept these concerns to herself, unwilling to tamper with her friend's newfound, hard-fought, high-priced contentment. In not speaking up, she knew she was giving up just a little on their ancient friendship. But a lesbian Katelyn was not a heterosexual Katelyn. She seemed sadly diminished to Arista. "And Serena never keeps you waiting?"

"She is constantly there."

"Like my characters are for me."

Inwardly Katelyn sighed. At least Serena was *real*, she thought. She worried for Arista, still so lost in the world of men, real and imagined; mostly, even the real ones, imagined. Arista would grow old alone, surrounded by her phantoms. When she could have had me, mused Katelyn, sadly, silently. "There isn't much sex in this one, Arista."

"I know, I know. Is that what's wrong with it?"

"I didn't say there was anything wrong with it. Besides, the problems of sex, and the implications of sex, and the results of sex are worthy subjects, too."

"Yes, yes," Arista agreed impatiently, "but I find that as I grow older I get farther, not closer, to writing the thing itself."

"Arista, you cannot write the thing itself. Sex is physical, not literary."

"That seems unfortunate." It was her turn to be pensive. "What character do you like the best?"

"Who's this Lester character?"

"Just that."

"I like Deerfinder."

"Ah. Your old self recognizes a companion in longing."

"He waits."

"They also serve, who only stand and wait."

Deerfinder did not hear the two women. He stood, arms akimbo, the very likeness of a cigar-store Indian, in the doorway of Maggie's shack, watching her sleep in the freckled arms of the white man Callahan. It was a half hour later when Fatpaws awoke, saw Deerfinder, experienced a moment of acute canine embarrassment, issued an obligatory bark, and slunk outside, leaving the three humans to their incomprehensible purposes.

"Deerfinder, you ugly iguana!" Maggie yelled in sudden angry awareness of the intrusion. "Get out of my house."

Jamie Callahan rolled over just in time to observe the appearance of a rare fissure in Deerfinder's usual stone-faced composure through which he caught a momentary glimpse of an interior struggle he had never seen before: red anguish churning against steel-gray pride. The crack congealed. Deerfinder was Deerfinder again, stolid and incomprehensible.

Deerfinder took one step backward, which carried him out, over the threshold onto the porch, but he retreated no farther. Maggie pulled a sheet around herself and came after him like an vengeful ghost. Deerfinder raised a hand.

"I come in peace."

She raised an arm as if to strike. He didn't flinch.

"Luke Sevensons sent me," he continued. His voice and eyes were as even as a horizon line. That stopped her, he thought, as Maggie suddenly sat down.

Callahan sat up.

Deerfinder stood still.

"Luke took his sweet time," Maggie responded, after she remembered to breathe. Her unbound hair brushed the floorboards; her thoughts brushed the past.

"He wants us in New York City as soon as possible."

"Who does Luke think he is, God?"

The old answers—and the old questions—about Luke curled in the air around them. Crazy old man, thought Maggie. "I am surrounded with crazy old men," she declared, and then stormed out of the cabin. Hurling away the sheet, she climbed naked into the pickup truck and drove away into the desert.

"When do we leave?" queried Callahan.

"Luke said as soon as possible. He doesn't have much time left." The Indian turned to leave.

"You never approved, did you, Deerfinder?"

"Of you and Maggie?"

"Of me and Maggie and Luke."

"You want to know the answer to that question?"

"No."

"You two drive her crazy."

"She'll be back. For God's sake, come in off the porch!"

Deerfinder edged back into the cabin with the wariness of an animal sensing a sharp-toothed trap. The deliberateness of his step made Callahan aware, in a way he had not experienced before, that the cabin was an enclosure— against the elements, against others. "Why are we going to New York?" he asked.

"There's bad news and there's bad news. Which you want first?"

"A drink. Then the bad news."

Deerfinder dutifully poured him a shot of whiskey, but when he passed it over to Callahan, he kept his hand around the glass, not letting go. The Irishman looked up inquiringly. Then Deerfinder spoke. "Eve killed herself." The whiskey spilled over both their hands.

"Oh, Jesus! So she finally jumped. Oh, hell."

"How do you know she jumped?" asked Deerfinder.

"Whenever she threatened me, it was always with a jump. Every time I turned around, she was opening a window. Looking down. Dropping things out. Why now?"

Deerfinder let go of the glass and shrugged. Callahan drank the whole of the whiskey down between sentences.

"I knew she was back in the Village again. I saw her on Bleecker Street a couple of weeks ago . . . and she saw me ... pretending not to see her ... and then she pretended not to see me ... and we were both, all in an instant, back in the old harness."

"There's a memorial service planned for her on the last day of this month. Luke's going to speak."

"That's what he wants us there for? I'm not going."

"No. You ready for the other bad news?"

"I forgot. Go ahead."

"Luke says he's going to die. First day of the new month. He doesn't want to die alone. He wants you with him, God knows why. He'll tolerate me if I bring you. I think he'd ask for Maggie, too, if he was sure she was alive. I got us all tickets." He gave Jamie time to absorb these revelations. "Now I'm answering the question you put to me about your ménage—about whether I like it or not—whether you like it or not." Deerfinder sat down on a straight-backed chair, somehow managing to appear just as tall as he did standing up. "You three strange people—Irishman, Swedishman, Indian woman. You three people very strong in spirit. Live many lifetimes together. Have many troubles. I think maybe you hafta keep sticking on each other all this life, next life, maybe few more lifes. Someday you work things out maybe. Also maybe not."

"You talking about reincarnation, Deerfinder?"

"He who would be born begins a journey of ten ten thousand years."

"Aren't you the wrong kind of Indian for that kind of rum Hindu thinking?"

"Buddhist."

"You're a Buddhist?"

"I took my vows in Taos last winter."

"What about the Great Spirit?"

"Great Spirit is Buddha."

"I need another drink. Don't get up. I'll get it." Callahan

swung out of bed and pulled on his pants, got whiskey, drank whiskey, and then began to do the dishes, his back toward Deerfinder; but the Indian seemed to look right through his skull.

"You crying, Jamie?"

"She was such a sad sad woman, my Eve. Her soul was all muddied up. Her colors were all gone to brown. Everything hurt her. Everybody hurt her. I did. Even little Elinor did. We loved her, but that was never enough. We didn't know how to stop hurting her, and as a result we waded in guilt up to our hips. Eventually it seemed best just to stay away from her, leave her alone. When she went off, it hurt like hell, but it was an incredible relief, too. She wanted to come back to us. Every few years she would call me or write me. I thought it was better for Elinor to keep Eve away from her. Maybe that was wrong. It became a choice between which kind of guilt I wanted to sink into." He paused, staring into the dishwater, noticing the rainbow of colors on the oily surface. "And Maggie Silvernails was a better mother to the child than Eve could ever hope to be."

"Elinor is coming."

Callahan wheeled around to face Deerfinder. "Elinor? Coming where? What are you talking about?"

"Henry Chang sent her Eve's obituary, and a long-winded letter about honoring her ancestors. So Elinor's coming to New York and she's bringing the kids. For Eve's memorial service."

"Not with bloody Brian O'Neill!"

"Bloody Brian O'Neill is her husband, Callahan. Makes sense she would come with him, but she's not."

Callahan was suddenly aware that hiding beneath his anger was a groveling fear. He was afraid to face his only daughter. He realized that of the two abandonments, his had been the worse in its terrible wrath and subsequent passivity.

He chose another tone of feeling, wondering what it would be like to see her, his beautiful honey-colored girl. "Elinor . . . home . . . with all those youngsters . . . where would she get that kind of money? The airfare alone would bankrupt Ulster. That bastard O'Neill wouldn't have it."

Deerfinder shrugged. "Everybody always love your Elinor. Somebody send."

They heard the truck roaring back toward the cabin. Callahan imagined the dust cloud swirling out behind it like the tail of a charging horse.

"You love Maggie Silvernails, too, don't you, Deerfinder?"

There was no answer spoken, only felt.

Callahan pressed on. "You two came to New York City together forty years ago."

"We came."

"And when she left, you left."

"We left."

"Were you ever lovers?"

"That's a white man's question."

"What's a red man's answer?"

They heard the truck door slam shut.

"Deerfinder, do you think Maggie will come with us to New York?"

"Does a bear live in the woods?"

"I believe the phrase is 'does a bear shit in the woods?' "

"I take Buddhist vows, remember. No dirty talk."

"What is the world coming to?"

It was a question that Luke often pondered, but seldom asked aloud, for he knew there was no answer for it.

"There be no answer for that," replied Methuselah,

shaking her head and scrubbing his back with the loofah. Luke sat in a lotus position in the round, tin tub on the kitchen floor. He was surrounded by tiny, white bubbles that were busy snapping and bursting and releasing the scent of orange blossoms into the steamy air. Luke had recently installed a modern bathroom upstairs in the farmhouse, with white tiles and silver tubing, but he preferred the ritual of the tin tub. He and Maggie and Callahan had had a matching set of tubs back in the Village days, in which they would sit and scrub and drink and talk and laugh and sing together; sometimes holding court with their nonchalant friends. Cool, it was then called. Mariah the cat approached, stuck her head curiously over the edge of the tub, and then marched haughtily away with a bubble on her nose.

Luke and Methuselah both chuckled.

"I was reading *Civilization and Its Discontents* last night," Luke informed her. "Isn't that a wonderful title? Very grand. Very grandiose. It's by Sigmund Freud. Do you know Sigmund Freud?"

"He daid," replied Methuselah, who tended toward the succinct.

"I mean do you know *of* Sigmund Freud?"

"Mighty smart Jew."

"You think so? So do I. He says—and I almost quote— that 'civilized society is perpetually menaced through a primary hostility of men toward one another.' You think that's true?"

"He know people cain't help being bad most the times they be bad."

"But do you think people want to be good?"

"Sure enough, they be happier when they be good. But the devil is in 'em fo' sure. Freud he call the devil by the name of id. That be a satisfying name, all right. You do something shameful, you say, 'I didn't mean to do it. Ol' id made me do it.' "

"You are a constant surprise, Maudie."

"Sit still, son. Bend your head and let me get behind your big, stickin'-out ears. You live as long as ol' Maudie, you be full of surprises, too."

"My ears do not stick out. And I will never be as old as you, my Methuselah. I'm going to die. The first day next month."

"Why you going to go and do that for? Plenty of time to be daid later on. Next year. Year after that. So on and so on."

"Funny. Arista Bellefleurs said something like that to me last time I worked with her." Luke shrugged. "Truth is, I don't feel I have much choice in the matter. Will you look after the farm for me?"

"Don't I always?"

"It won't be the same without me."

"No, I don't expect it will be. Be like it were before you was born. Who'll get the place now? I wonder. You, with not a child to your changed-over name." She shook her head disapprovingly.

"You want the farm?"

"I already got it."

"I mean do you want to own it?"

"What for? I got to clean it just the same and look after all these creatures, whether I own it or not." She waved in the direction of the pile of puppies sleeping near the door, and to the grown cat and dog nearby, who sat watching Luke's bath like it was animal television.

"You love to clean, and you love every beast that strays across your doorstep," he said.

"True enough."

"Well then, who do you want for company? You know

everyone I know. Who should I leave it to? How about that new youngster, Seth, with the flute. You like music. He'll be getting married in a few years and will need a place to raise a family in."

"No. He be off all 'round the world, that one."

"How about his mother? I hear she's a demon with a dust cloth?"

"Humph."

"Who then?"

"Maggie Silvernails."

"She daid . . . she is dead, Methuselah."

"Ain't."

Luke sighed. "She must be. Jamie Callahan went to New Mexico to find her at the beginning of last month. Yesterday I called Deerfinder and told him I was dying. I told him to bring Callahan back east. Now, don't you think, given the gravity of the circumstances, that Deerfinder would tell me if Maggie was alive?"

"Get up, Luke. Dry yourself off. Seventy years old and you still wet behind your stickin'-out ears when it comes to redskins. Your granddaddy shoot a few in his day. Now, *he* knew about Injuns."

"If Maggie were alive, do you think she'd take this place? Do you think she would come and live here on the farm?" The idea pleased him; the picture of her moving about in these rooms sloshed around pleasantly in his imagination.

"She be smart to take it, and Maggie be a smart woman. She too old for that city life and before long she be too old for the desert. Here, I take care of her. But maybe here, she miss you too much."

"I miss her, too."

"Not for long now."

Luke wheeled around, slopping soapy water onto the

kitchen floor. "You know something I don't know, Methu-selah?"

"Quite a bit, it be seeming to me." She pulled an un-opened telegram from her apron pocket and handed it to Luke; she saw his damp hand tremble, not with the infir-mity of age, but with the anticipation of youth. She smiled and shook her head. "Anatomy be destiny."

He ripped open the envelope.

"I can't believe it."

"It doesn't matter whether you believe it or not, Mr. Hackett," said the policeman. "You are under arrest. You have the right to remain silent. . . ."

But Ted did not hear the rest of the standard recitation, as handcuffs were clapped onto his wrists. He had grown up with Gus Reaper, now the Boar's Wood chief of police. Grim Reaper they had called him in high school because he would only wear black. Now he was neatly tucked into his blue uniform, a silver star glistening on his chest. Ted stood stunned while Timmy Matucek patted him up and down the legs by way of a weapons search. Only a few summers ago Ted used to hire Timmy to mow his lawn.

Ted found his voice. "Grim . . . Gus . . . please . . . tell me what this is all about. We're old friends."

"Do you have a passport?"

"What? Yes."

"You'll have to turn it over, and your driver's license, too."

"In the bedroom. Top drawer of my dresser."

"Timmy, go get them." Timmy left on his errand. "I had to get the kid out of the room, Ted. It's not protocol. But here's the deal. Off the record. You know Janet Joyce?"

"Of course, she's my daughter Holly's best friend."

"Well, she had some funny-looking bruises on her arms

and legs. The gym teacher noticed them when the girls were taking their showers."

Ted looked as bewildered as he felt. Grim reached out and patted him on the shoulder.

"Anyhow, this gym teacher had a talk with Janet, and Janet cries a lot and then says that you tried to touch her funny, where you shouldn't have done, and she fended you off and that's how she got the bruises."

Ted collapsed into a chair, stricken with guilt and fear.

"Ted, did you do this thing?" Grim asked. "You feel up this kid and knock her around a little?"

Of course he had, thought Ted. He must have done it to feel this guilty, this choked with remorse. But of course, he *hadn't*, couldn't, wouldn't think of it.

"Ted?"

"No. No, I didn't, Grim. I know exactly when it didn't happen. I mean I know what she's talking about. Only she's got it all wrong. Holly was right there."

"Ted. You're not making a hell of a lot of sense. Either it happened or it didn't."

"We were playing football. Touch football. Holly and her friends and I always played games like that while they were growing up. But not for a long time, because well, Holly thought she was too old for games, and then, last Sunday, she and Janet were over and out of the blue they said could we play, and it was just like old times."

"So no hanky-panky?"

"Grim, come on, we were in the backyard, right by the water, where anyone on the lake could see. The sailboat races were on. There must be witnesses."

"I'll check it out."

"Why would she lie? Lie about me? Why would Janet Joyce say a thing like that?"

"I don't know, Ted." Gus considered his old friend, the ever-rising star of the class of '62. Handcuffed now, he had sunk down into his chair so far he was almost gone. "Girls that age get funny ideas." But this, he knew, was not so funny. Ted's life would be ruined by these charges, even if, as he expected, they quickly proved false. Boar's Wood was too small a town, and sexual abuse was too big a charge. There would forever be a cloud of suspicion hanging over Ted Hackett. And Ted's business, his friendships, his whole life was built on the foundation of his flawless reputation, now defaced by the accusations of a thoughtless teenager. Accusations of physical and sexual abuse were all the rage these days. Schoolteachers complained that they were afraid even to pat a student on the back. Doctors hired nurses just to stand around during examinations. And his dentist wouldn't give gas anymore no matter what. It reminded Gus of stories he had read of Nazi Germany and communist Russia; about no one feeling safe; about angry young people turning over their own parents to the authorities. At the moment he was the authority and he didn't much like it. Timmy came back into the living room, with the passport and license.

"We'll have to take you in and book you, Ted. Likely as not you'll be released before nightfall. Ivy Sue will have to come and drive you home. We have to keep the passport and the license until this is sorted out."

"Don't want me to run away, huh?"

Gus shrugged.

"Where the hell would I go? My whole life is here."

"We believe there's nowhere else to go because we've both lived here so damn long," declared Oakley Klapper to Jerry Phails. "Why there's a huge city right outside Greenwich Village, any direction you go including up, and it has airports and train stations and . . . we could go anywhere.

Here we have nothing. Nothing." The two Village denizens were both well on the way toward determined drunk-
enness. Unawares, Eve had joined them, too. She hovered
warmly near Jerry.

"Easy for you to say," replied Jerry. "You can paint anywhere."

"But I can't paint any*thing*."

"And I can sing nothing."

"You sing like a God." This was Eve's opinion, too.

"I haven't sung in ten years. I didn't have it, Oakley, I
didn't have the stuff."

They were alone (or so they thought) in Oakley's ter-
raced apartment, far from the madding crowd celebrating
the opening of Oakley's latest show. Many people had
come to the gallery. Much white wine was drunk. Many
paintings had been sold. Oakley told himself he should be
happy, but he had found himself plunging deeper and
deeper into melancholy as the afternoon wore on.

"What happened to our dreams, Jerry?"

"I managed to accomplish mine, but only for a season."

"And I, never."

"But Oakley, you're doing fine. Most artists would kill
for your success. What is it you would like to do that you
haven't done?"

"I would like to be able to draw. I would like to be able
to paint what I see. Something of beauty. Something ugly.
Something real. All I can do is cover the canvas with my
unwieldy despair. No one knows what it is that I paint, not
even I. We know they are dark things. We know they are
unrecognizable things. We know that place within ourselves. I speak to this age. *Mi disperazione e su disperazione.*
Enough!" He struck his thighs with his hands, the sound
resounding, causing Eve to jump. "You never told me what
happened that night."

"I've never been drunk enough. But I am now. More champagne?"

"Tell me." Oakley held out his glass shakily. Eve steadied it for him.

"It was my first solo concert following my debut and my big success at the Met. I was the golden boy, the tenor of promise. I had chosen a selection of arias I knew exceptionally well, for although the audiences hailed me, I was very unsure, very unsteady in my confidence. I stepped out onto the stage. A stage like any other, an orchestra like any other, a conductor with whom I was friendly. There was a warm reception from the expectant crowd. The music started. I began to sing. The notes came and my voice, I was sure, was strong for the night."

Oakley was listening attentively. He knew exactly what had happened, of course. But he had never heard Jerry's own account of the disaster.

"Then I noticed, way in back, a moving figure. An usher? A latecomer. Maybe just a shadow. I will never know. For in that moment of preoccupation my voice wavered and then cracked. Can you imagine? Can you think of the horror? My voice was no longer mine to command. It was a thing unto itself. Alive. Slithering, wobbling, contorting itself further and further from the song. I stopped. The audience was silent. I knew not what to do. Then I heard a few faint claps of encouragement. Again, from the back. Clap, clap. Clap, clap. I tried again, but my voice wasn't even on the map. I looked to my conductor and there were tears in his eyes. Clap, clap. Clap, clap. The entire audience now. I tried once again, to begin again, but in that awful, punctuated silence my voice had died. Not a note came forth. My humiliation was complete. I've never had the guts to step forward and sing before an audience again. And always I hear, faintly, in the distance, around corners, on the other side of walls, under the mattress in the dark of night, in dreams: clap, clap. Clap, clap."

"And you don't know who it was, the latecomer, the shadow?"

"I think it was my mother."

"But I wasn't there," said Eve.

"Or maybe it wasn't," Jerry mused.

Oakley had gone pale and sober, facing his own cowardice. Which, he wondered, was worse—the humiliation of failure or the shame of cowardice? "Jerry," he said, putting down his glass, "it was me. I came late to the concert that night. But I never knew that my late arrival was the cause."

Eve watched her son as he struggled with this revelation. She moved closer.

"You were not the cause of my failure, Oakley. The cause is somewhere inside me, that dark place you speak of that I haven't even the courage to face. Perhaps something in my childhood . . . I don't know . . . perhaps my mother's abandonment . . . I'm no psychologist, and I don't want to be. Anyway, I've had a good life in spite of my lack of courage. I like music theory. I like teaching."

Ouch! thought Eve. Guardianship has its price. But at least I can do it now. I can look out for him, as I never could in life. She moved swiftly ahead to the recent future, arranging to keep him from harm's way.

"We never went to Luke, you and I," said Oakley. "We were the holdouts. And your mother, too, by all accounts."

"I was scared of Luke. He's uncanny."

"He knew you were afraid. I once talked to him about us—about my not drawing, your not singing. It wasn't at one of his . . . you know . . . things. It was just idle talk, late at night in the bar at the Algonquin. I was with him and Maggie and Callahan. You know what he said?"

"No."

"He said, 'Oakley, you are so damned disappointed in your life that you will not take one single step to end your disappointment.'"

"That's what Luke said?"

"Yep. So right in that moment I decided to approach Christian," confessed Arista.

"So Luke is behind this romance, too," said Katelyn, slowly shaking her head from side to side. "But, Arista, not with a preacher. You were raised by a preacher. It's incestuous, it's profane."

"My grandfather wouldn't approve of him either. He always said that Presbyterians had souls of the weaker sort. They were known to waltz, and occasionally rumba. Grandpa was a nut. Maybe you have to be a nut to be a preacher. Anyhow, I need to find out about this one. He's got charisma. There is going to be—are you ready?—a tea dance next week at the church house, and you, Katelyn my dear, my friend, my dear friend, are coming with me, for moral support."

"Immoral support, you mean. He's married, isn't he?"

Arista ignored the remark. "I want to see him close up. And rumor has it, he's a mean dancer."

The two women were enjoying an afternoon at the Caffe degli Artisti. Normal people were all at work, so they had the restaurant to themselves, except for Headstone Brown, who was lying peacefully on the floor.

"Mmm. Did you say a *tea* dance? Grown-ups don't go to tea dances. You'll have to find some other way to meet him."

"Grown-ups don't wait until they're married to get laid either."

"I know. I know." Katelyn sighed. "But Lester is hopelessly old-fashioned. I can't help it that he's a prude. Arista,

he loves me, and when I'm with him, I don't think about
Nelson Little."

"Mmm . . . ?"

"Well, I don't think about Nelson as much."

"A little bird told me that you arranged to see your unpleasant little Little just a little while ago."

"I knew you wouldn't approve."

"Not even a little bit."

"Enough, Arista. I couldn't stand the silence anymore.
Five years had passed without a word. Five frigid years. I
had to break the ice."

"So Buff Carrington told me. You broke the ice and
Greta Garbo broke the skin."

"Nelson was livid. I'm afraid he'll never agree to meet me
again."

"What? You're planning to make a habit of it? I thought
you were engaged."

"Don't say *engaged*. It makes me sound like a British toi-
let."

"Sorry. Why don't you bring your betrothed to the tea
dance? I'd like to get better acquainted with Lester."
Katelyn still looked hesitant. "Please, Katelyn," urged
Arista. "This guy is new, not just to Old Gray Presbyterian, but to New York. Nobody in our circle knows anything about him. Probably a few old crones at the church
do, but I can't talk to them. If I stand around at the dance,
I'm bound to pick up some gossip. Will you come?"

"No."

"No?"

"No."

"Is this the result of your est weekend?"

"No. I've got a better idea. Did you know Eve Callahan?"

"No. But I'm coming to her memorial service anyway.
Clayton, who as you know, is bewitched by oddity, met

Eve a few weeks ago and liked her. He wants me to go with him. And it's a rare chance to hear Luke Sevensons speak. He's usually so private at his gatherings. How did you know Eve Callahan? She was, from what I hear, a legend well before our time."

"It's a nasty sort of irony. One night a couple of years ago I called the suicide hot line. You know, the eight-hundred number? Over Nelson naturally. Anyhow, Eve was the volunteer I spoke to on the phone. When she found out I appreciated poetry she quoted Goethe for me: 'Life is the childhood of our immortality.'

"Then she urged me not to grow up too fast. It was so like something Nelson would have done that I decided I liked her, and I didn't want to disappoint her by offing myself. In return for the promise of my continued existence, Eve told me her schedule, the nights she was on the suicide line, and I began to call in on a regular basis. When I was in San Francisco for the poetry reading last summer, Eve and I got together for lunch, not a bad lunch either: prawns, pressed pheasant, shitaki mushrooms, and a rather crisp chardonnay. I don't think she noticed the food. She was busy reminiscing for me, telling me about the Village in the old days. She lived in the midst of the artistic community, but unlike so many others, she didn't kid herself. She claimed to have been born with absolutely no talent of any kind. Made terrible failures at poetry, evidently."

"How do people like that live?"

"In her case, she doesn't."

"Well, no matter what happens to us, we can write about it. You know, I can't imagine what it would be like to be hurt or depressed or sad and then have to go work as a secretary or as a housekeeper."

"Unless you love steno pads or Brillo pads."

"Do people love such things?"

"Somebody must. Maybe Buddhists do. Isn't everything all the same to them, everything equally worthy of appreciation?"

"Turn your attention to the moment and find enchantment in your ashtray. Don't they also say that all life is suffering?"

"I believe they do."

"They must never have sex."

"I believe they don't."

Katelyn was looking pensive. "Too bad Eve wasn't a Buddhist. God, I wish she'd phoned me before she jumped."

"I thought it was an accident."

"Father Mothersole at Our Lady doesn't think so. He's giving us a hell of a time about using the church. He doesn't want to host a service for a sinner. That's where your guy comes in."

"Christian?"

"Yeah. Do you think he would let us hold the service at Old Gray Presbyterian? We could go together and ask him. Jerry Phails and George Eliot Isaman could come, too. That way you could meet him in a group and it wouldn't be any more obvious than a tea dance."

"You're an angel."

"Not quite."

Outside the restaurant cars began to honk steadily. Peering out, the two single women could see a gaudily costumed limosine with a JUST MARRIED sign flapping happily over its behind.

"Arista, have you noticed that everyone is married to the wrong person?"

"Katelyn, please—"

"I don't mean Nelson. I mean Nelson is married to the wrong person, of course, but, well, Eve was, too. And I was. And you were—twice. Almost everyone I know who *is* married was in love with someone else first, and it didn't pan out, so later they got married and—although the match seems to work out for a while—somehow it's just not the *right* person because it was a second choice all along. Or maybe someone manages to marry their first love, and then, well, the romance fades out slowly into habit and then into boredom and then they think: I haven't lived, I was too young, I didn't know any better; and somehow the right person *becomes* the wrong person, but they stay married anyhow because they don't know what else to do; or they divorce, and if they divorce, then they marry a new person and then that one is the wrong one because the first one was *really* the right one after all and it didn't work out."

"Surely you know someone who married their first love and still loves them."

"No, I don't."

"Neither do I," admitted Arista.

"Maybe the real marriages aren't marriages."

"What do you mean?"

"Well. There's Buff and Quentin. Or Luke and Methuselah. They're inseparable. And you and I. We have a kind of marriage, don't you think?"

The idea made Arista vaguely uncomfortable, as many of Katelyn's ideas were wont to do. She shrugged.

"No. Really. Think about it. I'm sure that when all the battles are fought and all the men are dead, we'll end up somewhere together. The south of France. The north of Italy. We'll be these two eccentric old American *señoras* propping up the bar at the Piccolo Marina, and talking about what went wrong."

"Will nothing ever go right?"

"It doesn't look good, does it? By the way, Arista, have

you noticed that rather nondescript man who just came in, at the far table?"

"No. What about him?"

"He keeps staring at us. Or, more precisely, at you."

"Really?" Arista peered through the shadowy room at the stranger. She had just reached the age where, at medium distances, the edges of shapes were growing fuzzy. She would need glasses very soon, but at present she was fascinated with the change, wondering how to portray this soft-shaped world in her writing. She strained to see the man more clearly. "He has an interesting face . . . and he looks marginally familiar."

"He looks marginally creepy to me."

"Oh, no one looks interesting to you but Nelson Little."

"And Lester. You know, two romantic involvements are quite difficult for me to manage, Arista. How can you be attracted to so many men? There's Clay Grant; you've had an abstract crush on Oakley Klapper for ages; and now this preacherman—what's his name?—"

"Christian Davies."

"—and you're more than a little infatuated with Luke Sevensons. How do you do it?"

"There's nothing to *do*. When Marxie ran off with Harold, it broke my heart. Not broken into two solid, substantial pieces like yours—half left for Nelson and half for Lester—but broken into many pieces, shattered. So there are plenty of fragments to go around. Each piece is a whole piece, complete in itself, but small, and hard, with very rough edges."

"Then we must somehow heal ourselves, you and I—you more than me—or we'll never be able to love anyone fully again."

The idea irritated Arista. "Don't you think that *heal* is an overused word these days? Everyone is so busy healing they don't have time to live anymore. Maybe having your heart broken is part of life. Part of a good life anyway. Could you understand art or poetry if you hadn't suffered? Could you write it? Maybe instead of talking about being wounded and being healed, we should relish the experience of life in all its flavors and learn to accept, even appreciate, the changes."

"Appreciate pain?"

"Well, accept it."

"That's very est of you, Arista."

"Those are fighting words, Katelyn."

"Well, it's a sick idea."

"Sick? From a vendor of words, I hear sick? At least you could reach for masochistic or depressive or tragic." Katelyn was visibly upset now. "Oh, dear, I'm sorry," Arista was quick to apologize. "I didn't mean to strike in the vicinity of your work. Here then, forgive me and I'll give you another of my theories about why I can be divided by so many men. Let's see, how does it go? Oh, yes. I'm a bit of a whore. How's that?"

"Oh, stop it, Arista! Seriously, what's wrong with your relationship with Clayton? Most women would be happy to have him."

"Clayton's lovely. He's easy to get along with, like all men. Just give them everything they want and they're happy as clams. But he's young, so very young. He wants mothering, but the truth is he's some other woman's son. If I wanted children, I would have had them." She shrugged. "And in bed . . ."

"That's a sentence that needs finishing, my friend."

"In bed, he's . . ."

"He's . . . ?"

"Oh, I mean, it's nice. Nice. He's nice."

"One nice would have been enough."

"*Once* nice would have been enough. Katelyn, you know that for poetry—nice isn't enough. It's the same for prose. One needs a good strong thrust from time to time."

"I wouldn't know, actually. It's been so long."

"Celibacy has a different kind of thrust."

"About that, *you* wouldn't know."

"True enough. I don't think I could live without sex, so nice is better than death. The dissatisfaction is mutual, though Clayton seems unaware of his. Can you imagine how different the world would be if men were suddenly in touch with their feelings? Anyhow, Clayton has never needed me for much. He takes his inspiration and forms his meaningful relationships with large piles of mud and big mounds of clay."

"So did God."

"Nevertheless it's not flattering. I don't feel dirty enough. I'm not needed enough. And you know, there is something else. Clayton makes me feel old. When I'm in Clayton's arms, I see myself through his eyes, and what I see doesn't make me happy. I see the little lines above my lips, the widening waist, the waffle thighs, and it turns me off. I never knew how autoerotic my sexuality was until I took on a younger lover."

"And this preacher? He's older?"

"Even more worn-out than me. And he looks depressed. Maybe I can cheer him up."

"Haven't you cheered up enough troubled men to last you for a lifetime?"

"Heraclitus said, 'You can't step into the same river twice'—but I, Arista Bellefleurs, have discovered that when it comes to men, I can step into the same swamp again and again and again."

"Well, put on your galoshes, Arista. Anon, your marginally familiar stranger approaches." And she watched her friend with a wary expression.

Arista went white.

"Abigail? I mean . . . Arista?" ventured the man.

"Ted? Ted Hackett?"

"Oh, Abby, I was arrested . . . but I was innocent . . . so I ran away . . . and I've found you. I'm sorry. I'm so sorry," and he burst into tears.

At just that moment Mullahboy, hunched over the wheel of a taxi, swerved to avoid the path of a black cat, realized that he had lost control of his car, and though he began stomping furiously on the brake, found himself jerkily jumping the curb and slamming through the front windows of the shop situated just below the Caffe degli Artisti. The force of the collision knocked Ted Hackett across a table and onto the floor in a spray of shattered windowpane. The cab stopped abruptly, half in the café, half in the shop below. A few chaotic moments passed before they all realized they were alive and intact, though badly shaken and marked, redly, here and there with tiny glass cuts in unlikely places. Mullahboy sat in the taxi and wept.

"I'm sorry, I'm sorry," whimpered Mullahboy over and over with a lifetime's practice.

The waiter, after a few frightened questions, brought drinks to his shaken patrons and called the police to sort matters out.

"That was quite a spectacular entrance, Ted," commented Arista dryly. She was now dabbing at his wounds and his tears with a napkin. "Katelyn Wells, this is Ted Hackett. I went to . . . school with Ted, back in Ohio. Could you tell that cabbie to turn the engine off and stop caterwauling. My God, it's Mullahboy! We're all okay, more or less, and so is he."

"How do you do?" said Katelyn, wiping away at a fresh sprinkling of her own tears and nodding in Ted's direction. She got up shakily and went over to comfort Mullahboy, who was standing on the roof of his cab surveying the damage he had done and who seemed well beyond consolation. "Whatever is the matter with you? Are you hurt?" she inquired a little unkindly.

"Not hurt. I *keel* him," he wailed. "I'm sorry."

"You haven't killed anyone. Look, the man you knocked off his feet is sitting up and talking. And that dazed look on his face is love, not shock."

But Mullahboy was not to be distracted from his distress. He pointed to the center of the restaurant where Headstone Brown was sprawled, still as a corpse. "I keel *him*."

Katelyn started to laugh, and then went over to nudge Headstone. "Enough is enough now. You've scared the hell out of Mullahboy." But Headstone was immovable, until the waiter showed up with an ultimatum.

Headstone arose reluctantly and angrily delivered the waiter's epitaph: "By and by, God caught his eye."

Having failed to get a response from anyone, Headstone left the shattered restaurant feeling quite dejected. He walked along the street, past the head shops selling drug paraphernalia and the stone shops selling crystals, until he reached the newsstand on the corner where he bought a copy of The New York Times and began to check out the obituaries. This cheered him up quite a lot.

Meanwhile Ted lay where he had been thrown, propped up on one elbow, glad to be alive, and wondering who he was. He was apparently intact. He was looking hazily up into the smiling face of a beautiful woman. He didn't know who she was either. She had introduced him to the pretty woman as Ted Hackett from Ohio.

"I'm running away from home," he said aloud, thereby revealing the entire extent of his current self-knowledge.

He was badly shaken. His wife Indra's announcement that she wanted a divorce had come as a terrible shock. Perhaps some alcohol would help him think more clearly, though he could not recall that it had ever been helpful before. Nelson Little found an inch of good twelve-year-old Scotch remaining in a bottle toward the back of the cupboard and drank it down without bothering to find a glass. Why now? he wondered. Why wait through twenty-five years of marriage and the birth of three babies to spring the news on him that she was dissatisfied?

He had gotten used to being married, though he hadn't taken to the boys very much, conceived as they were in quick, nervous gestures. Poesy was different. It was his daughter who had stolen his heart. He found that it hurt too much to think about her.

Nelson rubbed his ankle where the stupid ravening gay dog had bitten him last month. The flesh was still tender. Damn dog. Damn Katelyn. Damn Indra. If it turned out that Indra was serious and the divorce actually came to pass, Katelyn would be sure to hear of it and she would be all over him with her buzzing, stinging feelings like a swarm of deranged honeybees.

In theory Nelson Little wanted to be alone. But when he was alone, he didn't know what to do with himself and always felt a little frightened, so eventually he would seek someone out—usually someone he didn't actually want to be with—and once in their presence, he would have to say or do something, and that led, inevitably, to one sort of trouble or another. Today an inconsequential complaint about the eggs had led to Indra Little's announcement of intended divorce. What had she said? Living with him was like living with a molding potato? Or was it a molting pigeon? Nelson made a point never to listen very closely to Indra.

He looked around their bedroom. It was full of junk. Dear junk representing a quarter of a century of marriage. Snapshots and souvenirs; an exercise bicycle that no one used; a large wicker hamper filled with soiled clothing; a dusty, broken stereo; several specimens of Indra's pocked, squashed pottery. There was trampled brown paper covering the floor. He hadn't gotten around to taking it up after last year's paint job, and Indra, in a silent contest of will, refused to remove it either. She no longer showed any interest in their bedroom at all. He was comfortable here. He sighed. He supposed Indra would want him to move out right away. He resigned himself to his fate. Now that he had decided to go, where could he go?

Nelson reached for the phone and dialed from memory.

"Katelyn," he said into her answering machine, "this is Nelson—"

He completed the message, deciding to pack up a few of his belongings. He was soon out of the apartment with a duffel bag full of rumpled clothing. The weather had suddenly turned warm for spring. He decided to walk through the streets of the Village in an uncharacteristic way, noticing his surroundings. It seemed bright and crowded and tumbledown and vital all at once. He was quickly overstimulated and tired, so he sat down at the edge of a children's playground that had been usurped by tall, black men playing basketball. He watched for a while, wishing he was taller, glad he wasn't blacker, listening to the rhythmic thonk of the ball.

He began to register a faint boredom, so he opened his battered, leather briefcase, intending to grade a few composition papers, but his eye fell on a small volume of poetry given to him by one of his female students. *Sonnets from the Portuguese* by Elizabeth Barrett Browning. Why did all the wretched girls in his class fall in love with him? He was without charm. Nelson opened the book at random.

I tell you hopeless grief is passionless. . . .

He knew this. Though he had told no one. He had mourned his tiny, stillborn daughter until there was no feeling left in him at all, for anyone or anything. Just mild preferences and aversions. Now he just went through the motions of his life as teacher, husband, father. What would he do if Indra really left him? What motions would he go through then? Those of a divorcé? Weekend father? Did it matter? He hoped, mildly, that Indra would change her mind. It might even be possible to influence her, though unlikely. He wondered for the first time in years what he might do to please her.

Suddenly he remembered that he had been put in charge of the two boys this afternoon, until Indra returned from her psychoanalyst. In his distraction he had left them all alone. He slammed shut the briefcase and began trotting in the direction of his apartment. If Indra ever found out about this lapse of responsibility, she would never forgive him. If Indra ever found out about almost anything he did, or was, or thought, or felt, she would never forgive him. A fire truck roared by.

I tell you hopeless grief is passionless. . . .

He knew this. The rest of Christian's life was full of passion, full of purpose, but not when it came to women. There, he was numb. Whenever he thought of loving, he beheld Grace, in his mind's eye—his lovely Grace of long ago—and was rendered passionless. Her flaming death had left a charred hole in the center of his heart that could not be unburned. Many women had loved him. He loved them back, but not as a man. He loved them as a saint would love them, chastely, from afar. He was their friend. He was their minister. Nothing more. Sometimes, with God's grace, chaste love was enough for them. Sometimes, not; and then, crestfallen, but not fallen, the women abandoned his congregation and troubled him no more.

He was looking over the upcoming calendar of church events. There was to be a memorial service for Eve Callahan, the woman whose death had had to be dry-cleaned off his trousers. It was scheduled for the last day of the month. The young self-righteous priest at Our Lady wasn't buying the Chinaman's version of an accidental fall. So when a contingent of Eve's friends had come to him and asked most humbly for the use of the sanctuary of Old Gray Presbyterian, he had acquiesced. He felt oddly indebted to Eve. He had begun his book in the down draft of her fall.

As he mulled over the details of the service he felt oddly troubled, though he could not find the source of his discontent. It was to be a twilight service. He had decided to follow his regular Presbyterian Order of Service for the irregular collection of people who would assemble to remember Eve. After the opening hymn he would give the call to worship: "There is longing in the high mountains . . ." That seemed appropriate. And then the opening prayer. The Sanctus, Prayer of Confession, and the Assurance of Pardon would be brief, though he was sure they all would need it. Then the standard two readings from Scripture would follow. He had chosen fine, accessible verses from St. Luke and Corinthians. In place of the Prayer of Thanksgiving, Henry Chang, the Chinese laundryman, whom he had first seen on the other end of Eve's shattered body, would read something from Shakespeare or the *I Ching*. That was weird, but not troubling. He enjoyed hearing new voices from the pulpit. He welcomed new souls to his church. In place of the Prayer of Intercession someone named Rabbi Barkowitz would say his agitated piece. The good Rabbi Barkowitz had been phoning all week from San Francisco, leaving a long series of short, excited messages at inconvenient moments for Christian, all of which had been taken calmly, but with increasing annoyance, by Alice May Patoon.

"You better put him out of his misery," instructed Christian. So the rabbi had been invited to say his piece. Someone named, rather strangely, Luke Sevensons, would deliver the eulogy. He was rumored to be a healer, whatever that might mean. Then Jerry Phails, a strikingly handsome man, who, in another set of rumors, was said to be the illegitimate son of the dead woman, would speak, rather than sing, the anthem. Oh, this was certainly not suburban Seattle!

At first he had not deemed it suitable to preach at the service, for he had known the woman Eve only in death, but her friends were curiously insistent that he should take an active part throughout the ceremony. He had agreed. There would be a closing hymn. And he would put the finishing touch on the service with his loveliest benediction:

> Go forth upon thy journey, Christian soul. Go in the name of God, and may he bring you at last to the land of promise, to the Country of the Great King.

There was nothing in the service itself to trouble him. He had only to choose the hymns. He would decide on them tonight, as a way of falling asleep. It was an old trick that seldom worked, but better than counting sheep. He knew over fifty hymns by heart. One for every year of his life. But what was the source of this amorphous anxiety? He let his mind ramble about for a bit. Ah. There it was, he thought. Woman coming.

Among the contingent of Eve's friends there had appeared a familiar face, a woman who introduced herself as Arista Bellefleurs. Doubtless it was she who had fired up the group about his sermons. He had noticed her in the gallery each Sunday morning since his arrival at Old Gray P. She was rapt. Once she had skulked about at a church reception, though she hadn't approached him. And once, with obvious reservation, she had taken Communion from his hands. It was a candlelight service, he remembered, because it was almost exactly at midnight when she had taken the wafer. The hesitancy had been in her eyes. What were her sins? Could she be saved?

After the brief meeting to arrange the memorial service he had walked her, slightly behind the others, to the door of the church. In those few minutes she had told him a remarkable amount about herself. She said she didn't actually know Eve Callahan, but most of her friends did. She said she was very grateful on behalf of them all, and that she was impressed with the intelligence of his sermons. She said her own childhood had been dominated by her grandfather, a Methodist minister. She said she was a writer, a novelist. She revealed that her name, Arista Bellefleurs, was a nom de plume. She gave her real name as Abigail Brainard. She did not say she was a believer.

Christian knew the signs of Incipient Feminine Emotion Heading Full Tilt in the Direction of His Person. He hoped that Christian charity would be sufficient for Arista Bellefleurs. He thought not. She appeared to be a sensual woman. He sighed. He would hate to lose her from the congregation. She had such a decorative face. He realized that he had begun to search her out each Sunday morning when he entered the pulpit. That was new. Usually he let the rows of solemn faces melt into a sea of warm anonymity, like passengers on a plane.

A breath of air, like the wake of an angel's wing, brushed through his stuffy study.

"Miss Patoon, if you please," he called.

"Yes, Reverend Davies." She stepped to the doors of his office.

"Do we have a church member by the name of Arista Bellefleurs?"

"No, Reverend Davies."

"Are you sure?"

"I couldn't forget such a melodious name, Reverend Davies."

"Of course not, Miss Patoon. How about an Abigail Brainard?"

"No, we have no such member."

"Thank you, Miss Patoon." Christian's Christian charity had been enough for Alice May Patoon. Simple devotion made life so much easier. He smiled a pleasant smile in her direction, saving the Clincher for tougher times, and she slipped out of the study and closed the doors, leaving him to his gentle musings.

So Arista Bellefleurs was a stray cat, was she? Probably agnostic, but bitten by the imagery, the lyricism, and the impressive longevity of Christianity. She seemed a little depressed. Maybe he could cheer her up. She was a writer. He wondered if she could help him with his book. Was he going mad? He remembered that they had stood together, reluctant to part, in the doorway of the church. Her friends: a woman named Katelyn Wells, the illegitimate nonsinger Jerry Phails, and another man with a great many names and pen names were already waiting on the street outside. She had extended her right hand. When he took it into his own, she had covered their clasped hands with her left, and he had covered hers with his. They had stood for a moment, their four hands crossed. "Keep in touch," he had said. He had never said *keep in touch* to anyone in his entire life! He felt as if he had reeled away from her, she from him. Christian could still feel the softness of her palm in his, her palm over his, the back of her hand under his. Smooth. Warm. Close.

Where, he wondered, was that breeze coming from?

He was wondered out. He felt a bit dizzy. He picked up the volume that Arista Bellefleurs had given to him. It was titled *I Am a Strange Flower*. He seldom read modern novelists. When he read fiction, he needed to be nourished. The modern writers were sparse. They starved his soul. He scanned the dedication, recognizing the name of the recipient with surprise.

To my brother and teacher, Luke Sevensons . . .

Why, that was the healer who was going to speak. He turned at random to a page halfway into the text. It revealed a rather shocking description of lovemaking between a woman and two men. His eyebrows went up. He reread the passage and felt another kind of rising, in long quiescent nether parts. She was an accomplished writer, that was evident. And a strange flower indeed! He made up his mind to avoid her.

When they met again, what would he say to her? So many years had passed. Katelyn was afraid. What if he wouldn't speak to her? What would she say to him?

Katelyn Wells approached the ancient house with trepidation. The street was crooked and cobbled and crowded with Saturday-morning shoppers. The smell of freshly baked bread and pastry lay, pleasantly trapped, in the warm air. It was her favorite part of Paris—old and cramped, the Ile St.-Louis. She was going to visit Sebastien. Her most secret, most ancient love. Everyone has one. Her hands were shaking. He would notice. She shoved them into her pockets. Then she took out her right hand. As steadily as possible she rang the bell. The bell shook with sound. There was no response from within.

His personal secretary, who sounded young and snottily competent on the crackling telephone connection, had assured Katelyn that Sebastien would see her. He had told her that Sebastien slept after breakfast until eleven sharp, then dressed and received callers or looked through his photographs until one o'clock, when he walked to the corner café for a light, late lunch. He was reported to be, at ninety years old, in excellent, if fragile, condition. Yes, he had been ill, but it was only influenza. He was quite recovered. She had been reassured.

It was eleven-thirty. She rang again. The door began to creak slowly open. She took a deep breath, preparing herself for the sight of him, but instead she found herself looking down with undisguised surprise at a pair of dwarfs who glared up at her with equally undisguised distrust from the dimly lit foyer. She recognized the seedy, surly look of a Parisian concierge, doubled, and halved in size.

"*Monsieur Sebastien? S'il vous plaît?*"

The little couple looked back and forth from her to each other, and then simultaneously pointed down the hallway to the courtyard garden and beyond. Perhaps they were mutes. They moved reluctantly aside to allow Katelyn to brush past them. Halfway down the hall she turned and watched them disappear, hand in hand, into the front apartment. Had they been each other's first and only love?

Behind the enclosed garden she found Sebastien's apartment door and rang again. Still there was no response. She began to worry. She knew now she was in the right place. And she had an appointment. After a few minutes she considered calling upon the dwarfs with her concern, but the thought of disturbing them again was daunting. She stepped to her right and, putting her hand against the glass, tried to peer through the window. It was too dark inside the hushed apartment to make out any details. Nothing seemed to move. What if Sebastien had died in his sleep? Or worse, had fallen, and needed some help? Perhaps she should go and telephone his secretary. No. Monday was his day off, he had said. She rang again, then knocked, then checked her watch. She paced a bit in the red-and-yellow garden, earth sticking to her shoes, and then, with more courage than she knew she possessed, pushed open the window and called softly into the apartment.

"Sebastien, Sebastien, are you there?"

There was no answering word from within.

Katelyn had loved Sebastien a long time ago. She had come to Paris twenty-five years before to study with him. She had been twenty. He had been sixty-five. They had been lovers. No one had ever known. Not anyone in the troupe, not Victor, not, in later years, Arista. No one but she and Sebastien had known, for they vowed never to speak of it. Often when she cried her most silent tears, they were for Sebastien. She let people assume that all her sadness was for Nelson Little or for her missing son or for her failed marriage. What did people know? Not half what they presumed to know. What did people care? Not half what they said they did.

Sebastien had been, was still, the greatest mime in the world. Katelyn had been his protégée. She had lived with him and for him. He had lived for his art and—as she was at the moving center of his art—for her. Together they had explored the silence, creating quiet changing worlds of meaning, of ever deeper feeling. Then Victor Wells, young and lithe, had joined the troupe. He had wanted her, and as youth would have it, he did. What a fool she had been! Sebastien, who Katelyn had imagined would be wise and forgiving, had been heartbroken. Like a mighty Jehovah he had reared up and sent her forth, an unspoken curse rolling down his outstretched arm and off his pointing finger.

She and Victor had tried to make a life together in New York City—inhabiting the kind of cheap rooms you could then get in the Village, terrible places. For a while they had made a slim living as street mimes, with occasional stage engagements, but the spine of her art was broken. With the advent of the baby, Victor had been forced to take other jobs. He became a salesman, first of shoes, then of hearing aids. As the years passed they found that they had very little to say to one another. When Victor found out about Nelson, he had left her, gracefully, without a word of recrimination. Then Amas had left her, too. She was sure that all the leavings were justified, fitting punishment for her betrayal of Sebastien, at the beginning of her life.

Sebastien had remained in Paris, teaching and performing. There was, she imagined, no shortage of protégés for a man of his energy and beauty. Sebastien had been her distant muse. She thought of him, dreamed of him, wrote for him, knowing how unlikely it was that he would ever read of her accomplishments. Even Nelson had not wiped him out. Then, only yesterday morning, she had read in the Arts and Leisure section of *The New York Times* that he was ill. In an instant she was packing, within hours she was on her way to him. There had been no thought, only impulse.

Katelyn pushed the window open wider and, with a quick glance around the garden to be sure she was unobserved, climbed awkwardly into Sebastien's apartment. It took a few moments for her eyes to adjust to the dusk within the sparsely furnished room. When her vision cleared, she found herself standing about six feet from Sebastien, who was sitting in a straight-backed chair staring directly at her.

"Sebastien?"

He did not move. Was he dead?

"Sebastien. It's Katelyn from 1967."

Sebastien blinked, very slowly. He was not dead. She saw no recognition in his eyes.

"I'm different now. But I was . . . I am . . . Katelyn Hemmingway. My name is Wells now. I married him. Victor Wells. You remember him. I'm sorry. I was your . . . your student. Do you remember me?" She strained to see the man she had loved, to recognize the body she had studied in every kind of stillness and every kind of movement. She saw only a wrinkled man in a wrinkled dressing gown—unknown, unmoving, staring silently into the empty space that fell between them. "Are you all right, Sebastien?" Nothing.

She glanced around the room, recognizing a vase, a painting from over twenty years in the past. She found another chair nearby and pulled it up before him. She sat down knee to knee with the aged man and waited. It was deathly quiet in the back apartment. She could hear only her breathing, his.

After a time she spoke to him softly: "Sebastien, I have come to apologize to you. I was very young, and very stupid to ever have looked at another man. Least of all Victor

Wells. You held within you all that excited and moved me. I loved you very much. But I thought . . . that you would tire of me. Discard me. I felt inadequate before the flame of your talent. You were so intense . . . so mature . . . so . . . sacred. You frightened me with your intensity. I frightened myself with mine. I adored you. You were my God." Her hand crept toward his, hesitated, returned to her lap, like a cat. "And my Satan. I felt I was burning up in your arms, burning out on your stage. What did I know? I was a child. I have not been happy. I have deserved my unhappiness, clung to it . . . because I betrayed you. I can never be happy in this life. I want you to know how sorry I am. Not for myself. I'm sorry for what I did to you, for my disloyalty to you, for my unfaithfulness to our art. I am sorry for my lack of trust. But believe me, there was no lack of love."

The old man did not speak. Nor did he move.

She remembered the wisdom by which he had lived:

Let me be silent, for so are the gods.

Katelyn got up and quietly pushed the chair back to its proper place. Then she knelt before Sebastien and bowed her head.

She did so with all the grace of her youth, with all the silent beauty of movement that he had taught her. Lower and lower she bent and kissed his ancient, naked feet. Katelyn slowly raised her head and saw a single teardrop course soundlessly down the ruined face of her lover. He did that better than she could ever have done! He was, truly, an artist.

Then she stood up and turned and climbed back out the window. The dwarfs were weeding in the garden, almost lost among the gently moving tulips and bending jonquils. They peered suspiciously at Katelyn through the foliage.

She left hurriedly, as she had come. The roar of the engines tore at her inner silence. She was returning to the world of noise, the world of words.

Airplanes, she noticed, had changed a lot in twenty years. After saying goodbye to Callahan and Deerfinder, Maggie Silvernails had spent a week alone in the desert, without food, without sleep. On the seventh morning she had seen a vision. Her spirit guide, the fragile fawn that had, since childhood, led her through this life, emerged silently from a clump of cactus and tumbleweed, gazing at her with the deep, sad eyes of the Great Spirit. Maggie knew that wordless communion was possible, questions she had never dared to ask could be answered. This time, with a boldness born of need, Maggie asked her questions as she peered into the glowing, brown eyes of the fawn. The silent answers resounded in her soul:

Why did you create this woman, Maggie Silvernails?

I WISHED TO BELIEVE THAT SEXUALITY WAS POSSIBLE, EVEN BEAUTIFUL, LATE IN LIFE.

But I have been in this desert for twenty years.

THE MIDDLE YEARS. NOW YOU ARE OLD.

Why did you leave me alone for so long?

I, TOO, HAVE BEEN ALONE A LONG TIME. SOMETIMES I DESPAIR. BUT IF LOVE CAN SEARCH OUT MAGGIE SILVERNAILS AFTER TWENTY YEARS, THEN THERE IS HOPE.

What am I to do now?

FOLLOW YOUR LOVE.

I have two. Three, if you count Deerfinder, though our bodies have never met.

THE TIME HAS COME. NOW YOU MUST CHOOSE.

What will you do?

WAIT. YOU'VE TAUGHT ME HOW TO WAIT.

I've given you that?

YOU ARE AN INSPIRATION, MAGGIE SILVERNAILS.

Then the young deer blinked and turned away gracefully. She had watched it bound into the sunrise. She knew she would go east. She packed up, carrying her latest canvases with her. Fatpaws was sent to prowl with the reservation dogs for a while. She felt fear for only one eventuality. What if Luke really died on the first of the month? Could she bear it? She could not sense it. The signs were not there. He must have made some mistake. She would talk with him, touch with him. He would live. She knew that back in Greenwich Village, there would be many reconnections to be made. Each would touch a scar on her heart.

The children were becoming restless now after so many hours in the air. But they were good about it, even wee Bren who had watched the movie and played with the repugnant airline food, and then, without complaint, had fallen asleep with his head in Elinor's lap. He looked as an angel might look. He reminded her of Paul when he slept.

Elinor hoped that Callahan would love his grandchildren; that his concern for them and her concern for them would form a bridge upon which they could meet after so many years of estrangement.

Her lovely daughter Bridget hoped for a meeting with the American boy Seth Hackett, having no notion of the vastness of the United States, the great distance between Ohio and New York. Bridget had written to him, telling him that her grandmother Eve was dead and that she was coming with her mother and all her brothers and sisters to the memorial service at Old Gray Presbyterian Church in Greenwich Village. Seth longed to see her. He had written an étude for Bridget. He carried it with him now, and he hoped to play it for her in person. The scandal that surrounded Janet Joyce's accusations, and the subsequent desertion by his father had left him feeling more alone than ever before. He hadn't known he could miss his father.

Seth had declared to his distraught mother that he refused to attend another dysfunctional-family meeting; then he had emptied out his savings and bought his airline ticket. He had never flown before. Soon he would be in New York City. He would go and look at Carnegie Hall, and at Lincoln Center, and at the Juilliard School of Music. Then he would find a room to rent, and then, by God, he would find Bridget O'Neill.

New York was huge, he knew, but the Village was small. He had read about the Village in the biographies of musicians and artists for years. It seemed a haven to him.

Perhaps, amid its ferment, he would find himself. Finding himself was the point of a temporary amnesia, the physician assured Arista when she asked him about Ted. The doctor went on to say that Ted Hackett would, most likely, come to his senses soon, remember who he was, and go home. The dysfunctional-family counselor assured Ivy Sue that her husband, wherever he was, would soon come to his senses and come home. The psychoanalyst assured

Ted Hackett that he would soon come to his senses and remember who he was and where his home was and go there. Ted himself wasn't so sure. Who am I? he asked. Do I really want to know? Who, exactly, am I? Buff Carrington answered his own question: I am a blind, dying faggot and this apartment house is on fire. If I crawl slowly and stay with Greta Garbo and don't panic, I may manage to survive, though the smoke in this stairwell is getting hotter and thicker.

Why, he wondered at such a time, was he wondering who he was? Perhaps it was in just such moments—moments of life and death—that the big questions arrive. The answers seemed quite small, everything considered.

He could hear the fire trucks converging outside the building. That was good. Whoever he was, the firemen might manage to save him. He had heard the other tenants on the floors below raise the alarm and leave the building in a trampling stampede. Quentin had not accompanied him on his impulsive visit to their friend Jerry Phails. Buff liked to sit in Jerry's apartment when he was talking librettos. Jerry lived alone on the top floor and this morning, surprisingly, he had not been at home. So it was just Buff Carrington and Greta Garbo who found themselves crawling for their lives, all alone against the elements and a concurrent existential crisis. What did it mean, after all, to be alive? Why did anything exist? And then he heard the baby's cry. The pathetic wail came from an apartment on the same floor on which he now found himself. He struggled to his feet, though the smoke was thicker, and pounded at the door, but there was no response from within, except for the continuing wails of the unknown infant. No, there were two cries, one a baby, one an older child.

"Hello, hello!" he called out, thumping on the locked

door. "Greta, speak!" and the dog began to bark roughly and noisily. No one came to help from either inside or out-side the apartment. He began to throw himself blindly against the door, hoping to break the lock. On the third try, just before he hit, the door swung open and he flew into the room, landing on top of a hollering two-year-old.

"Stop crying," he commanded, and the boy ceased his noise abruptly. "Help me up. I'm blind. Help me find your baby sister."

"Little brother," the coughing child corrected him, and led him by the hand to the infant's room. Buff noticed that the floors were strangely covered with paper. That would burn fast.

He swooped up the baby into his arms. The tiny morsel of humanity nestled into the crook of his arm naturally, and also stopped its cries at his touch. Gay men didn't of-ten have children, he knew, and Buff had mourned the lack of a family long ago. He had never known his own father. Now, in this terrible moment, he felt the desire for father-hood in one hot flash of longing. He would do his best for these children. "Now, hold on to the dog," he ordered the little boy. "So will I. She'll get us out of here." But as they neared the open door Greta balked and Buff could tell that what had been a smoky stairwell only a minute before was now a furnace of fire.

He kicked the door shut and asked the boy to lead him to a window. They were four floors up. With his free hand he opened the window and listened to the din below. He began to shout: "Are there firemen down there?"

"Are you blind?" came the reply from below.

"Yes. Where are you? Are you under the window? I am trapped up here with two babies."

"We're underneath you. We have a net. Wait a minute. Okay. Drop them down."

Buff hesitated. The warm baby was curled against him contentedly; the little boy clutched his hand and leaned against his legs. How could he throw them away into nothingness? His sons. Who were not his sons.

"Hurry up, mister! Throw them down. They'll be fine. We'll come up for you, but drop them first."

Buff felt along the window ledge. There was a window box in which young plants were growing. He could smell that they were tomato plants, already wilting from the heat. With one hand he pulled the obstructing planter loose and tossed it into the room behind him. Then he leaned out into the air and then, with something like a prayer, he let go of the trusting baby. He heard a roar of approval and relief from those below as the infant was safely caught in the firemen's net.

The door of the apartment burst inward from the heat and he felt the flames roaring toward them. He picked up the little boy and lifted him over the windowsill, but the terrified child clutched at him and he had to scrape the tiny fingers from his arms like melted wax from a candlestick. Screaming, the boy fell away. Buff shuddered, cold in the intense heat. Another sound of safe arrival rushed up to him.

"We're coming up for you, mister."

"No! Wait! Keep the net in place! There's no time!" Using all his strength, for he was greatly weakened by his disease, he seized the beloved dog and, before she had time to protest, hurled her out. "God bless you, Greta," he whispered as she went.

"The dog's safe, mister. Jump. Jump now."

He wanted to jump, but he couldn't. He had known from the first moment that he couldn't. It had taken all the guts he had to throw out the children and then Greta. He was a brave, blind man. But even blind men have their limits, their fears, their phobias. Buff was deathly afraid of heights he could not see. He could not leap into the void. The heat was incinerating. Behind him, objects began to explode. There was no oxygen left in the pulsing room.

He leaned, faintly, against the window frame, gasping for air and for courage. No, nothing could be worse than such a plunge—not even the flames of hell. His hair and the back of his shirt had begun to scorch. Buff covered his face with his hands and bit his lip against anticipated agony. Perhaps it would be an easier death than the slow deterioration of AIDS. He hoped he would pass out quickly. He hoped he would not scream. Buff Carrington closed his sightless eyes and prepared to burn to death.

And then he was gently, but firmly, pushed out of the window. He would never, in his brief lifetime, know by whom. As he fell through the blackness it seemed to Buff that for a moment he actually flew, and then he dropped gracefully into the net as if into the benevolent hand of God. In the instant it took him to fall he remembered who he was. The moment of grace was swept away in the commotion surrounding his rescue. The closest he would ever come to being able to describe the experience would be when, near death, having been given a book of Buddhist verse, he would find a poem by Han Shan, which he would memorize and recite aloud to all who would listen:

> In a flash, the violent mind stood still. Within without are both transparent and clear. After the great somersault, the great void is broken through. Oh how freely come and go the myriad forms of things.

Of course, by then, everyone but Henry Chang would think he was delirious, that the virus had invaded his brain. But now, bouncing gently in the weblike net, he heard only the sounds of celebration, mixed curiously with the sounds of grief as the residents of the blazing building realized that although they were all alive, everything they possessed was disappearing before their eyes.

Buff was allowed a brief reunion with the children before they were taken away to the hospital for observation. He would never touch them again, but the experience was complete for Buff. In the moment when he had saved the two boys, he had acted as a father. In the moment when he had been saved himself, he had been cared for as a son. And whoever or whatever had pushed him out of the window . . .

A few weeks ago, when he had returned to Quentin, after the long, cold, Ohio winter with Luke Sevensons, he had been ready to face his death. When he stood at the fiery window only minutes ago, he had been ready again. Now, on this overheated spring day, Buff was ready to live. He was eager to get home to dear, dear Quentin; and to Quentin's crazy boy, his pet boy, Mullahboy. Greta Garbo seemed energized by her airborne adventure and trotted happily along through the familiar streets with Buff in tow.

They had only gone a few blocks when a running, sobbing, limping man crashed into them painfully and, without a word of apology, fled in the direction of the conflagration. Greta growled, an unheard-of sound. Buff stopped walking and knelt down, patting the dog, offering reassurance. Fatpaws looked around at the strange surroundings. Human stuff.

Deerfinder handed him a hamburger. Things were looking up. This was a definite improvement over the reservation food! After their dinner they went for a walk, more of a trot, around a large, busy area with entirely new smells, where Fatpaws cheerfully contributed a few of his own.

Then they had climbed into a long box that started to move uncertainly, then faster and faster.

Fatpaws watched while the city and then the desert and then the city went by outside the box. After a while he lost interest and so he put his head down on Deerfinder's lap. Listening to the clack of the moving box, he fell happily asleep. It had been a good day with many adventures. He cinched the seat belt a little tighter. He loved adventure. And yet adventure had fled from his life.

Victor Wells knew this was due to a number of factors. For one thing he was no longer young, and for another he had been gifted with only a minor talent. No one gave a damn about mimicry. Not in this culture, if you could call this a culture. Also he didn't love anyone. That should free him up for adventure, he knew, but it didn't. He had become an ex-husband, an ex-character in the life of Katelyn and her friends. An ex–New Yorker. An ex-artist. An ex-factor. And he was lonely.

Loneliness depressed the hell out of him and kept him from considering anything outside of the ordinary. Yet, when the divisional sales meeting had been set for New York, he found himself pulled, pulled in the direction of the city where he had lived the longest and been the most unhappy.

Not always unhappy, he granted. His first trip to New York had been an adventure, oh so many years ago. And then there had been the tour through Europe. The performances in London. Rome. Paris. The treasure hunt of youth for exactly the right woman. The joyful flight back to New York with his nimble prize in tow. Katelyn, his first and only love, won from the old-geezer genius, Sebastien.

He laughed, startling the exceptionally prim woman in the seat next to his. How wordlessly happy they had been, he and Katelyn. And then Amas came along and grew apace. They had been poor and life had been full.

But life has a life of its own, he mused. Life stands up one day and shakes itself out like a dog, then bends over and empties its guts out. Everything you love is, in the end, lost. What had he left from all those years? A son he seldom spoke to. Great Daniel, their antique French poodle. A little more gracefulness than most middle-aged men possessed. A mouth full of unsaid bitterness. Eyes full of unshed tears. Unmoving memories. Why were memories always frozen, still? The plane soared and banked. He was going back. The ex-factor was going back to kick at his past. Victor would see Katelyn again. He leaned back and thought about sex with Katelyn. He ran his mind's eye up her long, perfect legs, happy at journey's end. He would have her again—win her back from Nelson Little.

Love doesn't make fools of us all, he thought; it makes us all love fools. He shivered. It was cold in the woods, even here in the tent Lester had staked out to protect himself from the evening air. He was nearing the end of his long spiritual search and he was beginning to understand the truth about his life. The quiet helped. Being surrounded by nature helped. The nearly forty days and forty nights he had been fasting had helped. He could hear his own inner voice quite clearly now. And other voices as well.

The voices told him he must marry Katelyn immediately. They warned that something was coming to take her away from him. Something evil. It couldn't be that fool Nelson Little. He had already usurped Nelson Little.

He would return today from the wilderness, proclaiming his true identity and making his long-awaited claims upon the world. An immediate marriage after all his talk of a long courtship would upset Katelyn, of course. But then

Katelyn was always upset. After a day like today, why shouldn't she be upset?

There had been four messages on her answering machine when she returned from Paris. Lester, to say he was returning from his extended retreat; the doctor with the disappointing test results; a message from Victor, her ex, informing her that he was coming to New York for a sales conference and asking to meet; and the unbelievable message from Nelson Little:

"Katelyn, this is Nelson. I'd like to come and live with you. Indra has thrown me out. I'll stop by sometime this afternoon and leave my bags with your doorman. See you tonight."

She didn't know when he had left the message. It was undated. It could have been anytime in the last three days. It could have been today. She would have cried, but that was finished. Nelson? Now? With a marriage being planned so carefully with Lester. How would Lester feel if he came back and found Nelson Little in her bed? Or supposing she and Lester managed to marry as planned—it now, suddenly, seemed impossible—how would Lester feel when she told him there could be no babies? He believed that the purpose of sex was to make babies. And what if she and Nelson were to get married and there could be no babies? Nelson loved babies. He had told her so.

She was only forty-five. Forty-five was too young to be told she was too old! Damn the doctor! It was a loss to age that was harder to bear than the dimming eyesight, the failing hearing, the thinning hair, the crinkling skin. Thank God for her son, Amas, wherever he was. He was now having babies of his own.

She supposed it was ridiculous—her a grandmother—

bemoaning the fact that she couldn't have babies. But she didn't feel like a grandmother. Since the arrival of Lester in her life she felt like a schoolgirl. Listening to Nelson's message, she felt like a woman in the fullness of life. Listening to Victor, she felt very confused.

Could there be a poem in all this? Perhaps Arista was at the Caffe degli Artisti. Katelyn grabbed her notebook and hurried to the coffeehouse. There, behind the newly repaired windows, she did not see Arista Bellefleurs, but she found George Eliot Isaman, Clayton Grant, Quentin Cox, Oakley Klapper, and Jerry Phails, all huddled around the clay model that Clayton was showing off. It was a mock-up for his sculpture of Eve Callahan, after her fall. There seemed to be no shortage of opinion, all of it enthusiastic.

"It's shocking!"

"Grotesque."

"Moving."

"No. It's the fact that she is so clearly *not* moving that's so upsetting."

"I love it."

"It will be terrifying in the life-size version."

"Where will you show it?"

"Not at a park or a gallery."

"Surely it will have to be dropped on a sidewalk somewhere."

Katelyn moved closer and observed the mock-up. She saw a woman crushed by life, shattered by her fall, yet still beautiful. As she remembered Eve. The head was turned skyward and she seemed to be saying, "Why, why?" Katelyn stared.

"No comment, Katelyn?" asked Clayton. He turned to Katelyn with little sympathy, for he thought of her as the girl who cried. Not wolf. Just cried.

"It's a good likeness, Clayton," she admitted, miffed at him, but too impressed not to give the compliment where it was due. "It should be displayed at the memorial service."

"I don't know," he considered. "Maybe. I liked the old girl. She was a bit of a chore to talk to, but, you know, she really could appreciate other people's lives. Everything she ever said about my work was supportive."

"She was good to me, too," affirmed Katelyn. "Does anyone know where Arista is today?"

"She's found God," said George, and then shrugged. All the men looked at Katelyn helplessly. They stood around the news of Arista's newest preoccupation exactly like men around a dead woman.

"She's at church," clarified Clayton.

"It's not Sunday."

"She's meeting with her minister."

"About Eve's service? I thought we had that all arranged."

"Is it? Then I can't imagine what it's about."

Katelyn could imagine quite a lot, and in detail. This latest crush of Arista's must have escaped Clayton's notice or he would not be so nonchalant. She had seen this phenomenon before; a man who was engaged wholeheartedly in his creative work simply lost track of the rest of his life—his diet, his bills, his relationships. Later, when the work of art was completed, he would look up, and be quite surprised to find himself sick or bankrupt or bereft or all of the above. "Maybe she's talking with him about her angel dreams."

"Her what?"

"She's been dreaming about a group of angels lately. They trouble her. And she thinks her shrink must have taken a vow of silence."

"I warned her not go to a psychoanalyst who had spent his youth as a monk," interjected George.

"Charles Agincourt is harmless," said Oakley. "I *think*."

"Anyhow, maybe this preacher will make sense of the angels."

"I'm sure whatever she's doing in church is keeping her out of trouble," said Katelyn protectively. She suddenly wished she liked Clayton better, but he was so briskly unsympathetic, so tightly self-involved. She felt that if she threw an egg at Clayton, it would bounce off him and break elsewhere. He was young, loved, healthy, good-looking, talented, rich, and male. A calamity of happiness. His good fortune had, so far, protected him from suffering, so that he was unseasoned by life, insensitive. Perhaps that was why he was fascinated with Eve Callahan, who had been seasoned and smoked and aged and processed like a sardine. Katelyn searched for something pleasant to say to Clayton and succeeded: "It's awfully good of you to put Ted Hackett up at your place until he figures himself out."

"Thanks, luv."

"How's he doing?"

"Strange. Fine. He talks to Old Nevermore, and to Dr. Agincourt. I think the raven answers him more often than the shrink does. He thinks. He helps out around the studio. He likes my work. He listens to music constantly. Classical stuff mostly. He wants to spend more time with Arista than she wants to spend with him . . . or me, for that matter. She seems to need whole eons of time alone these days. Ted's wife, Ivy Sue, is a pain in the neck. She phones practically every day. Wants him to come back to Boar's Wood. But he won't budge. I like him."

"He fancies himself an art critic," said Oakley Klapper apropos of nothing, "and he doesn't like my paintings."

"Or my books," said George Eliot Isaman.

"I don't think he's a critic. I think he's just trying to begin a new life. Everything is new to him. He says whatever comes into his head."

"Ted enjoyed my reading of *Henry the Fifth*," added Quentin with a touch of pride. "Sometimes he comes down to our apartment and sits with Buff or Mullahboy or Greta Garbo. He seems content not to do anything at all."

"Thinking is something."

"What does he think *about*? He doesn't remember anything."

"I wonder what it's like to feel completely new at the age of forty-five?" mused Katelyn.

"I wouldn't know," replied Quentin sadly, thinking of his deadly illness. It was still a secret from this group, though they had heard about Buff and knew his odds. He would probably not reach forty.

"I wouldn't know either," said George irritably. "I feel stuffed with some unidentifiable matter that's poking out in all the wrong places, like foam rubber from an old sofa."

"Sounds like you've started a new book."

"Yeah." He was dispirited. The writing of his intended masterpiece was again to be delayed by popular demand. "It's called *The Misplaced Coffin*."

As if on cue, Headstone Brown ambled in, carefully looked over the statue, and then quickly wove a small memorial wreath from the flowers on the table. This he placed near the miniature Eve, and then he sat down peacefully in a corner, his back to the living. His appearance unaccountably lightened what had been a darkening mood at the table, and the men began to talk of resuming their respective works.

Katelyn found that she didn't want to work. She

wanted to talk. She needed to talk to Arista before she went home. Home to Nelson? The thought took her breath away. She had waited five infinite years for a sign from Nelson Little. Now he was coming to live with her. What the hell was she doing here? In the Caffe degli Artisti? Why, all the waiting must have driven her crazy! Vaguely aware of the sirens in the distance, she bid a hasty farewell to the assembled artists and hurriedly left the Caffe degli Artisti. As she hastened past Old Gray Presbyterian she read the title of Sunday's sermon on the notice board. It said: *I Am a Strange Flower*. That was the title of one of Arista's books! It appeared that Arista was not doing *all* the seducing. And the relationship was clearly progressing if Arista was managing to get herself holed up alone with Davies. Perhaps the god of love with his tender wings and tiny arrows was, at last, looking out for both their interests.

Katelyn rounded the corner onto her block and quickened her pace as she went past the local library. Out of the corner of her eye she had noticed Florian Agincourt coming through the front door of the library and starting down the steps in her direction. She hadn't seen Florian for a while and she did not want to be distracted now. Not with Nelson at her door. Florian unchecked could go on for hours about big bangs and black holes. It was too late. He had seen her.

"Katelyn!" he yelled. "Congratulations!"

"Thank you," she called back, not knowing to what event he referred. Perhaps it was about Nelson. How did he know? She hadn't said a word about Nelson's message to anyone. She kept walking.

"Lester is a lucky man," he continued, gaining on her.

"Oh. Right. Yes. Lester. No. I'm the lucky one."

"So am I."

It was hopeless. He clearly wanted to engage her in conversation. She stopped and turned. Breathless, Florian caught up with her.

"I've just been notified, Katelyn. They're going to name the comet after me. The one I found. Agincourt's Comet. It should be visible to the naked eye by the end of the month."

"Then it is I who should congratulate you," she said. "That's wonderful news, Florian." He was grinning from ear to ear, which was uncharacteristic of this serious-minded man.

"Thanks. It means a lot to me. I'm more narcissistic than I could have imagined. I feel quite giddy about it, my little contribution to the knowledge of the universe. You know, Quentin's got some of his performances on film, and Jerry has his old recordings. You and Arista have your published works, and you've got Amas as well. Everyone in the damn Village has either got art or kids to carry them into posterity. Now I have something, too. Agincourt's Comet will orbit near the earth every one hundred and sixty-two years until it burns itself out, but that won't happen for centuries. I know it sounds silly, but that comet is my little morsel of immortality."

"Not silly. Not so little." As she mouthed the syllables of Nelson's name she panicked. What if he came to her apartment and she wasn't there and he changed his mind? But Florian was in full, if strange, flower.

"I feel like it's a reward for my faith in physics. I have always believed that in an expanding universe, a phase accompanied by, ruled by, entropy, it is man's mind that stands alone against the tide of dissolution; ceaselessly, relentlessly, hopelessly the brain makes order and sense, in spite of the knowledge that everything is destined to eventual collapse and destruction."

She could bear the delay no longer. "I'm glad your God has smiled on you, Florian. Congratulations. But I've got to rush. Be well, Florian."

"Look for my comet."

"I'll write a poem about it," she promised, hurrying onward. "Something better than 'Twinkle, Twinkle, Little Star.' "

"Twinkle, twinkle, little star . . ."

He sang the unfamiliar words that came floating back into his consciousness. He'd been out for a walk along the Hudson, watching the water and wondering what lay below its surface.

"How I wonder what you are. . . ."

He remembered a dark lake, then a weeping-cherry tree. Ted Hackett never knew when a stray memory would choose to surface. He thought this image might be the backyard of his house, the one Ivy Sue had told him about in her last plaintive phone call. He did not remember Ivy Sue, and she didn't sound very appealing on the telephone. He was not about to accede to this strange woman's repeated requests to come home, which he also didn't remember, and which she insisted was in a place with the god-awful name of Boar's Wood, Ohio.

Arista had told him that he was indeed married to this Ivy Sue person and that he did indeed come from this Boar's Wood place. Although he knew of no reason why Arista would lie to him, Ted couldn't believe it. Why should he? Nothing in his mind or heart informed him so. Arista had also said that they had once been lovers—long ago—though he couldn't believe that either. Arista was not his type. He was sure of it, though he wasn't sure what his type was exactly. Her confession had been an awkward moment for him. He didn't want to hurt her feelings after she had been so kind to him. But he had found no tender response to her revelation.

I wonder why my mind changed? he wondered.

I CHANGED MY MIND.

Who was *I*? Yet he wasn't complaining. He found that he was happy here. In Greenwich Village. He liked Clayton Grant, felt drawn to him. He liked Clayton's raven, Old Nevermore. He liked the variety of people who came and went from the sculptor's studio. He was challenged by the sessions with his psychiatrist, by the slippery climbs up the blank walls of his memory. Every now and then a foothold appeared. Why, just the other day he had remembered money. In the meantime he was learning about sculpture. He was learning about poetry. He was learning about music. He loved music.

He watched Katelyn Wells rush away down the street in the direction of her apartment. She appeared distracted and she hadn't seen him. She had been talking excitedly to the rather attractive man, who, having been left abruptly by Katelyn, was now standing alone on the sidewalk a few feet from Ted, smiling and humming "Twinkle, Twinkle, Little Star" to himself. Ted stepped forward.

"Hello," he said, extending his hand. "I'm Ted Hackett. Do you know me?"

The man seemed taken aback. "No. I don't believe so."

"Oh. Oh, well. I thought that because you knew Katelyn Wells you might know me."

"I'm sorry."

"Don't be. I've got amnesia and I don't know me at all. I'm on my way to my psychiatrist. His name is Dr. Charles

Agincourt." The man was looking more and more confused.

"Dr. Charles Agincourt is my twin brother."

Confusion was something Ted Hackett knew a thing or
two about. He smiled reassuringly.

"That's why you looked familiar. I'll tell him that I've
met you. I wonder if he will believe me? What's your name
then?"

"Florian Agincourt."

"I'm sorry I don't know you." He remembered that he
wanted to remember to ask Dr. Agincourt if he was gay.
Clayton had told him about homosexuals only yesterday
when he explained about Quentin and Buff. Perhaps men
were his type. The idea amused him. "Have a good day."

"Tell Charles they've named the comet after me."

"What's a comet?"

"A star with a wee tail," Megan answered Bren.

"It's dust and gas from far out in space," added Colin,
"and it orbits through the galaxy, and glows in the light of
the sun." Grady did an imitation of an orbiting comet
around Callahan's studio.

"Here in the newspaper it says that a comet is coming
toward the earth now and we can see it next Friday night,
the same night as Grandma's service."

"I think we should call it Grandma's comet."

"Eve's comet."

"Callahan's comet."

"It's called the Agincourt Comet."

The children had settled into Jamie Callahan's studio
like dust, comfortably into every cranny, as though they
had lived amid artistic disarray all their lives. At present
they were spread out over the Sunday *Times* in among the
paintings and the paraphernalia of his work. Callahan had

gone to pick up Luke Sevensons and Methuselah from Grand Central Station.

"You've got smart children, Elinor," said Maggie Silvernails. Elinor beamed over her brood.

"I love them so. They are all I want to do with my life."

"If you love them, what else is there to do?" The two women were joyful to be reunited, and they sat now where they had so often lingered during Elinor's growing-up years, at the scratched corner table near the old black stove. They enjoyed long silences while they soaked up the sight of each other and the babble of the children. The quiet times alternated with intense conversations about everything important in their unalike lives. "I knew your sons and daughters would be beautiful. I would like to paint them before you go back to Belfast. Would you like that, Elinor?"

"Yes. I would. Callahan plans to paint them, too. I hope they won't be spoiled by all the attention." Her face darkened.

"Tell me," urged Maggie.

"I have a picture of Paul with me. Do you think . . . Maggie, I love your paintings so . . . could you . . ."

"Paint your Paul for you? Of course I will, Elinor. You needn't be hesitant to ask me. It will be an honor."

"I'd ask Callahan, but I'd like Brian in it, too, and you know how Daddy resents . . . resented . . . my husband."

"Our old Jamie still has some growing up to do. Let me see the photograph."

"Here." Elinor took the small, framed school photograph from her bag and handed it over carefully. She handed over a wedding photo, too, with Brian looking happy and handsome.

Maggie was gazing sadly at the handsome, innocent face

of the lost youngster, finding bits of Elinor and Callahan and Eve and Brian scattered among his features.

"There's something else."

"What is it?"

"I'd like them painted with Eve. I've found a photo of her among my father's memorabilia and a feather of memory has drifted back to me. It's all I have of her." She watched Maggie closely, but the older woman showed no emotion. "I haven't hurt your feelings, have I?"

"No. How could I be hurt?"

"*You* raised me, not Eve."

"Eve made you. Eve carried you. Eve bore you. I've no quarrel with the woman who did that. I'm just sorry she hurt you."

"I've forgiven her. I prayed to be able to forgive her for years. But it wasn't until I got that cockamamie letter from Henry Chang telling me that she had gone to join her ancestors that I realized something." She paused, surveying her children. "Although she had left me so many years ago, she has really been a part of my life all along. She inspired me, in reaction to her, to be a good mother. Without complaint, her memory took the rap for all the unhappiness that came my way in life. I had made something of her absence. When I heard she was dead, I found I was through being angry with her. I was just sad, and then the forgiveness came. Like a gift. She's with Paul now. Perhaps she'll be a better grandmother than she was a mother."

"That often happens among the living. Why not among the spirits?" Maggie smiled. "I'll paint the three of them together, as you like."

"Maggie, do Indians believe in ghosts?" It was Bren.

"Some do. I don't."

"Aren't spirits ghosts?"

"No."

"What are spirits?"

"Like your angels."

"And the Great Spirit?"

"Like your God."

"Some boys at school said there isn't really a God."

"Wait until next Friday."

"Why?"

"You come with me after your grandma's service. We'll drive out of the city, out by the ocean, and we'll look up at the comet. Then you decide about God."

"Can we all come?" the other children chorused in.

"Yes."

Satisfied, the children went back to the newspapers, fascinated with the strange Americanisms in the writing, with the luxury of the advertisements, with the *amount* of news that their mother's country generated in one week's time.

"You should have seen Daddy's face, Maggie, when he first saw the children," said Elinor. "It was like a great wind had come across a blustery sky, smearing it all over with sunlight. He just lit up. He was afraid of me, I could tell. He's been a perfect bastard about Brian, and he knows it . . . but the wee ones . . . they left us no room for anger or fear."

"He didn't want to lose you, Elinor. Belfast is such a frightening place to our eyes. He couldn't forgive Brian for taking you there. Given all that has happened, you'll have to admit he had a point."

"He handled it wrong." Elinor stared hard at the photographs. "Belfast is a nightmare to my eyes, too." She straightened her shoulders. "Nevertheless it was Brian's home. The home he grew up in and loved. And it's been a home to me, too. Someday the troubles will be over. We have to believe that. Good God, even communism collapsed."

"Has it been very hard? The day-to-day living, I mean."

"Terribly hard. Brian left us only a wee bit of money. The neighborhood is devastated. The people are devastated. It's cold and it's damp, and there is so much hate everywhere. But in our home there is the thick, rich love that I learned at your knee, at Daddy's knee. What else matters?"

"I'll talk to Callahan."

"No, Maggie. Let him work it out for himself."

Elinor watched Maggie through another long silence, then she spoke gently. "Maggie, how can you be so calm? Luke should be here any minute now."

"So be it."

"Aren't you excited? It's been twenty years."

"It's been one minute. Then another."

"When I was little, you taught me that love is timeless. That love prevails over all the laws of time and space, over all the ways of life and death. That love just *is*."

"Love demands all, and has a right to all."

"Who said that? Shakespeare?"

"No. I did. But Beethoven said it first."

"Are you nervous, Luke?"

"No, Jamie."

Luke put his suitcase down next to Methuselah's and stood as straight as his accumulated years would allow. He fingered the turquoise charm that hung from the gold chain around his neck. He was standing with his old friend and his old servant outside the door of Jamie Callahan's studio. He was about to see Maggie Silvernails for the first time in a young lifetime. The sound of children's laughter trembled through the door.

"My grandchildren, Luke."

"We are fortunate men."

"There have been days we would not have said so."

"We have always had the work that we loved. And each other. Out of that joy has come all the rest."

"I love my work, too," declared Methuselah, "and if one of you two boys will open dat door, I can get on with it. Cain't be chilluns inside without plenty work to do."

"Right you are," said Luke. But he didn't move.

Neither did Callahan.

Neither did Methuselah.

Luke began to sing, very softly:

> *"Come, you wing-eds,*
> *Come, you wing-eds,*
> *Tell me what I need to know*
> *Show me where I need to go . . .*
> *Come flying things."*

In response, the door opened slowly, smoothly, revealing Maggie Silvernails. She seemed to glow with a golden inner light, wrapped in a silken caftan, framed by the warm colors of the studio behind her. Luke extended his hand and she took it gently, stepping out into the hallway without a word. Their eyes caught and held one another. Jamie and Methuselah stepped past them, turning, joining Elinor and the group of fascinated children inside the studio. Luke and Maggie also turned, but in the opposite direction. They walked down the hall together, then down the stairs. And they were gone.

"Are you all right, Daddy?"

"Gray."

"Come and talk with me." Elinor took her father by the arm and led him into his own home as if he were a stranger. "The children have missed you. Hello, Methuselah. It's been a long time."

The two women shook hands warmly. Though pleased

to see one another, they were distracted by Callahan's quiet disquiet. Not so the rambunctious children.

"Hi, Grandpa."

"Was that Uncle Luke?"

"He looks old."

"He didn't even say hello."

"Where did they go?"

"Are you Methuselah? Mommy told me about you. I'm Megan."

"You be named for Maggie, I reckon."

"And I'm Doreen."

The doorbell rang, and they all stopped talking to wonder who was there. Had Maggie and Luke returned? Callahan took a deep breath and answered the door. Deerfinder stood outside. The children gaped. He was in full Indian regalia: leather, beads, feathers—the works.

"I have come to meet the sons of Elinor Callahan O'Neill. Also the daughters," he announced. "First I unwrap my own papoose." He slipped a large knapsack from his back and set it down at his feet with effort. The children had gathered around, mesmerized. Deerfinder unbuckled the bag and flipped back the flap. Out wriggled a slightly bewildered dog, who looked around, wagged his tail, and then with a yelp of delight, trotted over to Bren, the person nearest his own size, to be patted.

Fatpaws was pleased that his ride through the strange city on Deerfinder's back was over. He could smell that Maggie Silvernails had been in this new place, and that pleased him, too, for it promised her return. He had missed her.

Deerfinder was now ready. Raising a small, stretched-hide drum, he tapped it rhythmically and began to dance. His moccasined feet made their way around the studio as a chant of celebration went up. "Hiya, Hiya, Ho," he sang. Fatpaws sang, too. "O, How, O . . ."

"Well. Come right in, Deerfinder," welcomed Callahan, somewhat belatedly, shaking his head in disbelief. "You're certainly a mood breaker." And then he began to laugh, releasing them all from tension.

"Let's get you a drink."

"Yes. Tea would be lovely," Arista agreed.

"I'll ask Miss Patoon to bring some in," said Christian.

Arista felt awkward and nervous here in this precise study. Everything was polished. Everything was in place. Everything was proper. It reminded her of her childhood—second childhood—after her grandfather, the Reverend Elam Brainard, had taken her from her father's broken-down trailer. Arista remembered a narrow, noisy chaos that was her first home only vaguely. The Reverend Brainard had rescued his granddaughter when she was four. Arista's father had not been rescued and had disappeared.

She remembered little of her father. He had seemed to consider her some sort of plaything, tossing her up into the air, catching her just before she hit the ground, laughing at her screams. Or driving the car very fast along the rutted back dirt roads while she huddled on the floor of the backseat. There hadn't seemed to have been a mother, though women came and went. And rather curious men.

Her parents were never mentioned in the parsonage. She had lived with Grandpa Brainard and Uncle Rudy; her three great-uncles, Shadrach, Meshach and Abednigo; and dear old Aunt Viola—amid Bibles, ancient books, strait-laced curtains, and mahogany furniture. Her grandfather, a gentle man about the house, was always kind to her and gracious to others. He never had a bad word to say about anyone, but once a week, on Sunday mornings, he told the

Methodists in Boar's Wood, Ohio, in no uncertain terms, that they were all going straight to hell. He had held little Abigail in his thrall until sex and literature had set her free.

Now she was feeling trapped again. She felt herself to be in the presence of an entirely good man. She knew this was a fantasy. She knew it must be an idealization. She knew such misapprehensions came with states of infatuation. But Christian's goodness was real to her now and she was disarmed by it. She didn't know what to do. She couldn't come on to him. None of her familiar moves were available to her. Her cynicism failed her. Also her seductiveness. Clearly a romance was impossible.

He, on the other hand, seemed completely at ease as they sat across from one another at the study table. He was wearing a suit, a staid tie, cuff links of gold that flashed in the shaft of sunlight falling between them. His wedding band flashed, too. There was an immaculate, starched handkerchief in his pocket. He was smiling. A guileless smile, a child's smile. It was irresistible. She smiled back, suddenly aware of how long it had been since she had smiled, fully, in pleasure, into the face of another person. Her rare moments of happiness, she realized in a flash of gold, were something she kept hidden, almost as if she was ashamed of happiness.

The study doors parted. An enormous woman came in.

"Ah, Miss Patoon. You have outdone yourself."

"Thank you, Reverend Davies."

"Thank you, Miss Patoon."

What was going on in that woman's mind? Arista wondered. Her happiness flitted back into the shadows. The secretary set down a silver tray with a matching silver tea service, delicate china cups, a plate of cake, and napkins with real lace trim. The aroma of strong Earl Grey tea and pungent lemon drifted around the study. Alice May

Patoon, whom one would expect to lumber out, miraculously drifted away. The doors shut.

"I am very particular about tea. Shall I pour?"

She nodded. He poured. She helped herself to milk and sugar.

"Now, where shall I cut?" he asked. The glinting knife was poised over a thick slice of lemon cake.

"You will be able to determine a great deal about me if you cut it unevenly."

"Whatever do you mean?"

"Whether I choose the large or the small piece will give evidence of my character."

He sliced the cake precisely in the middle. "I think I will choose . . . to take my pleasure in your pleasure," he replied, presenting her with the cake.

Arista felt dizzy. Why weren't they in bed?

"Thank you," she said, taking a plate. His precision told her of a restrained sensuality. The cake was delicious. The smiles were back between them.

"I have admired your novel."

"I, your sermons."

But he did not let the conversation turn to himself. He went on a bit, speaking of specific characters, uses of imagery, meanings she had not known were in her lines. She was impressed with the intelligence he had brought to her work. She thanked him, feeling off balance. Then he leaned forward and presented his request. "I have something more ambitious than my sermons in mind at present." Tritely her heart skipped a beat. "I am attempting to write a book. Drawn from my own experiences. I asked you to come today in the hope that I could persuade you to watch over my work, rather like a guardian angel."

"How could I be of help?" She needed some time to take his offer inside herself.

"Well, we both love words, don't we? We both read and read. Is that true? Have I guessed right?"

"Yes."

"Well, I thought, as you have taken such an interest in my sermons, that you might take an interest in my book. Read it as it goes along, comment, criticize, suggest. Like a fine editor would do. It is a lot to ask, I know. I could arrange to pay you"—he watched her closely—"if you wouldn't be insulted."

"I would rather not be paid."

He nodded.

"But I have no experience with nonfiction," she protested, knowing the protest would not be accepted. "I've never attempted it. I'm not sure I'm the right person for the job."

"Would you *like* to help me?"

It was the same question that Ted had asked her, in almost the same tone in an entirely different context. Dear Ted Hackett, who was not Ted Hackett until he could remember who Ted Hackett was—or was he Ted Hackett whether he remembered himself or not? In response to Ted's question she had poured out everything that she could recall of their shared childhood and adolescence, all the little details of his home and his parents that came flooding back to her from she knew not where. The memories had reawakened long-buried longings for Ted, yet when she turned to look into his eyes, he was so uncomprehending, so un-Ted, that she found herself still longing for him, though he was but an arm's length away from her.

Christian pressed. "Does the answer require such deep thought?"

"No. Yes. I would very much like to help you." There was no guile in her response, she thought. No mystery. What was happening to her? Had she forgotten how to be elusive? Had her crush crushed all subtlety out of her?

"Then there could be no better choice." He pushed a few sheets of neatly typed script across the table. "This is the beginning."

She looked from the manuscript to the expectant face of Christian Davies. She felt the impulse to brush back a lock of his extraordinary hair from his broad forehead. Daringly she did so, and as she touched him she felt two small pieces of her heart rejoin. She was going to love this man. She dropped her eyes, and they fell upon the page. It was titled *Sermons in Stone.* It began:

> Of the 144 people who got on the plane with me in Chicago, 127 of them were dead when I crawled out of the smoldering fuselage into a corn-field near Davenport, Iowa.

Good God, she thought, the things that have happened to people that you never know.

He watched Arista absorb the first sentence, wondering what secret event had broken her, as the plane crash had broken him.

She read his mind. She had never read anyone's mind before, but his question brushed up against her brain as if he had spoken it; so she answered him.

"My second husband, Marxie, whom I loved very deeply, left me for another . . . older man. Later I found out that the man he left me for was my own father. When that gender and generation of Brainards failed to satisfy him, Marxie killed himself."

How could she be other than a strange flower? thought Christian. She had grown in perverted soil. And yet she drew him, against his intuition, against his common sense into her garden. He extended his hands across his manuscript, palms up, relaxed—and she took them. His hands closed gently around her hands.

"I am sorry for your troubles," he said simply, warmly.

"I am sorry for yours," she replied.

She had felt the warmth of his hands once before, the day they had scheduled the church for Eve. His hands were as soft and warm as she remembered them. Here in the quiet, in the sunlight, she wished her hands would melt, wished that they would flow into him like molten bronze into a waiting mold. There was a sudden knock on the door. Startled, they pulled their hands apart like little children caught in a forbidden act.

"Just a moment, Miss Patoon," said Christian, getting to his feet.

"It's urgent, Reverend Davies."

"So is this," he whispered, and leaned down to kiss Arista Bellefleurs, who was stunned, then responsive, in turn. Their lips parted and their eyes met. I am going to love this woman, thought Christian.

"Come in," he said softly to Arista.

Alice May Patoon came through the doors rather jerkily, and in obvious distress.

"Reverend Davies, may I speak with you alone for a moment?"

"What is it, Miss Patoon?" His very personal and very private secretary shot a meaningful glance in Arista's direction. "It's all right. You may speak in the presence of Ms. Bellefleurs. She will be helping me with some of my writing." There was a pause while Ms. Patoon took in the unexpected information. A tic below her eye, a flaw in her large but perfectly arranged appearance, allowed them to see that the news was unwelcome. Arista watched her ef-

fort at composure. It was awesome. Ms. Patoon pulled herself up and shut herself down at the same time. When she
spoke again, it was in a level tone of voice. Her face was
calm. Nothing ticked. If unwelcome news was to be the order of the day, then Alice May Patoon was equal to it, she
thought. Was he?

"There is a young man outside. He is wearing robes and
sandals. He is carrying a shepherd's crook. His name, he
says, is Jesus."

"Oh, Good Lord!" exclaimed Christian.

"That's what he wants to be called."

In a different dimension of the same room Grace Davies,
Eve Callahan, and Paul O'Neill beamed. Then, as one
mind, they swept southward. Their graceful passing quiv-
ered the long white curtains that covered the open windows that punctuated the darkened room that enclosed the
exhausted, enchanted bodies of the naked lovers, Luke
Sevensons and Maggie Silvernails.

"Ah," said Luke, "There they are again" as he was
touched softly by the breeze.

"You cannot go with them, Luke. Not yet," said Maggie.
"I felt them, too, but I need you here, on this earth, my
love." She could not be closer to Luke than she was at this
moment, given her present form.

"Can I say no, if I'm summoned?"

"They only lead us. They don't command. You can take
your own sweet time in this, like you do in all else."

"The call is very strong."

"You are very strong. Together we are stronger still."

"Until I held you again, my Maggie, I wanted to follow
them. I had had enough of this life. Now . . ."

"There is only now."

"The eternal now."

And the evening light came through the veiled windows, reluctantly. Only its subtle changes marked the passing of time. As the light faded, so did Katelyn's hope. Nelson Little had not come. She sat in the lobby of her apartment building where his luggage should be. She felt enormously sad, but enormously calm, for somewhere, around the edge of her grief, like redness around the eyes, she sensed the faintest irritation. It was boredom. There was a redundancy to this disappointment that even she could feel. If she grasped at the straw of her distress and pulled, she knew she could be free of him. Would she? Could she be other than despairing? Could she do anything other than wait? Who would she be? To whom would she then be attached?

There was Lester, wasn't there? Solid, respectable, sensible Lester. Young. Only thirty-three. And, of course, he had a flaky side, too. Didn't everyone? Except for the terse message on the machine, she hadn't seen or heard from him for over a month, and he had been peculiar before he left. Absences of this duration were common in her relationship with Lester. He went on retreats. Not religious retreats exactly, but meditative withdrawals. He was listening for something, he explained, which he could not hear above the cacophony of conversation or the blaring of city sounds. So off to the tranquil woods he went. There existed nearby, within hours of the city, a variety of enclaves that welcomed such pious pilgrims: a Buddhist monastery near Woodstock, a Catholic brotherhood in the Ramapo Mountains, a New Age tribe that traipsed about through the state park system setting up temporary villages of canvas teepees and Porta-Johns. Lester would return from these inner excursions thinner and paler and more ethereal than when he had left. Also more considerate and more compassionate in his actions. Also less forgiving of the failures and deviations of others. She sighed. He was better,

Katelyn was sure, than most men. Certainly better than Nelson, better than Victor, better than nothing. Really?

She knew she had a stake in continuing to love Nelson Little. Emily Dickinson said it best. She took out her pocket Dickinson to read the familiar poem, though she knew it by heart.

> They say that 'time assuages'—
> Time never did assuage—
> An actual suffering strengthens
> As Sinews do, with age—
>
> Time is a Test of Trouble—
> But not a remedy—
> If such it prove, it prove too
> There was no malady—

Once begun, she could never stop suffering for Nelson—not ever—for she knew it would prove that all her pain had been false. She had held on to her suffering for Sebastien from the same sentiment. Sentiments change.

The book of poetry fell from her hand, opening to a less familiar verse:

> I felt a funeral in my Brain,
> And mourners to and fro,
> Kept treading—treading—till it seemed
> That Sense was breaking through—

Was the funeral in her brain for Nelson? Could it be that sense was breaking through at last? She stood up suddenly, startling Biggs Howard, the weary doorman.

"If anyone comes for me, Biggs, tell him I've moved away."

"Anyone, Miss Wells?"

"Anyone at all."

"Where should I say you've gone?"

"Tell him anything that pops into your attractive head."

"Shanghai?"

"I've never been there."

"Shanghai vely intelesting city," explained Henry Chang. My glandmother there."

"Your grandmother? How old *is* she? You're no spring chicken, Henry." Katelyn sat on a high stool in the back room of Henry Chang's laundry, watching him iron shirt collars with enormous grace and eye-tricking speed. She was very glad to be where she was, amid all the clothes and steam and sudsy smells, here, with Henry on Bleecker Street, and not sitting, barren, in her apartment—worse, in the lobby—waiting for Nelson.

"Glandmother immortal," he said with conviction, then launched into his explanation: "My glandmother did not so much enjoy her mother, though hold vely much respect for her. She respectfurry hate the old bitch. So my glandmother not so eagel to join ancestors yet."

"Is this grandmother the one with the teapot?" Katelyn inquired.

"Yes. Yes. The vely one."

Katelyn remembered the story fondly. Henry had told it to her twenty years ago: Henry's grandmother, while still a young woman, had been a servant in the house of a wealthy tea merchant. Early one morning she had been called to serve tea to her master as he hurriedly prepared to attend a meeting with an even more wealthy American trader. She was frail and the teapot was heavy. As she approached the table the teapot slipped from her hand and shattered, splashing hot tea over her employer's gown.

Protocol of the time required the merchant to beat her properly, which he did at some length. This and the need to change his robes caused him to be late for his appointment, thereby angering the American, and losing the sale. As a result, the American trader was delayed in Shanghai while a new purchase was arranged with another merchant and he was forced to postpone his passage back to New York. As a result of the later sailing, the American did not drown when the ship he had originally booked went down off the Cape of Good Hope. As a result of his escape from watery death, the American returned to his country, prospered, married, fathered many sons, one of whom produced a son who grew up to become a president of the United States. As a result, Henry Chang considered President Kennedy as family, and still, many years after his death, wore his campaign button proudly.

"Maybe I should go to Shanghai."

"Just got back from Palis. How is old Sebastien?"

"How the hell do you know about that?"

"Henly knows."

"He's old, but he still has all his powers."

"What did he teach you, old Sebastien?"

"Not to cry anymore. You know, I don't have any idea what to do with my life now that I'm back."

"You do what you do. Wait for Nerson."

"I've been waiting a long time."

"Not rong enough. Maggie, that old squaw, she know about waiting. She wait in the desert for twenty years. Not too rong. She with Ruke and Carrahan now in Virrage. Deelfindel come back, too."

"Luke Sevensons is in town? Oh, what a relief! I need to work with him now."

"Ruke he knows about waiting, too. Eve Carrahan, she get fed up with waiting. She go clash. That not good thing."

"I've never considered suicide. Well, once. I was lonely enough to be forgiven if I'd tried."

"Can't jump out the window and go up. You wait for rong man. You should wait for Victol. I say wise thing to you now. Victol stirr roves his Kateryn."

"Henry, that is surely the strangest thing anyone has ever said to me." She shook her head in negation. "Strange though, now that you mention it, I hadn't heard a word from Victor in ten years, and just today I got a message from him."

"Absence makes the heart glow fondel."

"That's an old saw, Henry. And I don't believe it. I suppose you will claim that Confucius said it."

"Henly Chang's glandmother said." He smiled.

"Really?"

"She heal it from Confucius when she was vely young."

Katelyn's laughter at Henry's assertion was cut short by a disheveled young man carrying a handful of dirty shirts who barged into the shop, looking furtively around as though he had stolen them.

"Why, it's Mullahboy. I hardly recognized you. You haven't shaved. Are you growing a beard?"

The distracted Mullaboy ignored Katelyn and spoke anxiously to Henry. "I see a woman. Out there." He pointed wildly toward the street. "I theenk she ees mamma mia."

"Must be that Itarian woman. Came in yestelday. What name?" He stopped ironing and flipped through a pile of receipts stuck on an iron nail. "Selena Lomano?"

Mullahboy looked confused.

"Serena Romano," said Katelyn.

"Oh, no. Oh, God. Incha Allah. Mamma mia. She finds me!"

"Don't you like your mother?" asked Katelyn, too curious to be overly polite herself. By the confused look on Mullahboy's face, it had never occurred to him that the words *like* and *mother* could be arranged in the same sentence.

Henry answered for him. "Murraboy roves his mamma. Mamma roves her Murraboy. She came in and says, 'I am searching for my son. He's clazy, climinal, and queel, but I rove him.' She speak with accent. Vely hard to undelstand."

"*Sì, sì,*" he agreed. "Where can I hide, Henry?"

"Give those to me." He took the soiled shirts. "*I Ching* say: 'To leturn again will not cause distress. Fliends leturn and it is not a mistake. Lepeated cycles are part of the tao, just as seven days blings a leturn.'"

"No capeesh."

"Go home."

The boy appeared enormously relieved at the suggestion. He turned and left without another word.

"I wonder why he's so afraid of his mother?"

"She eregant woman."

"Arrogant? No, you said, elegant. Oh, Henry, have you ever thought of working at reversing your *r*'s and your *l*'s?"

"Would sound funny."

"Which home did you mean to send him to, Henry? Rome, or his home here, with Quentin and Buff?"

Henry shrugged. "Where is home?"

"He claims to have no home," said Detective Finger, looking back and forth from the cardboard box to his partner, Sergeant Dooney. The man in the Frigidaire box was a new addition to the block. They couldn't see much of him through the handle holes punched in the cardboard.

From what they could tell he appeared to be rather well dressed for a homeless person.

"What's your name, mister?"

The man looked out through the holes blankly, as if the question had no relevance to him or to his situation.

"Look," explained Sergeant Dooney, "This is important. I don't want to give you no trouble. You can live in this here box until my retirement if you want to. The street's yours as much as mine. But we need to know your name for the record. Case there's trouble, or we need to get you to a hospital someday. So, now, what's your name?"

"Little."

"Little what?"

"Little. Nelson."

"Sounds familiar." Detective Finger shrugged. "Okay, Little Nel. Have a good night." And the cops moved away down the block.

Deep in the box Little Nel was muttering poetry:

> *"Thy soul shall find itself alone—*
> *Alone of all on earth—unknown*
> *The cause—but none are near to pry*
> *Into thine hour of secrecy."*

"There's more and more of these homeless guys," complained Detective Finger, shaking his head sadly. "What's wrong with this country?"

"That one looked educated."

"A lot of them do when they first hit the street."

"Then the street gives them a different kind of education."

"It doesn't take long before they look like they lived in a box their whole lives."

"I hope he'll be all right."

"He hasn't been right since the fire," said Quentin. "The superheated air that blew him out the window also seared his lungs."

Quentin, Clayton, and Ted stood around Buff's bed, deeply concerned. Buff was having difficulty breathing. He knew it wasn't the aftermath of the fire that burned in his chest. It was his illness. He had pneumonia. He didn't complain. Since the fire he had had the odd feeling that he was living an extra life. That every minute he experienced since he was pushed out into the black, bottomless air was a gift to be relished, whether it brought pain to his body or the winning Lotto numbers.

"I think you should call an ambulance," he directed. "I'll be better off in the hospital."

"That bad, Buff?"

"I don't know, but everyone I ever knew who went to the hospital and got there in time to have their life saved has told me they should have gone a lot sooner." He stopped talking for a moment and gasped for more air. "I always vowed to go sooner, not later. But, you know . . . it's a hard decision to make . . . to choose to put yourself into the hands of strangers . . . it's frightening . . . to know your personal priorities will instantly become unimportant . . . to feel your pain and know that to a medical staff it will be, simply, data . . . and yet . . ."

"Okay, Buff," Quentin interrupted, "I'll get you to a hospital."

"I've checked. Mother Cabrini Hospital will let Greta Garbo stay in the room with me."

"You've checked?"

"We've known this was coming, Quentin."

"What's he talking about, Quentin?" Clayton had gone pale.

"AIDS."

"What's AIDS?" This from Ted.

"I'll tell you about it later," said Clayton. "Right now we have to get Buff some help." And he walked shakily to the telephone and dialed the number that was written in both pen and braille, taped to the receiver. He came back shortly, still pale, but collected. "They'll be here in ten minutes. Is this the first pneumonia?"

"Yes." All but Ted knew the statistics. Usually men survived the first and second bouts of pneumonia. After two the outlook was grim. Few could prevail over the third onslaught. Many developed other, more terrifying symptoms as well: palsies, sarcomas, brain lesions.

"Clayton, we both have it."

"You too, Quentin?"

"Yeah. We've been through all the minor stuff already— the rashes and thrush and sweats. I've had one bout of pneumonia, too. With luck we'll go out together."

"You call that luck?"

"We call the years we have been together luck—good luck. The rest, well, we'll see."

"I'm glad you told me. What can I do to help you guys?" Clayton's own tears were in his eyes and in his voice now.

"Nothing special. Just keep being our friend." Quentin and Clayton embraced. It was the first time they had done so. Clayton felt his inner world begin to break apart.

"There is something specific you can do for me, Clayton," gasped Buff. "You brought a work-in-progress down from the studio. You wanted our comments. Let me hold it." Clayton, who in the face of Buff's illness had forgotten the clay model, picked it up from a nearby table and brought it to the sick man.

Buff grasped the statue eagerly. "God, you can't imagine

how much I love sculpture," he said. "Paintings are the devil's own invention in a blind man's world. But this, I can *see*. Oh! This is good." His fingers ran quickly, then slowly, over the piece, questioning it, finding the answers. "It's a beautiful object made from a tragic moment. And it works. Thank you, Clay."

He tried to hand the statue back to its maker, but he was too weak. In the distance he could hear the sirens call. "Don't be afraid," he said to the three men standing around his prone body, as if the statue had grown to a lifelike size and he was in Eve's place. "I haven't hit the sidewalk yet."

He reached down to pat the dog. He had known many dogs on his journey. Amas Wells had learned exactly how to judge the merely curious beasts from the truly ferocious ones, and the trickster dogs who appeared to be kindly only to bare their teeth after you lowered your guard. Amas was being doubly careful now that Illuminada was carrying the baby, papooselike, on her back. This dog was friendly.

"Don't be afraid," he said reassuringly.

"I'm not afraid, Amas."

He had planned to stay in Milwaukee for a while to let her rest. Surprisingly it was Illuminada who wanted to begin walking again. She hadn't liked the restriction of the hospital or the small room he could afford to bring her home to. And she wanted Walker out in the air. Walker had taken to their leisurely way of life like a baby trooper. The rhythm of their walk lulled him into calm or sleep when he wasn't at Lumi's bounteous breasts.

"That dog looks as if it means to come along with us."

"It will drop back. They always do." It was a little dog, young and exuberant. It had a rich, chocolaty coat with a correspondingly sweet disposition. There was a white stripe down its forehead and muzzle, giving it a slightly daffy look. It was alone and wore no collar and seemed delighted to have found some company on this peaceful, piney stretch of road alongside the Wisconsin–Canada border. The dog had begun trotting beside them, with occasional excited excursions into and out of the nearby underbrush.

"No," she declared. "This dog is ours."

"We'll see."

"What shall we call it?"

"Oreo."

And they marched on for a while, laughing at the puppy's antics and enjoying the calm of the warm morning. Several miles later it was Illuminada who broke the spell.

"I want to go home, Amas."

"What!" He stopped in his tracks. "To Hammond, Indiana?"

"No. To your home. To New York City. To the Village. To Katelyn. I want Walker to see his grandmother."

"How long has this been brewing?"

She smiled. "Since Milwaukee."

"You've never been to New York. You've never even met my mother. This is some kind of romantic fantasy. And why not visit your own mother, if you want the baby to have a grandmother?"

"I've met *her*."

"This is nuts. Why do you want to do this? I thought we were happy."

"We are happy."

"Then why do you want to ruin everything? My mother *cries* all the time. When she's not crying, she writes poetry that makes *you* want to cry."

"That's why, Amas. Our baby, our Walker never cries. I think he will make her happy. I think we will."

He squatted in the road, patting the grateful dog, breathing deeply, gathering his thoughts and feelings together. At last he looked up at her. "It's a beautiful thought, Lumi. It's loving. It's what I should expect from you. But it won't work." He shook his head sadly from side to side. Illuminada looked unconvinced and disappointed. "I'll tell you what. At the next town I'll call Luke Sevensons. I'll talk to him about the idea. Luke always helps me figure out what I should do." He shook his head again while the heedless puppy cavorted around his knees. "It just won't work." And then he did something he had never done before. He kicked a beer can out onto the roadway.

"Amas!"

"I'll get it." Distracted, he stepped out to retrieve the can without first checking the oncoming traffic. The speeding car swerved, but not enough. As Amas was struck he heard his spine crack. As he was hurled through the air he wondered if he would die. As he hit the pavement he knew that he would live. As he lay on the pavement he raised his head and looked down the length of his unfeeling body. "What will our life be like now?" he whispered.

"I don't know what our life will be like, but we must *try!*" Luke was speaking. He and Jamie and Maggie were huddled, like three conspirators, around the old kitchen table in Callahan's studio. Sometimes their hands sought each other through the maze of paintbrushes, coffee cups, open books, silver nails, eyeglasses, and drinking glasses half-full of Irish whisky that littered its worn surface. The harsh smells of turpentine and old coffee grounds mingled with the soft aroma of melting candle wax. A single taper in the center of the table, now burning low, lit the three faces, giving them an eerily youthful appearance.

They had the place to themselves. Elinor and Deerfinder

had taken the children to see the Statue of Liberty and then out for dinner. Methuselah had gone to visit her grandmother in the Bronx. Fatpaws was asleep in the corner.

They did not feel alone. It was Callahan who spoke of it first.

"I have dreamed of this reunion for twenty years," he mused, "and now I feel the presence of our younger selves around this table. So many younger selves. Luke, you expressed the same sentiment two decades ago, and the decade before that, and the decade before that as well."

Luke shuffled the empty cups around, appearing mildly embarrassed.

Callahan continued: "You always declare that you are willing to try to give up jealousy, but you can't."

"If we could all give up the jealousy—the pain—"

"But we can't."

"So far."

"So far."

Maggie was looking over Callahan's shoulder through the flickering light to his current painting, a boisterous canvas full of grandchildren. It was hotly red with the intensity of his love. Jamie was looking past Maggie to her easel, where the portrait of Paul and Eve and Brian glowed in a soft, gray sadness. Luke was looking at his two best friends and was thinking that he would die for them if he could. And he could.

Maggie read his mind. "Don't think of death, Luke. We always think of it and it never helps."

"Maybe it never helps because one of us never dies."

"I have never seen you so morose."

"I am old, Maggie. I am tired."

"How can I help?"

"I don't know. My work always helps. My work is to

help. But I've never been able to help, here, with you"—he turned to Jamie—"and you—where it matters the most."

"That's not true," countered Callahan. "You've helped us each a hundred thousand times over."

"But I've never been able to help *us*. We three. We band of lovers. We love and we hurt and we rage and we forgive and we love and we hurt and we rage and we forgive endlessly, endlessly, endlessly. There is no way out of the box—"

"So it has always been." That from Maggie.

"—except into the box."

"No, Luke! Nobody dies for anybody else. We all agreed. We live this out. We see what it brings."

"You died, Maggie. You died in the desert for twenty years."

"I lived. You knew it, old man."

"I knew it."

Callahan abstained from this latest skirmish.

"You didn't come for me, Luke."

"No."

"Why?"

"It wouldn't have helped. In the meantime I could help others."

"Have you worked well these twenty years, my Luke?"

"Yes, Maggie."

"I, too."

"And I," Callahan joined them.

"The canvases we've painted, the people you've helped—that's what the love brought us, in its way."

"All those years we stayed apart!"

"And now?"

"Each other's old bodies."

"So wonderful."

"So wonderful."

"So wonderful."

"And all the old feelings."

"So terrible—"

"*And* wonderful—"

"As before."

"Do you remember the time we were in Venice together?"

"Bellini, Tintoretto, Titian—"

"Jamie, Maggie, Luke."

"And in the gondola. There were the two seats at the back, tight together and romantic; and the other little chair off to the side—"

"We didn't know how we should sit."

"And Maggie, you kept jumping back and forth between the two of us—"

"—rocking the boat."

"And we were laughing so hard because it was all so unfair and all so not unfair."

"The water was inky, black."

"And the lights spilled across it like jewels."

"Back and forth you went, from one seat to the other, finding no peace."

"The gondolier was confused."

"He didn't dare sing."

"How we laughed."

"But what do we do *next?*" They could hear the knife in Luke's voice, piercing through their happy recollection to the hurt that lay beneath.

"What we agreed upon," said Jamie. "What we all agreed upon so many years ago. We keep living and we keep working and we keep loving and we see what the love brings to us. And whatever that is, we accept it. Nobody dies. And Maggie doesn't have to choose."

They waited then, in ritual silence, for Maggie to say her oft-repeated words: *I could never choose.* But this time the words did not come. The two men looked at one another alarmed, and then at Maggie.

"This time I will choose," she said.

"When, Maggie?" This from Luke.

"Soon. You will live to know it." They felt the rightness in her voice and were afraid. "But for now it is as before," she reassured them.

"I love you, Maggie," said Luke. His eyes were full of tears.

"I love you, Jamie," she responded.

"I love you, Luke," said Jamie. And they sought one another's hands again across the cluttered table as the candle flame sputtered and went out in the hot, wet remembrance of itself.

Part Three

The
NIGHT WATCHERS

Behold a sacred voice is calling you,
All over the sky a sacred voice is calling.

—BLACK ELK

"There are a *lot* of characters, Arista," said Katelyn.

Arista, who had been idly stroking the cat and ineffectively shuffling papers at her worktable, snapped forward into alertness at the sound of Katelyn's possibly critical voice. "Can you keep them all straight?"

"Straight?"

"Oh, don't be so touchy."

"Yes."

"Any other comments?"

"I'm not sure about your guy. Christian. What's all the fuss about?"

"Handsome. White hair. Tragic past. Charismatic. Not enough, huh?"

"No. Not for me."

"Probably not neurotic enough. I'll work on him." In truth, more work was always worthwhile, thought Arista, but also, in even more truth, Katelyn wasn't the best judge of men these days. Not that she ever had been. "Do you have anything else to say about the book?"

"Not yet. I'm too involved for comment at present."

"It's awfully ladylike, for me, don't you think?"

"Well . . . yes. But it's still pleasantly wicked."

"And shouldn't I be making more of a statement about society? Shouldn't I be offering wise prescriptions to a dying culture?"

"We're not dying. Aren't *we* society? Aren't we culture?"

"We are the lunatic fringe of a lunatic culture."

"I don't feel like a lunatic."

"Result of a double negative."

Katelyn was suddenly serious. "Arista, are you happy with him?"

"Yes."

"You're not frightened?"

"Of what?"

"I suppose that answers the question. When will he be back?"

"Dinnertime."

"I'm glad you're happy."

"So am I, Katelyn, so am I."

"Who would have thought it?" Katelyn shook her head gently from side to side.

"The Katelyn I wrote would understand."

"The Katelyn you know does understand." She smiled and then returned her attention to the manuscript. In a moment she looked up again. "But he's a strange choice . . . even for you, Arista."

Maggie Silvernails had made her choice, too.

She had only to implement it. First she wanted to be certain that Luke survived past the first day of the month; that was tomorrow. And she needed assurance that Callahan and Elinor had made their peace with one another. Then she would speak.

She sat alone by the black water in this, the darkest

hour of the night, watching the Hudson River struggling for its sloppy life against the excretions of the city. There were homosexuals nearby, making love on the docks, under the docks. She hoped they would be safe, though she knew they harbored no such hopes, poor boys; struggling for erotic life against the power of the mother. Too much water here, she thought. Maggie rose and walked steadily back to the core of the Village.

She knew that somewhere in the shadows Deerfinder lurked, keeping a watchful eye upon her, keeping her safe, but not, this time, intruding. He had been so as a boy. What did the white men call him? A brave. Yes, Deerfinder was a brave. He thought she hadn't noticed him, all these years, slinking about, standing steadfastly between her and all manner of trouble. A brave fool. She knew he lived for Maggie Silvernails. A brave dear fool. But since the end of his childhood he had lived in regret. Deerfinder slipped silently along the Village streets, pondering the nature of regret.

He was an Indian man born into a world long ago lost to Indian men. What was there for him in America? Reservation poverty, migrant-labor poverty, army poverty, Injun politics; that, too, impoverished. Drink. He had stayed reluctantly clear of drink, except occasionally with Callahan. There was artistic poverty, too. Yet always there had been Maggie Silvernails to enrich his being, to quicken his spirit, to love, and to love him in return.

In their youth she had been his religion. Every day had been filled up with her lightness. Until the year when they were old enough to marry. Oh, Maggie, he thought with deepest regret, why did I not strike like lightning and make you my wife of this earth? There had been the scholarships. Couldn't be turned down. Chance of a lifetime. So they said. So they thought. The golden moment had slipped away from them that youthful summer as the city beckoned in the wings of autumn. There, in the shadow of the university, the white men had claimed her. The nature of regret was pain, Deerfinder decided as he watched Maggie Silvernails from the darkness, returning, unafraid, to Callahan's studio. Another realm lost to this Indian man.

Deerfinder pondered a saying that Luke had read to him recently, something Henry Chang had brought to his attention from the *I Ching:*

> Changing inspires confidence only after it is accomplished. It is only then that we realize our exceptional progress. There is an advantage to correct persistence. Regret disappears.

Could change be accomplished? Could regret disappear? There was no way to change the past. The future? Change to what? A white man? A younger man? A bolder man? Wait a minute! thought Deerfinder as he realized that even though Luke had read the passage aloud to him, it was still a dose of Henry Chang advice. He stopped thinking about it immediately and turned his eyes outward to admire Maggie's fine profile.

If he were a better Buddhist, he would be able to loosen his lifelong attachment to her. Then there would be no longing, and there would be no regret. He had to admit that as Buddhists went, he wasn't a very good one.

He remembered the Buddhist initiation ceremony he had undergone the previous year. Tibetan men. Red, brown men. Exiles. He had felt an immediate affinity for them. The translation of the sutras were poor and the initiation instructions incomprehensible, but at one point in the ceremony he understood he was to choose a flower from an arrangement near the altar, approach the guru who stood peacefully in his flowing, saffron robes, and throw the flower onto the mandala that was being proffered. The place where the flower came to rest on the intricate pattern would tell him which aspect of the Buddha would rule this lifetime of his soul.

As he approached the altar Deerfinder prayed for a sign of peace, for wisdom, for compassion. He threw the flower. Wrath! Anger was to be his lot in this life. The Tibetan medicine man took one step back, away from Deerfinder. In so doing his robes brushed the altar candles and up they flared in saffron fire and smoke.

Deerfinder quickly began to beat out the flames while the attending monks threw water from the flowerpots onto their beloved holy man. The guru was unhurt. The guru was unfazed. Impressive. Deerfinder was reminded of his own stoic people. Deerfinder was reminded of the fiery, protesting Buddhists of Vietnam. Yes, he thought, we are of one spirit.

The guru quickly resumed the ceremony, holding out the mandala for the remaining initiates. Deerfinder obediently returned to his lotus position. He had received his sign. He was powerful angry.

But Deerfinder believed that he had one chance left, and that belief held him attached to Maggie like a tick to a dog's ear. He was determined to outlive both Luke Sevensons *and* Jamie Callahan. Not that he didn't love them. For all his jealousy he wouldn't bring rain down onto their parade while they walked the earth; but he would dance one helluva dance on their graves when they were under it.

If Luke was right about his own demise, Deerfinder would be dancing tomorrow. Then there would only be Callahan. Luke Sevensons was sure now that death was the best of all possible solutions. He had worked it all out in his mind. Maggie would never be able to live with a definitive choice on her conscience. (She would choose Luke, of course. Maggie loved him. Always had.) He would save her from that impending guilt. And she could be happy with that old rogue Jamie, once Luke had been respectfully laid to rest. He would never be out of their thoughts, though. That idea amused him. Yes, he thought, best to die. He didn't want Maggie to grow old all alone in the desert.

He supposed it would be his heart that would take him out. Cardiac arrest could arrive on schedule. There was no time for cancer or strokes to work their wonders. Just as well. It was peculiar to see the light of dawn this morning. Not his last. Tomorrow would be his last. The penultimate dawn. He was glad he would have today, to appear at Eve's memorial service. He could say goodbye to her, and to all the rest of those assembled. He would say goodbye silently, in his heart, for no one believed he would die. Not that knucklehead Callahan. Maggie had her doubts. Luke had none. The conversation had been too explicit:

TIME TO GO, LUKE.

So soon?

I CAN GIVE YOU UNTIL THE FIRST OF THE MONTH.

Why now?

IT'S FOR MAGGIE.

Well, that's all right then, isn't it? By the way, are you Thor?

I GO BY THAT NAME IN SCANDINAVIA.

I thought so.

ANY OTHER QUESTIONS, LUKE?

Quite a few actually. I suppose now they can wait.

CATCH YOU LATER.

The night following that conversation produced a terrific storm. Luke, lying awake pondering his fate, had burst into laughter at the first clap of thunder and had kept on chuckling for so long that Mariah the cat became impatient and went to sleep with Methuselah.

"What all dat commotion 'bout last night, Luke?" Methuselah had asked him, a wary look in her yellowed eye as she served up his breakfast. "You be laughing louder than God half the night."

Luke just laughed some more and munched his grits, but later that day he had begun to put his affairs in order and pack for his last trip to New York City. The first day of the month suited him fine. He would work until the last minute, of course, following Gurdjieff, as he had done since his youth. He was looking forward to a good talk with Gurdjieff.

Work as if everything depends on work.
Pray as if everything depends on prayer.

Story of his life. It had been a good life. He had passed along the advice whenever and however he could. He got up and stretched, appreciating the luxury of the small hotel room. Good, heavy furniture. Shining brass lamps.

People always thought of Luke as spiritual, unattached. But he loved the material world. He wondered if he would miss it. He decided to call Callahan and make a last-minute try at getting himself believed. He had dialed the number and heard the first ring before he realized he might be disturbing Jamie and Maggie. Maggie sure hadn't been with Luke in the night. Her absence had been acutely felt and Luke understood her decision as a sign—that she refused to recognize him as a condemned man. Tough as nails, his Maggie. So what if he woke them up! They'd survive it. And they'd survive him. The phone was answered by Bren.

"Hi, Uncle Luke."

"Hi, Bren. What are you up to this morning?"

"Mr. Agincourt is helping us build a telescope to put up on the roof of Grandpa's building."

So that was to be the lay of the land, was it? Florian Agincourt and beautiful Widow O'Neill. He approved. He was glad he had sent Elinor the plane fare to come back home. He could hear shrieks of excited comment in the background. Morning at the Callahan residence was clearly in full swing. "Let me talk to your ornery grandfather."

"Grandpa Callahan, it's Uncle Luke," shouted the child. Lucky my hearing is failing, thought Luke.

Jamie took the phone cheerfully. "Did you ever think you'd live to hear that?"

"Glad I took the trouble, but I needn't have. That boy could wake the dead."

"I'll send him around to you tomorrow. Seriously, Luke, you've given up that dying talk, haven't you?"

"No."

"Damn."

"Where's Maggie?"

"Sleeping late. She was out half the night. Came in at dawn like a stray cat. I thought she was with you."

"No such luck."

"Good."

"Tell her I would like to see her tonight. After the memorial service, would you?"

"We're *all* staying with you for the twenty-four hours after the service." There was an air of one-upmanship in his tone. "We're all driving out by the ocean to see Florian's comet. Then we're not letting you out of our sight until you come to your senses."

"Really?" Luke was touched. But he wanted to be alone with his love. "Who is *all*?"

"Maggie, me, Deerfinder, Methuselah, Elinor, even some of the old boys—Oakley and Jerry, George, Florian, of course. The kids, too."

Fortunately, thought Luke, there was still time to negotiate; and if all else failed he would kidnap her.

"Uh. Great . . . fine . . . I'll see you at the service."

Clayton Grant hung up the telephone. But he didn't feel great, and he didn't feel fine, and he didn't know how he was going to face Arista, let alone tell her they were through. How could he? With no warning. Just take in a big slurp of air and say, I'm sorry Arista, but I'm sleeping with your old lover Ted Hackett now?

He groaned at the thought. He would have to tell her sooner or later. Better sooner. No, better later.

Clayton turned to look at Ted, still asleep beside him. Weathered. Strong. Hard edges everywhere. Clayton had felt a rightness to their lovemaking that surpassed all of his previous experience with women. The only thing he had ever wanted to grab hold of as much as Ted was clay. And to think they were both virgins. Kind of. At least they wouldn't kill each other. He was in some kind of sexual shock, he knew. And his whole life was in disorder now, he supposed. But he loved Ted. He wondered if there was any possibility of going back.

NEVERMORE.

Old Nevermore was loud this morning, Clayton noted. He was clearly ready to be up and gloomy. Clayton left the rumpled bed reluctantly and took the cover off the raven's cage. Clayton often had morning conversations with his pet, who always, unlike people, responded predictably.

"So there's no going back, is there?"

"Nevermore," said the raven right on cue. Clayton chuckled.

"No more women?"

NEVERMORE.

Why did this happen to me? he wondered.

I WAS ANGRY.

Clayton wheeled around to stare at the bird. What!

I SUPPOSE I SHOULD APOLOGIZE FOR PLAYING FAST AND LOOSE WITH YOUR LIFE. CHANGING YOUR SEXUALITY LIKE THAT WHEN YOU LEAST EXPECTED IT, BUT I REALLY WAS ANGRY.

Why?

IT WAS THE MIDDLE OF THE NIGHT AND I WAS LONESOME, AND YOU WERE BUSY WITH ALL YOUR PROJECTS, OTHER PEOPLE. YOU NEVER SEEMED TO THINK OF ME AT ALL.

"Why are you talking to me this way? You're a raven," Clayton whispered.

AMONG OTHER MANIFESTATIONS. YOU DON'T LIKE IT?

"I'd like to get back to normal. Okay? Would that be possible?"

YOU MEAN NORMAL, AS IN HETEROSEX-
UAL NORMAL?

"No. I mean normal, as in I-don't-hear-voices-coming-out-of-my-bird-cage normal."

ALL RIGHT. BUT FIRST, DO YOU FORGIVE
ME?

"Yes. Yes, of course. Whatever you say. Whatever you want."

STORY OF MY LIFE.

Clayton sensed that the uncanny incident was over. I hope nothing like that ever happens to me again, he thought.

"Nevermore," said the raven.

Clayton wondered briefly if he should make an appointment with Charles Agincourt, but immediately decided that this hallucination was too personal, too deep to share with a psychoanalyst, with anyone. Except Ted. The thought cheered him.

Still shaken, he returned to the bed, where Ted was just awakening with a smile.

It was only then that he became conscious of the firmness of his decision. It wasn't just a mood. He would retire. He would give up being a shrink. He wasn't very good at it anyhow. He should never have left the monastery.

Arista Bellefleurs was lying restlessly on his fake leather couch. She had been coming here every weekday at nine in the morning for the last five years. Had he helped her even one little bit? And now these angel dreams! She was bedeviled by angels. Was she worse? How could he tell her that the analysis was over? With no warning. He would have to think of some way to break the news. Some way that was therapeutic.

"You know, Dr. Agincourt, over the years I've had repetitive dreams," she was saying. "There's that old narrow house with the green wallpaper that I get lost in from time to time. But these angel dreams are unprecedented. They're a whole saga of dreams—the same characters, a continuing story. What do you think they mean?"

Dr. Charles Agincourt had no idea. He was remembering a time many years ago, in what seemed like another life, when he was a novice in the monastery and he had had a series of visions—also of angels. He had hoped that perhaps God was sending his winged messengers as a sign, to mark his specialness. His abbot had listened impassively and then recommended more hard work out-of-doors—always with a hat—and less solitary prayer for a few months. The visions stopped. He certainly couldn't tell this woman to put on a hat and go hoe potatoes.

Charles knew that if he were a Jungian analyst, he could tell her that angels were archetypal and thereby reassure her, in whatever peculiar way people are reassured when they are told that they have archetypal dreams. But Charles was a declared Freudian. How many angels can dance on the head of a penis?

Arista was used to the cavernous silences of Dr. Agincourt. She went ahead and filled in her own meaning: "I guess the religious symbolism is an indication that Christian's narrative has somehow taken hold of me. I'm falling in love with him, you know."

No response.

She was thoughtful for a while and then continued. "The dreams began right after I heard about Eve Callahan's suicide. And what spooks me is that the angel named Grace Davies, Christian's dead wife, was in that very first dream. I have the date in my journal. It was weeks later when Christian first told me about his wife. She—Grace, I mean—wants me to marry Christian. In the dreams, I mean. I know it must be a coincidence . . . dreaming her first . . . before I knew about her. I'm sure you can explain it to me."

No response.

"Well, how about this? Christian often preaches about God's grace, and so I suppose I made up a character in my dreams named Grace. But it's uncanny, don't you think?"

No response.

"And I know that Grace represents the part of me that wants to marry Christian. After all, it's my dream."

No response.

"*A soft answer turneth away wrath.*"

No response.

"That was a proverb. I've been saving it for you for months."

No response.

Arista sighed, giving up. Charles Agincourt was thinking of another proverb:

Even a fool, when he holdeth his peace, is considered wise.

Arista dutifully continued her associations: "And what about the younger angel—Paul? He says he's Eve Callahan's grandson. He seems so real. What if he turns out to be a coincidence, too? What if she really has . . . had . . . a grandson named Paul? I'm going to ask someone about her grandchildren at the memorial service this evening. That sounds crazy, doesn't it? Do you think they could be *real* angels? Could their appearance mean something dire? Are they preparing me for death?"

"You're asking me a whole host of questions today, Arista. I sense that you are blocking your own associations with these questions."

"Really? What could I be blocking? Let's see ... I was saying that the dream characters seem real. They make me feel a little crazy these days ... and that I'm falling in love with Christian ... love ... falling ... Eve ... sin ... the last time I fell in love ... I mean, *really* ... was with Marxie ... and I got hurt so badly I wanted to kill myself ... I thought about jumping out a window, but I didn't ... I went on living somehow—"

"You are saying that the suicidal ideation, symbolized by the angels, is still alive within you; and therefore you're afraid to fall in love again. Afraid that if you get hurt again—say, by this new man, Christian—you may actually kill yourself."

"Am I?"

No response.

Charles Agincourt was lost in his own associations. Everyone knew that good interpretations worked both ways—served the analyst as well as the patient. Was *he* suicidal? Had his angels warned *him* not to love again? He hadn't loved again. Not after God. Oh, he had *liked* Freud well enough. But it wasn't a passion with him, as it was for some of his colleagues. Without his love of God had he found life worth living? Not really. He had carried on. It was the best he could do. God had been a dreadful loss. But once the angels had vanished, it didn't matter how much Charles had prayed. There was no response.

"Maybe I'll never recover from losing Marxie to Harold."

Oh, what was this woman on about? he thought. Men, men, men. What did she know of loss?

"I hope I never lose you!" she declared. "What a depressing thought. What a depressing session!"

Charles felt the guilt slam down on him, like the lid of a coffin. "We have to stop now."

"Good." Arista got up and slid into her shoes. On the way out she turned to her psychoanalyst. "Are you going to the memorial service this evening?"

"I'll see you tomorrow, at nine, Arista."

"Oh, loosen up, Charlie."

The door closed behind her and Charles Agincourt dropped his head into his hands. He would never be able to tell her. He would never be able to tell any of his patients. He could never leave them. He would be trapped here in this fake leather life, a shrink forever.

OH, LOOSEN UP, CHARLIE.

She chuckled. What a thing to say to him! Still as she left the office she felt oddly off center and mildly irritated. This was not an uncommon feeling at the end of her sessions. More and more she questioned the value of her analysis. The treatment was one in a long series of attempts she had made to bring some order to her inner life. People used to go on long sea voyages when they were in emotional turmoil, she knew. Following such a prescription, Arista calculated that she would have been at sea for all of her adult life, excepting the short intervals when she had been in love with someone. Charlie was only half-right about her. She wasn't afraid of being in love. All the craziness and contradictions of being in love made an inner sense to Arista. She felt healthy *only* when she was in love. Of course, she was afraid to get hurt again. That seemed sensible, too.

Christian kept preaching that loving Christ would bring order and meaning to her existence. She wasn't sold. She would much rather love the middleman. Christian Davies, she knew, was a strange choice . . . even for her. She remembered his kiss. So tender. She must be getting soft in her old age, she mused. Her irritability settled in her stomach and she felt a little ill. As the cab pulled away from the curb she felt her queasiness increase, but she was aware of no way to get from La Guardia Airport to midtown Manhattan, except by car. The cabdriver was young and, to Ivy Sue, he had a greasy, slightly overcooked look. He might be Italian or Syrian. He resembled the terrorists whose newspaper photos Ivy Sue had seen and then worried about before hesitantly boarding the plane to New York City.

Suddenly he spoke. "My name is Mullahboy. What's your name?"

Ivy Sue, who had never been addressed in this way by a stranger, did not know what to do, so she answered. "Ivy Sue Hackett."

"You not from New York?"

She was sure now that he was looking for a way to rip her off, just as she had been warned by her concerned neighbors when they heard of her plan to fly east in search of her family. Grim Reaper had passed along a tip on Ted, and she had decided to follow it herself. Seth, as she had guessed for a long time, had his heart set on New York. She was determined to find them both and bring them back to the dysfunctional-family therapy she believed would save them all. Maybe Holly could come home from boarding school, too.

"I'm from Ohio, but I come here often and I know my way around."

"So is good."

"Uh. Yes." She hoped that would end the conversation. She needed to concentrate on soothing her upset stomach.

"I be here two months already. You have husband?"

"Of course I have a husband," she replied somewhat defensively.

"Too bad. I make good husband to pretty lady like you."

This was going from bad to worse for Ivy Sue, on whom the idea would not dawn to ask for an end to the interchange. "I'm old enough to be your mother."

"No. You too young, too pretty, lady. You have children?"

"Two." No one had called her a pretty lady for a long time.

"Not many children. Need more."

"No!"

"Yes. It's better with many children. I will have many children."

"Good for you." She thought she might need to throw up.

"My grandfather have many many children. My father have many children. His children have many children. They all live together in village," lied Mullahboy, who was beginning to enjoy himself.

"Greenwich Village?"

"No. In . . . Arabia. I, Mullahboy, am my father's favorite son. He send me to America to make plenty of monies for the rest of family. He say, 'Mullahboy, you make monies, then you come back home to Arabia with pretty woman and make many children.' "

"Well, good luck to you." Perhaps it was the heat bearing down on her already beleaguered brain, but in that moment Ivy Sue produced a fantasy. This was a very unusual occurrence for Ivy Sue, and it shocked her quite a bit. She saw herself arriving with this dark, young man in a dusty desert village. She was greeted by a clan of curious relatives and then gifted with native clothing. She could hear the murmurs of approval from the men in the family, the quiet jealous whispers of the women as they admired her blond hair and fair skin. She and Mullahboy were then shown to their new home, a small square house under a palm tree. Inside the walls were of mud . . . flies spotted the . . . "Can you let me off here please?" she questioned urgently.

"This not Manhattan, lady. This is Queens."

She had never heard of Queens. "Nevertheless let me off here, right now, please."

Mullahboy pulled over abruptly, causing her another lurch of distress. Ivy Sue climbed out awkwardly with her suitcase. Mullahboy gratefully accepted what was an enormous tip while Ivy Sue wondered fretfully if she had given him enough. She had no idea what she would do now.

She sat on her suitcase for a while trying to calm her churning stomach and mind. The neighborhood in which she found herself appeared ominous to her Midwestern eye, mostly ill-lit stores selling cheap goods to swarthy people. And the street was badly littered.

With relief she noticed a green railing surrounding some stairs that led down under the sidewalk. The sign indicated Manhattan trains. She had been warned about the subways by the same well-meaning neighbors who had warned her about the taxis, but no empty cabs seemed to frequent this place, no cabs at all, and she felt as if she was beginning to attract unwelcome notice.

With considerable trepidation she lifted her suitcase and descended the subway steps. She was soon sweating with the effort and the anxiety. Oh, this was all Ted's fault! she thought. No. It was that evil Janet Joyce and her filthy lies that had brought this disaster upon them all.

Ivy Sue knew that no amount of scrubbing would ever

make her life spotless again. Yes, the charges against Ted had been dropped. Yes, the odious adolescent had recanted and apologized, publicly, privately. But Ivy Sue knew that the human mind was a dirty mind. As long as the Hacketts lived in Boar's Wood, Ohio, people would talk. People would gossip: there goes Ivy Sue Hackett did you know about her husband Ted he was the one who— The prospect was ghastly.

Perhaps she was making a mistake, trying to bring Ted back. For it was Ted who had managed a way to wipe the slate completely clean. But what else was she to do? She had no handy can of amnesia to spray over her life.

The subway was the opposite of everything Ivy Sue cherished. It was dank, and dirty, and noisy, and smelly, and dark. But it was home to him now. Nelson Little sat with his back against a grimy wall in an abandoned corner of the Sheridan Square station and wondered when he would get something to eat. Since Indra had told him about the fiery death of his two sons, he hadn't cared much about food. And he had developed a phobia. He could eat nothing cooked. Raw food could usually be found with a bit of effort. But he was very tired.

Sleeping was the only thing he could do competently anymore. He had no dreams, only welcome blackness. When he was awake, he thought a lot about death. But Nelson Little, like Hamlet, was suspicious. It seemed likely to him that death would be worse than life, that he, and every other soul on this godforsaken planet, was on a spiral going down, down, down into an eternity of worsening hells.

He heard footsteps approaching his secluded corner and assumed it was some new variety of trouble. He braced himself. Headstone Brown, all in black, was walking ominously in his direction. He was holding out his hand.

What did he have to lose? He extended his own hand, finding the answering grip reassuring. George followed Luke Sevensons hesitantly into the small bedroom in the Algonquin Hotel. George Eliot Isaman was not in the habit of accompanying strange men to their bedchambers. But this was a special occasion. Katelyn had won him an exceptional private session with Luke. George had never worked with Luke before and he wished, in the anxiety of the moment, that he had canceled the appointment. He knew he should be appreciative of Luke's attention, not apprehensive. But Luke struck him as weird.

When George had arrived at the hotel, Luke had been sitting in a wing-backed chair in the overstuffed lobby opposite an impressive grandfather clock. Luke was talking to a cat who sat, transfixed, at his feet. Excusing himself from the feline, he had looked up at George quizzically, nodded, extended his hand, and then suggested they go to the privacy of his room to work. The cat stepped gracefully aside. The whole scene had given George the willies.

He seated himself on the only chair in the room, and Luke sat down in a cumbersome fashion on the small, ornate brass bed.

Quiet overtook them. Luke waited. Very slowly George began to relax. Luke's gaze was not threatening. His eyes were large and interested and accepting, not accusatory or impatient. George had seen eyes like that once before, somewhere. Where? he wondered. When? Recognition came to him. They were his grandmother's loving eyes, from childhood, when she beheld her little Georgie. He had the curious sensation that Luke had lost some of his materiality, so that his grandmother, long dead, could arrive and peer out through his eyes at her grandson. George felt like crying.

"Who is it?" asked Luke.

"My grandmother."

"Tell her what you want." There was no derision in his voice. They were speaking as though this were a normal conversation about ordinary matters. "You can tell me, too, while you're at it."

"I would like to write a great book. And I think I finally know what it is that I want to write about, but the idea seems so blatantly obvious, so obviously ordinary, that I'm not sure it's worth bothering. I don't know if I can bring any greatness to it."

"Tell me about it," said Luke.

"Well, the other day I was on the movie set where they've begun shooting a movie based on one of my novels. It's called *You've Got to Be Kidding*."

Luke gave him a questioning look.

George shrugged. "Okay, it's a junk novel, it doesn't count, it's not what I want to write, it's what I *do* write."

"Everything counts. Go on."

"I was having a fight with the director about one of my characters. The character's name is Sincera. Anyhow, I had wanted to make Sincera a little unlikable, so I had given her some atrocious table manners. The actress playing Sincera was throwing a fit about that. She didn't want to look like a pig on screen, and she had the director all charged up and ready to drop the whole bit. I didn't approve of the change. I thought that if Sincera wasn't somehow repulsive, then her whole character, and most of the plot, didn't make any sense. Now here's the thing: I had stolen the idea from a man I had never met, but disliked intensely. I'll have to go back a little. . . ."

Luke nodded encouragingly. But George had the creepy feeling it was his grandmother who was listening. Would dear old Millie Cheetwell approve of what he was about to reveal?

"Don't mix up love with approval," said Luke.

Jolted, George went on with his narrative. "I once had a love affair . . . many years ago. The woman I was sleeping with wouldn't leave her husband for me. I was very much in love at the time and I wanted her for myself. You understand?"

Luke understood.

"Anyhow, I had never met her husband. She refused to talk about him, so I couldn't even imagine what he was like or why she would prefer him to me. As it happened, I heard from some mutual friends that he had slovenly table manners. It stuck with me. I really hated him for that. I imagined him acting in uncouth ways in restaurants, reaching across other people's food for the butter, wiping his mouth with the back of his hand, embarrassing my lover. Well, to make a long story short, it didn't work out with her. She and her ill-mannered husband left the city. Don't have any idea where they are now, but there I was, years later, on this busy film set, having this heated argument with this famous director and this idiotic movie star over whether my character Sincera should eat scrambled eggs with her fingers or not. So you see, I want to write about how we all go through life and we never know what things we do, which things we say, will influence the lives of other people. I mean we assume that heroic actions or great thoughts will have an effect, but sometimes it's the tawdry bits, the habits we don't even think about, like our table manners, that take on a life in someone else's world. I want to show how one tiny event, totally unknown to us, leads to another and another—"

"That everything counts."

"Exactly. But it's an old idea. It's all been said before."

"Isn't every story just one thing leading to another?"

"Well. Yes. But I want to write about how we are all in

each other's stories, in ways we wouldn't guess, couldn't imagine. I'm the character in your story and you're the character in mine. But we don't know where we'll turn up. We think we're living out our own lives, but we are actually, when we least expect it, animating other people's narratives."

"As in Henry Chang's grandmother's teapot story?"

"Why, yes. That's a perfect example."

"What would your grandmother say about all this, George?"

George was thoughtful. He looked again for her presence. It was uncanny. It was as if she sat just behind Luke in a beautiful garden, peeking through Luke's eyes into the rumpled room in which they sat. She was as he remembered her: serene, loving, interested.

"She would say to me, 'Write, Georgie, write what you think. Write as well as you can. I'll read your story.'"

"Will you be able to write it now?"

"I wish she was here, really here, to read it."

"How do you know she's not?"

"She's dead."

"Have you ever been dead?"

"Not that I recall."

"Then what do you know about it? Write it for her. See how it goes."

"I usually write for my mother."

"Ah."

"Ah?"

"There's the block."

And George thought of his mother, so alive, so eager for the next book, so pleased to show it off to her friends, so uncritical of its content. She never actually read his books. "If I wrote for my grandmother, I wouldn't have to rush. I couldn't. It would have to be good. She'd actually read it. She'd have thoughts about it. I wish she was really here."

"She is with you until the end of the age."

George felt himself suddenly eager to be gone. To be home. To begin working.

"Time to go?"

"Yes. Luke. Thanks."

"Can you let yourself out—and the cat in? We weren't quite finished."

George Eliot Isaman left the Algonquin Hotel with an unaccustomed lightness of heart. The day seemed bright with promise.

Jamie Callahan turned a corner and smacked directly into George Eliot Isaman.

"Sorry."

"Sorry."

"Lost in thought."

"Me too."

"Going home to write."

"To paint. Later."

"Just saw Luke Sevensons."

"At the Algonquin?"

"Yes. He's helping a cat now."

"Did he help you?"

"Yes."

"What are you going to write?"

"A novel. I'm going to call it *The Unbearable Lightness of Being*."

"I think someone else wrote a novel by that title."

"Couldn't have."

"See you, George."

"See you, Callahan."

Dr. Charles Agincourt came down the block just as the two men went their separate ways. He waved in both their directions and then stood looking around uncertainly. He called after Callahan: "Do you know which block the Algonquin Hotel is on?"

"Right around the corner, Charlie." Callahan wondered what a psychoanalyst could possibly have to talk to Luke Sevensons about. He gave up the notion of checking on Luke. Luke was clearly in fine form for a dying man, and he wasn't, at least for the moment, with Maggie.

Callahan had enjoyed his leisurely stroll uptown from the Village. It did him good to get out into the real world from time to time, he thought, to see how the other half lived. He had been thinking all during his long walk. Actually, he admitted reluctantly, he had been worrying. He felt change in the air. There *was* change in the air: the arrival of all the kith and kin for starters. Luke's threats. Maggie's decision to make a decision. What if she chose Luke? She couldn't do it. Maggie loved Callahan. Always would. He moved his hand across his face. Her amber scent, from this morning's lovemaking, had lingered on his fingertips.

With an unbearable lightness of step he turned and walked back in the direction of the Village.

He was done with worrying. There were too many things you couldn't know. But there were a few things you could! Ted Hackett knew that he loved Clayton Grant. He knew that he had once loved Arista Bellefleurs and that Clayton had once loved her, too. He knew he had once loved and married someone named Ivy Sue. He knew he had two children with her—Seth and Holly—though he had never met them. He knew how babies were made. His psychoanalyst had told him, but the idea seemed foreign to him. He knew his name was Ted Hackett. And that was the list of his life. Life felt very good and very simple to Ted.

"Do you think I will ever remember my life in Ohio?" he asked Clayton.

"Nevermore," said Nevermore.

They both laughed. It was long past time to get out of bed. They had to dress for the memorial service. They were meeting Arista outside the church.

Clay continued to fret about their inevitable conversation. He could only hope she would take the announcement with good grace. He didn't want to hurt her.

Arista, meanwhile, felt as if she had been kicked, hard, exactly in the center of her stomach, with a steel-tipped boot. She doubled over and went down onto her knees, breathing hard, reminding herself that pain passed.

She had felt this variety of agony several times before, at the onset of flu or an attack of food poisoning. In her distant past there had been an inflamed appendix that had resulted in surgery. She began to shake and a slimy cold sweat covered her body. Frightened, she pulled herself up by the overwrought leg of her writing table and made her way to the bathroom, where her insides seemed to come up and out all at once. Afterward the pain subsided a little and she was able to stagger to the bedroom, cursing what seemed a terrible flu.

Two hours later she was worse. Miserable with fever and nausea, she had struggled around the apartment in an ever-deepening depression. She couldn't think, she couldn't write, and worst of all, her ability to fantasize seemed confined to a series of ever-more-distressing physical disasters. If she wasn't better by tomorrow, she decided, she would concede defeat and go to a doctor. After all, she had responsibilities, obligations. As it was, she would have to forgo the memorial service. And the dinner! What a disappointment.

In the very next moment another stab of pain doubled

her over. This time she could not unbend herself. She was afraid she might loose consciousness. I must get help, now, she thought, and began to crawl toward the door of her apartment. She heard herself cry out in anguish at each hunching movement. The tortured-animal sound embarrassed her, but there was no one else to hear.

She reached the door, and by an act of will pulled herself up, this time by the knob. She stood leaning against the frame, trying to find enough strength to walk. All of her energy was being burned in order to stay conscious, to keep breathing. In time—she didn't know how much time—she managed to open the door and fall through the rectangle of new space into the hallway. The pain, unbelievably, was worse; bad enough to overrule her self-consciousness. She cried out again and again until, at last, another door appeared to open and an unknown neighbor was spinning in her direction. Why don't I know my own neighbors? she wondered.

The next thing she knew she was burning with summer heat, pressed into the back of a stifling, speeding ambulance, though it melted and re-formed into a hay cart as songs from her childhood surrounded her. She and her friends sang on and on into the night. Eeyi, eeyi, ooh. But why was she in so much pain? Why didn't Ted stop the jolting hay ride and help her?

"Help me," she gasped.

"We will help you," said the young doctor.

"Please, can you give me something for the pain?"

"We can't do that just yet, miss. Not until we know what is happening to you."

"Hurts."

"Hold on."

And the young doctor pushed on her abdomen and dissolved. She was in another room, with X-ray equipment and a black man in a white coat.

"Can you slide over onto this table?"

"No."

"I'll move you."

She groaned, straining for consciousness, as he lifted her from the stretcher, but the tiny bump onto the metal table was too much for her and she howled through the series of shifting procedures.

"Good luck," said the X-ray man as he held the foggy pictures up to the light. There were splotches of white all over her dark insides.

She was wheeled back to the young doctor.

"Can you hear me, Miss Bellefleurs?"

"Yes."

"Do you know where you are?"

"Hospital."

"You are in the emergency room at St. Vincent's Hospital."

"Pain. Flu."

"No. Not the flu, Miss Bellefleurs. You have peritonitis. There is infection throughout your abdominal cavity. Something inside you has ruptured."

"What?"

"We won't know until we get in there."

"In where?"

"We need to perform emergency surgery. Now. As soon as the team is assembled."

Dim memories from the childhood operation arrived, carrying with them intense foreboding. There would be the unbelievable surrender of her privacy to strangers, already under way, the smothering of her spirit with anesthesia, the invasion of her body by men and instruments, the chill awakening into helplessness and pain, the terrible cut puckered with tough, black stitches, nausea, weakness, dependency, and more pain. "Will I die?"

"If you don't consent to the surgery, you will die."

"And if I have the surgery?"

"You have a good chance. An ulcer may have ruptured."

"I don't have ulcers."

"Then the tear is somewhere in your intestinal track."

"No appendix."

"You told us that."

"Did I?"

"Yes. When you first came in. Now please sign this consent form. No. Try to read it first. There. Dr. Day will do the surgery. You're lucky. He's the best there is."

"Please give me something for the pain."

"Miss Knight will be in shortly to prep you for surgery."

Arista snorted, but her sense of humor was cut short by a spasm of pain.

"She'll give you something. Is there anyone you need to call first? You'll be groggy after the injection."

"Yes." She was wheeled over next to the nurses' station, where she could reach a telephone from her stretcher. Nearby she could hear other voices going out on other phones, collecting the medical staff, preparing the way, for her operation.

Katelyn's answering machine came on.

"Oh hell!" But of course she would be out for supper and then to the service. Or vice versa. Or something.

She waited for the beep, spoke into the hiss of tape: "Katelyn, it's Arista. I'm at St. Vincent's. I have to have surgery right now. Something inside broke. Not my heart. I hurt like hell. Can you come up here in the morning? Okay? Don't tell anyone else. Not Christian. Not Ted. Not Clay. Okay? If I live, we'll figure out what to do next." Leaving the message seemed to bring her some slight relief, so she continued: "The intern says I'm lucky, the surgeon is good. But what else *would* he say? 'Good luck, the surgeon on call this evening is all thumbs'? And Katelyn. I love you a lot."

She lay on her stretcher panting, enduring, trying to distract herself with her surroundings. The emergency room was a clashing composition of hard surfaces and soft bodies. The green-tiled walls glared under the harsh fluorescent lights. In corners, complicated machinery with pumps and dials waited to be put to urgent, unsavory purposes. There seemed to be about a dozen dark-skinned people lying in alcoves on metal stretchers, with IVs in their arms. Some were in restraints. None moved. From time to time they were approached by clusters of light-skinned people with stethoscopes and clipboards and expressions of concern. There was a ruthless-looking security guard pacing by the door watching his watch. There was blood on the floor nearby.

Another young doctor approached her. He was carrying a purse.

"Mrs. Bellflowers? I'm going to go through your handbag and list the contents. Then I'm going to put everything—and your street clothes, your watch, your ring, and your purse—into this plastic bag, seal it, and give it to security. You'd better watch, because you'll have to sign the list. Okay?"

"I need something for the pain. My insides keep trying to be my outsides."

"They haven't given you anything?"

"No."

"I'll see if I can get you something. Hold on to this." And he handed her her purse. Where did it come from? She didn't remember bringing it. And where were her clothes? She was dressed in a faded blue hospital gown.

Who had undressed her? She lay clutching her purse and moaning softly, trying not to move.

The second young doctor returned with a nurse in tow. "We better do this fast." The nurse prepared to give Arista the injection in her hip, rolling her to the side and hitching up the gown in full view of everyone in the emergency room. No one seemed to notice, and she noticed that she didn't care. She knew that at this point she would have crawled naked down the corridor to get some relief. How did mankind survive for all the centuries before the invention of anesthesia? Without ways to stop the pain?

"One pen and a notebook . . . one lipstick . . . one comb . . ."

Arista watched a large, black garbage bag swallow her possessions one by one. If she died, who would even know to retrieve them? Who would want them? She should have made a will. She signed the list. Nurse Knight wheeled her into a nearby enclosure and whisked some green curtains shut. She was left alone there, in what appeared to be a storeroom. Her eyes ran around the shelves of medical paraphernalia. Who thought all this up? she wondered. On a high shelf she noticed a cardboard box. It was marked in crayon: AMPUTATED PARTS. She shuddered. What was she doing here? How could it be that this was happening to her?

Knight returned. "I'm going to scrub you up a bit with this special soap and put a catheter in. It will only take a minute and it won't hurt." In the midst of the embarrassing procedure the green curtains parted and the first young doctor entered.

"How are you doing?" he asked, ignoring her compromised position, taking her wrist, and beginning to count her pulse before she could answer.

"Better." The nurse finished the insertion of the catheter

and then painted Arista's stomach with iodine. She began to prepare an IV. "Are you an IV nurse?" Arista challenged.

"No."

"Would you call one, please?" They might have taken over her body, but she still had a brain.

"Time is of the essence," intervened the young doctor. "Shall I do it?"

"Yes."

And he punctured her vein efficiently.

Nurse Knight tucked Arista's hair into a plastic cap and called for a porter. In her mind's eye Arista saw herself as she was at this moment. What an ugly corpse I will make, she thought.

"We will take you to the OR now," said the young doctor. "We'll stop along the way so you can talk to the anesthesiologist."

"Thanks."

And the journey, seen in so many movies, began: along corridors, around corners, the ceiling flashing by overhead, a queer sense of importance accompanying the entourage—doctor, nurse, porter, patient. Were these to be her last fleeting images of life? Was the end just minutes ahead of her, lurking in the darkness of anesthesia? Was her death to be called a surgical accident? An unexpected heart attack on the operating table? An irreparable disaster in her abdomen? She was only forty-five years old! She was supposed to live to be ninety. Wasn't she? Wasn't everybody? This could be *it*. Who, left behind, would be bereft? No one. Sad? Yes, many people would be sad—Katelyn (but Katelyn was always sad); Clay (more shocked than sad); Ted (if he managed to remember her); Christian (yes, if *he* remembered her); George (sentimentally); Luke (with acceptance)—and they would all go right on working, and playing, and eating, and sleeping and making love while their sadness slowly faded into the business of their living and was forgotten.

It was okay to go, she realized with sudden relief. No one would really be harmed if she died. That was a surprise. Shouldn't she be sad to know how unattached to life she had become? How unattached to others? No. She wasn't sad at all. She was free. Liberated from life. Unafraid to die.

The stretcher came to an abrupt halt. A kindly-faced, gray-haired man who seemed to glow incandescently leaned over her.

"I'm Dr. Agincourt. I will be your anesthesiologist."

"My psychoanalyst is Dr. Agincourt. You look like him, and my friend Florian."

"My brothers."

"I knew they were twins."

"Triplets."

"I'm what's left of Arista Bellefleurs. Pleased to meet you."

He took her hand in a reassuring fashion. "My first name is Winston. Do you have anything to tell me? Or any questions about the anesthesia?"

"Please be sure I'm out, Winston."

"That's my job," he assured her cheerfully.

"And please be sure I come out."

"That, too, is my job. I've read your chart, and your medical history. Anything you haven't told us?"

"I don't know. I don't remember the admission interview."

"Then let's hope you habitually tell the truth." He asked a few specific questions, checking them against the chart. She liked him. "Okay, I'll let you go now. I'll see you in the OR."

The stretcher swung into motion again.

She had discovered, during her ordeal, that she—unlike many others—did not want to live if it meant living in pain. Suffering, like unhappiness, was an enemy. She knew others could accept these twin realities as part of life. They could make peace with unhappiness, accept suffering. She knew it was wise to do so. She could not. There were moments in the last two hours when she had considered death her oldest friend, lost these many years as she wandered the earth. And she had been eager for reunion. Could death *be* God?

But supposing the doctors could fix her? Supposing the pain was gone and she had regained her health. Yes, then she wanted to live. Certainly, yes. But what, if there was no one to whom she was inextricably attached, did she want to live *for*? She wanted to write. She wanted to write another novel. No one else could write her books. She had ideas that were hers alone, as yet unrecorded. Of course she wanted to see how her relationship with Christian would turn out. But it was the novel, *only* the novel, that called her to life. How strange, she mused. All these years I thought it was men, but it's the work that matters after all.

With the full acknowledgment of her attachment she felt the momentary liberation vanish. In spite of her marination in the pain medication, she registered fear. She didn't want to die. The ceiling seemed to fly by endlessly, the corners grew sharper as they rushed around the turns. She groped through her life experience for a word of wisdom, for solace, for a moment's grace on this grotesque ride toward mutilation. No poetry could reach her here. She was moving too fast. Only terror could keep pace.

She gripped the stretcher, willing her thoughts to slow down. What would Luke Sevensons tell her to do? He would encourage her to accept what was happening, not to fight, to let her feelings flow, to change, not to get caught in a fight with her own body, her own circumstance. Her heart was pounding and she was hot again. If she accepted her feelings, what would follow? A new feeling always followed acceptance.

She let the heat and the pounding take her. Anger followed. She didn't want this to be happening. She wanted to be home. Or out with her friends. After the surge of anger came the pull of longing. Who was it for? Someone. No one.

The fear was returning. She took a deep breath, trying to accept it. She couldn't accept fear! She wanted comfort. What would Christian say? There was something from the Bible, the New Testament, from that first sermon, repressed these many months. It was an assurance. How did it go?

My God, in his loving kindness will meet me at every corner.

Yes. That was it. Could she believe that? Christian did. Funny how she thought of his words, not of his kiss.

My God, in his loving kindness will meet me at every corner.

They turned into the OR. Was He here? Was It so? Was there a God at this corner? She had a sudden realization that if He was, she should stretch out the hand of her mind to meet him. She tried.

It was a big room, with a domed ceiling. Very bright. Very cold. There were strangers here, in masks, in gowns. They moved instruments and machines around. They murmured softly among themselves. She was not one of them.

She was the other. The stranger. The patient. They moved her from her stretcher to a cold metal table, where they peeled off her gown. Sheets draped her lower body. She was naked from the pelvis up. Her arms were stretched out to either side and fixed at the wrists, ready for needles, ready for tubes.

She was completely helpless now, at the hands of these strangers. Who were they? she wondered. Where had they come from in the middle of this evening? What lives had they led that brought them to this moment? To what homes would they return? To what concerns—children, lovers—concerns that would be of equal importance to their work here tonight? Arista was their work tonight. In another age, in another place, she would be tied up in this fashion and surrounded by strangers for death; in another time, in another place, for torture. But in this time, in this place, she was here to have her life saved.

"We meet again." It was the glowing Dr. Agincourt. His eyes, above his mask, were warm and reassuring. Was this her answer?

My God in His loving kindness will meet me at every corner.

It was thus that Christian reassured himself. He had been edgy all day. He approached the altar in preparation for the twilight service. He would light the candles himself. He held the long, white tapers in his hand. They were splendid objects, made for the worship of God. Behind him he could hear Little Nel snoring on a back pew. He would have to awaken him soon. A village character who called himself Headstone Brown had asked permission for the homeless man to take refuge in the sanctuary. He had told Christian, speaking in his peculiar succinct rhyme, that this particular man wouldn't last another week on the street.

> *"Here lies the man known as Little Nel*
> *Without a home*
> *He'll go straight to hell."*

"You mean this man is failing at *homelessness?*"

Headstone had managed to communicate that Little Nel was too high-class, too educated a person for street life. He appeared to be a cultured man in the midst of a nervous breakdown, but he was quite docile and somewhat clean.

Left in the quiet of the church, Little Nel had soon nodded out on the back pew. Christian smiled ruefully when he noticed the pangs of jealously he felt for the man's ability to sleep so long and so well. Man's nature is truly fallen, he thought. At least mine is, if I can covet this poor man's one solace.

In spite of a clear conscience, sleep was elusive to Christian. He approached his bed each evening as if he were about to embark upon a safari or a space journey. He never knew what the dark of night would bring. He fell asleep easily enough, but within an hour he would waken, crashing into consciousness without thought, seized by a wild, unnamed terror. Or the fire dreams would come—fire sermons amid incinerating churches in flaming cities in blackened countries. From these he arose, hot, and sweating with fear. The rest of the night would then become a battle for sleep—an hour here, an hour there. He was saved from utter, ongoing exhaustion by his afternoon nap in the church study. In those few stolen minutes (for Alice May Patoon thought he was at prayer and she would rather die than disturb him), he slept the sweet sleep of an angel.

Well, not always an angel, he corrected himself, for sometimes his dreams were erotic.

Perhaps, mused Christian, these afternoon slumbers were a kind of prayer, a meditation in which he clung to life and to love. For except in these fleeting dreams, sexuality had become meaningless to him. Words only—fat, round, squashy words heard from troubled parishioners, or skimmed in a novel. When he poked at them, the words collapsed like soufflés. He watched images of love at the occasional movie. They carried no feeling with them. And without feeling, could sexuality be said to exist? Christian awoke from these stolen sleeps as from the dead, rested and renewed. He had once consulted a psychiatrist about his insomnia. "You are sexually frustrated," said the doctor. "You are impertinent," said Christian Davies.

The memory of that embarrassing consultation wove itself into his anxiousness. He expected a difficult night tonight. Arista Bellefleurs was coming to dinner; coming to his apartment. A candlelight dinner. Mrs. McGee, his cook and housekeeper, had been excused for the evening. Surreptitiously he had reset the dining-room table with the good, gold-rimmed china. He had held the long, white tapers in his hand, then placed them in the candlesticks that once had been a wedding present. Christian would light the candles himself.

Christian Davies had never entertained a woman alone in his home before. He had gone from his mother's house in Belfast to Dublin College, to the seminary in Cork, to marriage, without ever having the occasion to live alone. Since the death of Grace, he had taken the majority of his meals in solitude. He always insisted on well-prepared meals and good wines at his lonely parsonage table, lean stew beef and whole-wheat dog biscuits for Caleb—and the church committees that considered such concerns had complied. He, in turn, considered this fair compensation for the dozens of congregational dinners over which he presided with unrelenting cheerfulness, while swallowing overcooked roast beef or underdone chicken with luke-warm tea. At such communions he offered up silent prayers of intercession, pleading for a divine intervention in the approaching gravy, a godly finger in the soup. Never had these particular prayers been answered. Others were.

As Christian completed his preparations for the service Alice May Patoon sailed into the sanctuary and announced that Luke Sevensons, Rabbi Barkowitz, Jerry Phails, and Henry Chang were assembled in the conference room awaiting his instructions. Her voice was absolutely even, but her eyebrows had arched almost to her hairline. They must be quite a group, he thought.

"Thank you, Miss Patoon."

"You're welcome, Reverend Davies." There was a moment's pause. "Reverend Davies?"

"Yes, Miss Patoon?"

"He has a rattle."

"Who has a what?"

"The old man, Mr. Stevenson . . . no . . . Sevensons . . . he has a rattle."

"It must be him, don't you think? The man from the train. Oh, Alice May!" he cried. Her announcement had filled him with delight. He had never called her by her given name before, and in the instant of her reaction he realized there was more to Alice May's feelings for him than secretarial loyalty and Christian duty. She looked as if she'd been suddenly overinflated with helium. He imagined her bobbing about in the upper reaches of the sanctuary. "Oh, Miss Patoon, my dear Miss Patoon," he corrected himself, returning her to normal size. Time for the Clincher. He flashed her his glorious smile and watched as her features nestled into contentment. That would tether her for a time. He could return safely to protocol. "I'm just delighted! I'm sure it's the man from the train." And he darted out before she could reply to his incomprehensible statement.

Alice May sank down on the front pew and felt things: confusion, anxiety, warmth, anger, longing. Love? It was a most unwelcome succession of experiences. Rattles and trains indeed! She took a deep breath and concentrated on the rows of flaming candles. She suddenly wished she had a fireplace. She had never wished so before. She envisioned herself stretched out before its hot, orange mouth, wearing a thin, white negligee, a glass of red wine nearby, and nearer still, Christian Davies. Her head snapped back in dismay. This would not do! Oh, why had the previous pastor, that cantankerous old fool, gone to glory without so much as a by your leave, leaving her vulnerable to this new man who was always billowing about the place—a man who was always smiling. It wasn't seemly. Alice May felt very uncomfortable. She needed to purchase some tighter foundation garments.

It was at that moment of discomfiture when she became aware of an exotic sound emanating from the back of the church. A snorting sound such as a pig might make. She looked around, but could see no one. She listened more intently. Why, it was someone snoring! She got up and began to make her determined way down the aisle.

The memorial service was scheduled to begin shortly. The friends of the deceased would be arriving, expecting a funereal atmosphere conducive to grief and meditation. She must awaken the sleeping person, whoever it was, and send them on their way. She felt yet another unwelcome feeling: fear. She stopped. The snoring-snorting sounds continued. What was there to be frightened of? It was only a tramp, most likely, a wino who had wandered in and fallen asleep in relative safety. Or possibly a parishioner, one who had, after a hard day's work, nodded off in the midst of their evening prayers. She assured herself that she was perfectly safe with Reverend Davies and the other men so nearby. But danger seemed to emanate from the back pew.

She could see the peril, like a shimmer of air above a heated roadway. She had a premonition that if she moved any closer, if she looked upon the face of the sleeping man—for surely, these ungodly sounds could only exude from the sinus cavities of a man—if she woke him up and gazed into his unknown eyes, her life, she was suddenly sure, would change forever.

Alice May took an enormous breath. Was she losing her mind? she wondered. First she had been bedeviled by erotic visions of Reverend Davies, and now she was beset with premonitions of evil. Perhaps she should go home, tighten her corset, and rest. It was after five o'clock. She didn't have to attend the service. But she was curious. There was nothing at all to be curious about at her home, where everything was familiar, and extremely neat. But here, she felt, energies were collecting, as if for some pagan rite. Why, anything could happen. And so she was drawn inexorably toward the sound, toward the man, toward her fate.

She peered over the penultimate pew, into the last one. Why, it was Assistant Professor Little! She had taken a short course in medieval poetry with him just last year at The New School. At the moment he appeared to be in rather bad shape. There was a bruise over one eye, and he hadn't shaved for a while. His clothes were rumpled and dirty, his shoelaces were untied. Instantly all of Alice May's premonitions were forgotten, and a great spasm of tenderness overwhelmed her.

THIS COULD BE A MISTAKE.

In spite of the clarity of the injunction, Alice May ignored the inner voice. For although she had given years of faithful service to Old Gray Presbyterian, she, like most people, did not believe in a personal God. Oh, she admitted some force, some benevolent power that had put the whole shebang into motion, but not the kind of being who would pay attention to the likes of an Alice May Patoon.

THAT, TOO.

"Wake up," she said softly, her whole life now changed. "It's time to go."

• • •

"It's time to go."

Seth rolled over lazily in a twist of clean, white sheets and was smiling up at Bridget, even before he opened his eyes. Bridget smiled back at him, first upon the fragile, fluttering lids, and then into his bright, blue eyes.

"Won't your mother be worried about you?" he asked.

"I called her late last night, after you fell asleep."

"Was she angry?"

"At love? Mother, mine? She may be a come-again Catholic woman, but she's a child of the Village, and she married for love."

"Funny. I've never thought of my mother as a child, or about why she married my father. Come to think of it, I've never thought of my mother at all. I wonder who . . . how she is?"

"You should ring her up, Seth."

"Whatever for?"

"To tell her how you are, where you are."

"She'd only ask if the room was clean."

Bridget took a breath and then a risk. "Maybe tell her who you are."

"She installed soundproofing against that possibility long ago."

"Then tell her who you're with."

"She'd only ask if *you* were clean."

"Pure as the driven snow, I was."

"Do you mind very much not being a virgin anymore? I mean, being that you're a Catholic and all."

"I've never been happier."

"Do you think you're pregnant?"

"Yes."

"Yes?"

"Do you mind?"

"How could I mind? I hope you are pregnant. I hope it's a girl. I hope it looks like you. What shall we name her?"

"Pauline."

"Good." And they snuggled together in absolute contentment. "Just think, Bridget, our lives will never again be the same. How will we live?"

"Happily ever after."

"Making music and love and babies."

"And money."

"Yes. I suppose we will have to make some money. For the babies. Should we worry about it?"

"We're too young to worry about money."

"Isn't it strange to be starting out our new life together by going to a funeral?"

"Seth?"

"Yes, Bridget?"

"I love you."

"I love you, too. I wonder . . ."

"What do you wonder?"

"I wonder if old people can remember these feelings, this kind of . . . enchantment?"

"We will have to grow old and see."

"Will we ever be old?"

"Only if we're fortunate. I wonder why she did it?"

"Who did what?"

"My grandmother. I wonder why she killed herself?"

"Does it hurt you?"

"Yes. I would have liked to have known her."

"You will in time," said her brother Paul, though he couldn't be heard, only felt.

Eve, meantime, was reflecting that Bridget would never have met Seth if she hadn't fallen out the window; and Pauline and Patrick would never be born. It was pleasant to have some idea how these matters worked. She watched benevolently as the two young people hurried themselves along to her memorial service.

When Eve had first heard about the arrangements at Old Gray P., she had felt self-conscious in a disembodied sort of way. "I feel a little foolish," she remarked to Grace, "everything considered."

"IT IS I WHO CONSIDER EVERYTHING," God reminded her.

"But you are going to attend?" pressed Grace.

"Oh, no," declared Eve. "I would feel too much like Emily in the last act of *Our Town*."

"Oh, here comes Clayton Grant," Grace exclaimed. "Isn't he a heartthrob?"

Clay entered the church carrying the latest, somewhat larger clay mock-up of the sculpture inspired by the crash of Eve Callahan. He appeared very handsome in the twilight. His arm muscles were taut and his strong hands held the sculpture firmly.

"I hope it won't disturb her grandchildren too much," he remarked to Ted.

"She should have thought of that before she jumped."

"Ted, don't be so unfeeling!"

"Am I?" They sat down together in a middle pew. It made Clayton feel uneasy to sit so close to Ted in this place, absorbed as he was in the anticipation of Arista's arrival. She hadn't been on the church steps as planned. He sat restlessly peering around the sanctuary, enjoying the unusual space and light.

"People really come here every week," he whispered with amazement in his voice. "Grown-up people, who actually believe in all the claptrap about God." He remembered the voice of the raven. Couldn't be, he thought, though he was ruffled.

Other mourners had begun to file into the church. Clayton recognized most of them, not one of whom, he knew, ever set foot in here on a Sunday morning.

There was Quentin Cox, as handsome as ever, with Buff Carrington leaning on his arm. Buff was looking frail and ill after his brief hospital stay. There but for the grace of God, go I, thought Clayton, without noting the discrepancy of his position. Greta Garbo, sedate as ever, led them to an empty pew.

"My God," said Clayton, "look at that. It's Katelyn Wells, surrounded by men, and she's smiling!" Katelyn had come in holding tightly to Lester, whom she had just gotten released from Bellevue, on a temporary pass, to attend the service. "He does look a little like Jesus," Clayton observed.

"Who's Jesus?" asked Ted.

"It's a long story."

Katelyn was accompanied by a tall, wiry man that everyone either knew or guessed was her ex-husband, Victor.

Victor was helping their son, Amas, who was walking with a cane, negotiate a seat in a middle pew. There was a beautiful young woman with them, too, carrying a baby.

"That must be Katelyn's grandson," said Quentin to Buff. "And he sure doesn't take after Katelyn. He's laughing and chortling as if his arrival in this family was a large private joke." Buff was not yet too weak to laugh. "And they seem to have two small dogs with them stuffed into a satchel. What a congregation."

James Callahan, looking strained, arrived next. He was accompanied by a magnificent red Indian couple, a younger, paler woman herding a flock of attractive red-haired children, and an elderly black woman. Quentin did his best to describe them.

"The black woman is Methuselah," Buff informed him. "She takes care of Luke, the farm, and everything else she comes in contact with, as far as I can see."

"And there is that dear, distracted Florian Agincourt," Quentin added. "I believe he's with the Callahan contingent, too. I haven't seen him in ages. Isn't his comet due tonight? And there's his brother Charles! With that muddy-handed potter, Indra Little of all people. Wasn't Charles her analyst? I don't see George; but that's not surprising. Nobody has seen George since he started work on *The Unbearable Lightness of Being*. Do you know he's decided to keep writing under the name Cheetwell? Wants to rehabilitate the family name—"

His narration was suddenly overpowered by the first bellowing chords of the organ prelude played by Biggs Howard, Katelyn's doorman, who doubled as Old Gray Presbyterian's organist. Other Village oddities, including their dear, daft Mullahboy arrived. Mullahboy had a stray cat with him, an unlikely-looking woman with a suitcase. The eyes of both Mullahboy and the woman were darting wildly about, all over the congregation. They sat down anxiously together in the back pew. Quentin was curious.

"What's all this about?" Ivy Sue whispered to Mullahboy, who had rather gallantly come back to rescue her from the Queens subway platform only a few minutes after her anxious descent.

"You say you looking for my friend Mr. Ted Hackett. He probably come here. Everybody coming to Eve Callahan's funeral."

"This is a funeral? Who's Eve Callahan?"

"I fear maybe my mamma, she is come here looking around for me, also, too."

"From Arabia?"

The music grew louder, making further talk impossible. The church was too full and too dim for Ivy Sue to determine if Ted was among the mourners. Almost immediately she noticed that a dirty, disheveled man was sleeping further along their pew, his head in the lap of a fat woman. The woman, who had a pruny, pinched look stuck in the midst of an otherwise smooth, friendly face, glared at Ivy Sue intensely, as if to deflect her stare.

In fastidious compliance, Ivy Sue turned her eyes back to the rest of the congregation, and in so doing she experienced an unexpected shock. Forward only one pew, and to the right of her, she saw her missing son, Seth, who sat placidly holding hands with a unknown red-haired girl. By the look of his lips he had been practicing a lot. Before Ivy Sue could begin her approach, the Reverend Christian Davies entered the pulpit followed by three strange-looking men, who seated themselves, rather uncomfortably, in the high-backed, brass-buttoned chairs arranged in an arc behind him. Another man entered the choir loft. The first chords of the opening hymn were sounding.

> *"Our God, our help in ages past,*
> *Our hope for years to come . . ."*

Christian was pleased with his selection. The choice had been between this old chestnut and "Creation's Lord, We Give You Thanks That This Your World Is Incomplete." This hymn sounded right tonight.

> *"Time, like an ever-rolling stream,*
> *Bears all its sons away;*
> *They fly forgotten, as a dream*
> *Dies at the opening day."*

As the singing continued Christian surveyed the congregation. A wary group, he surmised. Unbelievers to a man, and a few undecided women. And where the devil was Arista?

She knew only that she was somewhere frigid and that she was in unfathomable pain. She forced open her eyes, looking up out of the swirling darkness. Grace Davies, Eve Callahan, Paul O'Neill, and Winston Agincourt hovered at the end of the bed. She remembered where she was, what had happened.

"I'm glad you all survived the operation," she gasped as the pain clamped her eyes shut again.

"What did you say?" It was Dr. Agincourt.

"I'm cold."

"We'll get you a heat lamp."

"Pain." She felt as if she had been saying that for days.

"Yes. We can give you something, now that we know you're conscious. It will take a minute to work."

She felt as if she had been hearing that for days. "Hurry." She opened her eyes again. A nurse was preparing an injection. The angels and Dr. Agincourt were gone.

"I think I'm in love with him," she said.

"Right, dearie," said the nurse, and gave her the needle. She went black again. When she woke again, she was warmer and she could stand the pain if she didn't move. Only Eve and Paul were standing by. She glanced around to get her bearings. Intensive-care unit.

"Did something go wrong?" she asked.

"No, but it seems that way," answered Eve. More blackness then and another awakening, this time with enough consciousness to be scared. There was solace somewhere, but she couldn't remember where. Oh, yes. It was somewhere near Christian. What was it he said at the start of the service?

"Be not afraid, you are God's children in your Father's world. . . ."

The congregation was beginning to settle down. But there was still no Arista.

"Let us pray," said Christian, troubled by her conspicuous absence. About half the heads bowed. The others looked around uncomfortably, then stared at the napes of other people's necks. Oh, why did they fight so? he wondered. And against what? All the love of God.

"Almighty God, Thou has made us for Thyself, so that deep calleth unto deep. Seek us. Find us. Call home our hearts to quietness. For we are weary of the half-light and the half-life, and we long to be at peace with thee."

As the peach of a preacher asked merciful God for the forgiveness of their sins, Quentin Cox considered the nature of sin. Was it really an abomination to be gay? To Quentin, the love of mankind had been natural, joyful, and therefore, good. He could not believe, as so many now proclaimed, that contracting AIDS was a wage of his sin. Consider his dear Buff. Buff was the best of men. Surely he did not deserve to suffer and die. But then, who did? Quentin would have liked to believe in miracles, to pray for one; but to believe in miracles would require a belief in God, and therefore in sin, and he wasn't about to give that kind of ground, not now.

Glancing around the sanctuary, he noted the mean-spirited whiskey priest, Father Mothersole, slunk into a far corner of the church. From the pulpit the minister was assuring them all of God's pardon. Quentin considered the nature of hypocrisy.

He reached down and patted Greta in an attempt to restore his fragile equilibrium. He was easily upset these days. He didn't want his diagnosis to make him bitter. He wanted to go out as a loving man. Life was making love harder and harder as he and Buff got sicker and sicker. The reading of the first lesson was announced: Corinthians 13, 4:13, from the New English Version. Quentin listened.

> "Love is patient; love is kind and envies no one. Love is never boastful, nor conceited, nor rude; never selfish, not quick to take men's sins, but delights in the truth. There is nothing love cannot face; there is no limit to its faith, its hope, and its endurance. Love will never come to an end—"

This bit of religion he knew to be true.

> "In a word, there are three things that last for ever: faith, hope, and love; but the greatest of them all is love."

Everyone stood for the doxology:

> *"Praise God from whom all blessings flow,*
> *Praise Him all creatures here below.*
> *Praise Him above ye heavenly host.*
> *Praise Father, Son, and Holy Ghost."*

Right on, thought Buff Carrington.

Father Mothersole, here solely out of curiosity, noted that there was a great deal of standing up and sitting down to the service. He disapproved of all these damned Protestants, who never deigned to dirty their knees. And he disapproved of the rabbi (who, he had heard, was some kind of gay-rights activist) and the crazy men in the pulpit, too. Even the singer wasn't a singer. His faith, the true faith, had given him much to disapprove of. He felt it his Catholic duty to disapprove well. The preacher was onto the second lesson. This time King James, this time St. Luke.

> "Judge not, and ye shall not be judged: condemn not, and ye shall not be condemned: forgive, and ye shall be forgiven—"

Got him, thought Christian Davies, watching with amusement as Father Mothersole slouched deeper into his pew.

> "—For with the same measure that ye mete withal it shall be measured to you again.

"In modern parlance we would say, what goes around comes around. Thanks be to God for his word."

Christian shut the Bible and sat down in his thronelike chair. Little Henry Chang stepped forward.

"I lead one rine from *Hamlet* by Shakespeare for my friend Eve Carrahan: 'To be or not to be, that is the question.' "

And he smiled broadly at the accomplishment of the flawless phrase. "My fliend Eve maybe she decided answer is: not to be. I don't know. Now I read from"—here he took a deep breath—"Henry Wadsworth Rongfellow: 'There is no death. What seems so is transition.' "

Another smile, large enough to be seen in the farthest reaches of the balcony where the angels were thought, by some, to sit.

"How did you know?" Shakespeare asked Longfellow.

"That is the question," replied Longfellow smugly.

Henry Chang bowed low to the congregation, then continued. "Ruke Sevensons lead now, so you undlestand."

He handed *The Book of Changes* to Luke Sevensons, who stepped forward to read from the *I Ching* for him. He looks fine, thought Jamie Callahan, and winked at the worried Maggie. Then Luke toppled over.

There was a moment of stunned surprise. Then a great commotion hurled itself at the pulpit.

"Is he dead?"

"He can't be dead. It isn't the first of the month yet."

"Is there a doctor here?"

"He's breathing."

"I told you."

"Stand to one side, please. I'll do what I can. I'm only a psychiatrist."

"Call an ambulance."

"Henry Chang already went for one."

"I suppose it's his heart."

"He doesn't look good to me. The poor bastard."

"Don't talk that way in a church."

Luke Sevensons struggled toward consciousness cutting through the underbrush of voices with a machete of pain. There was something he needed to say.

"Maggie, Jamie," he gasped.

"We're right here, Luke."

"Take the children to the sea."

"What?"

"Like you planned . . . tonight . . . to see Florian's comet. It's important."

"Don't be absurd, Luke. We're coming to the hospital with you."

"Last wish. You have to grant it."

"That's bloody unfair, Luke."

"Going to ride out on the comet's tail. Want everyone to see it."

Luke passed out again. This time his breathing stopped. Dr. Charles Agincourt searched frantically for a pulse. Hardly had his heart missed a beat when Maggie and Jamie were at work. Callahan pinched shut Luke's nostrils and bent back his head. With short steady bursts, he blew air into Luke's mouth. Maggie pushed rhythmically on Luke's chest every fourth breath. They worked purposefully, perfectly together for what seemed like several minutes, the three of them like one being. Maggie chanted softly under her breath. "Come you wing-eds." Deerfinder tapped a moccasined foot on the thick, almost-red carpeting. "Come flying things."

Christian recognized the whispered chant and began to pray silently for the life of the old man he had just refound and was not willing to lose again so soon. Grace descended. Christian knew. Luke responded and began to breathe, Jamie to cry, Maggie to smile. The rest of the congregation, still seated, was unsure what to do. In the back pew, Alice May Patoon began to hiccup uncontrollably, emitting short, little yips at regular intervals. Rather than be wakened, Nelson Little rolled over and fell off the pew, which woke him up abruptly.

Where the hell am I? he wondered. There were a lot of feet shuffling around his head. He was under a row of benches. Christ! There was that vicious dog, Greta Garbo. And there, crawling around amid all of the feet, were his two sons, Edgar and Allan, as large as life. This was the weirdest dream he had ever had. And the cruelest. Except it didn't feel like a dream. His head hurt where it had bounced off the floor, and a large, hiccuping woman with a tic seemed determined to join him down underneath the benches. He heard sirens. Not fire. Not police. Ambulance. What was going on?

A mournful, beautiful melody, played upon a flute began to fill the air.

"Seth Hackett," he heard someone say.

The music paused, continued.

"Luigi Romano!"

"Mamma mia!"

"I've comma from Roma, Luigi."

"I thought your name was Mullahboy. Oh, my God, Seth, there's your father. Ted! Ted! He doesn't recognize me. Who is that man he's with?"

"Clear the aisle, please, stretcher coming through." He recognized the voices of Sergeant Dooney and Detective Finger.

More hiccuping. More music. More yipping from other dogs.

None of this made any sense at all to Nelson Little, who was trying to crawl to his sons through the forest of legs. Greta Garbo began to growl ominously at his approach.

Oreo and Great Daniel squirmed out of the carpetbag next to Katelyn's feet to see what all the fuss was about.

"Oh, damn, the dogs got loose."

"Yip. Yip. Yip."

"I'll get them. Katelyn, you still have great legs."

"Get away, Victor. You still move like a god. Just get the dogs."

"What's going on?" asked Buff Carrington. He and Quentin Cox stood anxiously in the waiting room outside the intensive-care unit at St. Vincent's Hospital.

"There was a brief heart failure during the first surgery," Dr. Day explained. "Then her blood count revealed a post-surgical infection was brewing. It happens in a small percentage of these cases, where there was so much infection to begin with. We had to go back in, but she's fine now. All her vital signs are strong and there's no fever. We expect her to be moved out of intensive care as soon as we have a room available. I can let you step in here for a minute, but not with the dog, I'm afraid. You understand."

"No, we'll wait until she's in her room. How long will that be?"

"Don't know for sure. We're short of beds, with AIDS and all."

"And Luke Sevensons?"

"You know him, too?"

"Yes."

"You two gentlemen are having a bad night."

"You could say that."

"I can't tell you much. Touch and go. At present he's holding his own. We don't know yet how much damage his heart has sustained, and there appears to have been a small stroke. We'll know more in the morning when the test results come back from the lab. Reverend Davies is with both of them right now. They're resting as comfortably as can be expected."

"Thank you, doctor. I'll go and call Katelyn."

"No need," said Buff. "Katelyn had to get Lester back to Bellevue, before they stamped him overdue or something, and then she's coming here. Let's stay until she arrives."

The two men sat down, assessed the institutional decor in their respective ways. "I don't want to die in one of these places," said Quentin, speaking for them both, "surrounded by tiled walls, vinyl furniture, plastic flowers, fluorescent lights, and dirty metal ashtrays."

"Most people do."

"Why do they have to be so god-awful then?"

"Try not to think about it."

"But that's why they're so grim. Nobody thinks about hospitals until they're stuck in one, and then it's too late."

"Maybe it doesn't matter . . . at the end. Maybe the only interior decor that matters then is what's in your head."

"Of course you're right. It's your friends, the people you love and who love you back that matter. Not the furniture. Still, I would move these couches so that they face the window, and then bring in some ceramic planters and real plants—"

"Quentin, Buff, how are they?"

It was Katelyn, and now, although she had plenty of reason for it, she wasn't crying. Come to think of it, Quentin realized, he hadn't seen her crying in quite a while. Buff briefed Katelyn on the medical situation.

"You guys must be exhausted. Mullahboy is outside with the cab. He's got company: his mother (she's lovely, by the way; her name is Serena, but she's about as serene as a tornado) and Ted Hackett's wife (now there's a piece of work) but he's waiting to take you home."

"He certainly knows how to collect trouble."

"How did his mother ever find him?"

"She went to the police. Apparently she's had occasion to do that before. Anyhow, they had him on file because of the accident with the cab."

"How is he?"

"You'll see. I hope it won't upset you too much."

"What?"

"He appears to be in love."

"With his mother?"

"With Ivy Sue Hackett. Besotted. I thought he was . . . well . . . you know . . . gay."

Quentin shrugged. "Don't ask me. I never laid a finger on him. Well, the occasional snuggle perhaps."

"Same here," added Buff. "Greta, too."

"I'm going to go in to Arista now. What a night! Goodbye, you two. Enjoy the next episode, whatever it is. I'll call you tomorrow."

"Thanks, dear. Oh, and Katelyn, there seems to be a shortage of hospital rooms."

"I'll put Henry Chang on it. By the way, Quentin, when you get outside, look up. Florian's comet has arrived. It's glorious."

Glad to be out in the brisk, night air, Quentin looked around for their awaiting chariot. There was no sign of Mullahboy and his entaxied harem. He shrugged good-naturedly and looked skyward. "I wish you could see it, Buff."

"Next life. Greta, old girl, can you see the comet for me?" Greta swished her tail against Buff's leg, in just the same arc as the tail of the comet. "Oh, it's lovely," said Buff. Quentin reached for Buff's hand.

"Excuse me, gentlemen. You must be Buff Carrington and Quentin Cox." Startled, they turned and recognized the look and sound of the man emerging from the hospital. "I saw you two"—he patted the dog—"three . . . in the congregation today . . . and again upstairs."

Christian Davies introduced himself nervously. He seemed to have something he wanted to say. After an uncomfortable pause he went ahead.

"I stepped outside the intensive-care unit . . . for a breather . . . a few minutes ago. I couldn't help overhearing what you were saying . . . about not wanting to die in a hospital. Forgive me, but I know about your illness from Arista. I hope you don't mind that I know. There is something I thought *you* should know; something about Eve Callahan."

Buff and Quentin looked confused.

"I'm not doing this very well. Please let me stumble on. Rabbi Barkowitz, the man with us in the pulpit today who didn't have the chance to speak—he's from San Francisco. He came to tell Eve's friends that she had devoted the last few years of her life to people with AIDS. Evidently she founded a hospice out there, a place for gay men to . . . round out their lives."

"You mean to die." This from Quentin.

"Yes. To die. She designed and endowed an environment that is beautiful, and dignified, and respectful of the sensibilities of the young men who are now dying so many years before their time. I've seen the photographs. It's much more like a home than a hospital, yet it has all the medical necessities, especially those that make a very ill person's life a little easier. She was here to oversee the completion of a similar hospice in the Village. Rabbi Barkowitz will stay and do that now. He's hired Headstone Brown as an assistant. It will open next month—

and carry her name. I'm sure she would want you to consider it ... when the time comes ... if it comes ... I pray for a cure."

The two men were speechless.

"I hope I haven't embarrassed you. We ministers have a way of butting in a little too much sometimes."

"No. You're kind to tell us," Buff assured him.

Quentin unbent a bit, too. "We're just surprised. About Eve."

Christian smiled. "I think of a person, even a close friend, as a book in which I've only been privileged to read the footnotes. Well, thank you for letting me tell you that note about Eve. I'll go on now. It's been a long day." He nodded toward the hospital.

"How are they?"

"Arista is in pain. Luke is unconscious."

"It's been a long night."

"But it's magnificent, isn't it?" said Seth. He and Bridget had walked off down the beach, a long way from the others. The two young people needed to be alone with each other for a while. The day and evening had brought so much that was new to them that they were only now beginning to absorb it all. They sat on a smooth, flat rock that still held the heat of the sun, high above the sea, watching the comet, and feeling as if they owned the universe.

"Would your father be happy for us, Bridget, if he knew?"

"Da? Yes."

"How did he die? You couldn't bring yourself to write about the details at the time."

"It was just too much to bear, after Paul and all. I can tell you now, but it's hard."

"Don't then. I can wait."

"No. I want you to know. My da was a good man. A

hard worker, a loving father. He had always stayed well clear of politics. That's not an easy accomplishment if you're born on the Falls road as he was. But he saw the devil in the Troubles early on, and the devil was just evil spelled with a *d*, or so he used to say. But after Paul was killed ... he was different ... I think, devil or no, he wanted to do something ... revenge ... it's a man's devil, I think ... that need to strike back.

"He got mixed up with some wrong people. IRA types. I think he saw something he shouldn't have seen or heard something he shouldn't have heard. If I know my da, he probably objected to some killing they were planning or some wickedness they had already done. Anyhow, they ... these men ... just walked into our kitchen one night. There were four of them. They had hoods on. They were carrying guns. We were all there having our dinner. Except Bren, who had gone to bed early. Da knew right away that they weren't going to kneecap him, that it was all up for him. 'Don't hurt my family,' he said. 'We're just here for you, Brian O'Neill, so if you don't try nothing they'll be all right,' they told him. 'Not here,' he said. 'Step out back then,' they told him. And he just got up and went out there. At the door he turned and gave us all a look ... one by one ... such a look as I'll never forget. They let him do, then they gave him a push out. One of them stayed behind to keep a gun on us. We heard two shots. Then a thump. No one moved. No one cried. Then they walked past us through the kitchen and out of the house and left."

"My God."

"That isn't all."

Bridget wiped away a tear and sat quietly for a while. Seth held her hand and waited.

"As they were leaving ... going up the walk to the street, there was another shot. Mother had gone out the back, of course, but we children were still in the kitchen afraid to move. At the sound of the shot, Colin said, 'That's Da's rifle, from upstairs.' We crept to the front of the house; scared we were, but mostly past feeling anything at all. Three of the gunmen were running down the street, one of them was lying on the sidewalk. They had just left him there . . . their mate."

"Was he dead?"

"Yes. Bren had killed him."

"Little Bren."

"Yeah. He had heard the commotion from upstairs. He looked out the back window and he saw them kill Da. He says he didn't even think then. He just ran into my parents' bedroom, and got Da's gun and shot at them."

Seth was silent.

"That's how it goes there, Seth, the killing from father to son. It seems nothing can stop it."

"I'll never let you go back."

"No. It's over for me. I hope it's over for all of us, but you don't know what a night like that does to your mind. I'll always be afraid that one of the boys will go back. There's still the three other killers left loose. Them with their cowardly hoods."

"Why did your mother stay in Belfast after that?"

"I don't know. I think she was paralyzed kind of, afraid to move, afraid not to move. And stricken, of course. Da was the world to her. And she had a fight on with her own da back here, and no money. We agreed among us not to tell who had killed the gunman. He was a punk from the Divas Flats, only a kid himself. The Ulster police put it down that one of his own gang had killed him. We were afraid of a reprisal for a while, then we realized how humiliated they must be. They had to have figured it was wee Bren. Only four years old."

"I'm sorry about your dad."

"Yeah." Again they were silent. Then Bridget took a deep breath, determined to change the mood. "What are you thinking about your dad?" she asked.

"Oh, well, that was quite a shock. It was like someone planned a surprise family reunion for me at Old Gray Presbyterian. Missed Holly, though. And what a surprise . . . Dad . . . with that man. He seems nice enough. I thought Mom was going to have a heart attack, but Luke had already had one. And who was that man she went off with? The Italian or Arab or whatever he was?"

"Luigi Romano, his mother called him."

"I guess she would know."

"Everyone else called him Mullahboy."

"It all happened so fast, and I couldn't give it my full attention. I was so worried about Luke. Still am. It didn't seem to matter very much that my father didn't know who I was, or that he was gay."

"How do you feel about it now?"

"Awesome," said little Bren, trying out his first Americanism. He stood, gazing at the comet, next to Maggie Silvernails.

"It grows more beautiful by the moment," said Maggie, taking Callahan's hand into her own. With her other hand she reached up and brushed across the heavens—up, up, up, down, down, down—following the arc of the comet's tail.

"How long will we be able to see it?" asked Doreen.

"About three weeks," said Florian, his voice full of pride.

"Can they see it way back in Ireland?"

"She wants to know if her boyfriend, Sean McKinney, can see it."

"Don't tease her, boys," said Elinor. "Yes. Even in Ireland people will be looking up and seeing it burn across the sky. Does Ireland seem so very far away to you now, Doreen?"

"A long way. I wish Paul and Da could have seen the comet."

"Who's to say they can't?" asked Maggie. Still holding on to Callahan, she knelt down among the children.

"But, Maggie, you know that Paul and Da are dead," Megan declared.

"Then they can see the stars close up."

"Really?" Bren's eyes were wide. Then they narrowed in suspicion. "Ah, Maggie, how do you know for sure?"

"Sit quiet, Bren. Look up at the comet, and over there at the Dog Star, and there at Orion. The knowledge you're seeking has to come and find you. It can only do that when you're still. It will fly into you on silent wings and make a nest in your heart for wisdom to grow up in. Sit quiet and see if any knowing comes to you." He looked at her skeptically. Maggie was aware, of course, that Bren knew more than most children would ever know about the mysteries of life and death. Still she challenged him. "You're probably too young."

"No, I'm not," he protested, and the other children chorused in that they weren't either.

"So then try," said Maggie.

They all sat down like a row of clams along the dark shore. Maggie pulled Callahan down next to them.

> "Come you wing-eds
> Come you wing-eds
> Tell me what I need to know
> Show me where I need to go
> Come, flying things."

As Maggie continued to mesmerize the children with her soft song-chant, Callahan loved her and Elinor moved away, a little closer to Florian.

"It's breathtaking," she whispered. "I'm so proud of you." She, too, now held tightly to the hand of a man she loved.

"I didn't create it," he replied happily. "I only found it."

"Sometimes the best things are the found things."

They were together then—family, friends, children, old people, listening to the roar of the ocean, the silence of the stars.

"What's that sound?" asked Jamie.

Far off, way down along the shore, they made out the faint sound of Seth's flute.

"That's 'The Dance of the Seven Suns.' Seth wrote it for Luke. He told me so," said Colin.

"And me," added Grady.

They had all been thinking, silently, of their stricken friend. The song seemed to give them voice.

"Do you think he's riding out on the comet's tail?" It was Maggie.

"No. He lives." It was Deerfinder.

"I've never known him to be wrong." It was Callahan.

"He be wrong most all the time." It was Methuselah.

"Then let's start back." It was Oakley Klapper. "It will be morning by the time we reach the city. Maybe we'll be allowed to visit him."

"Wait." It was Florian. "Seth has changed his song. And there is singing somewhere, too."

> *"Twinkle, twinkle, little star*
> *How I wonder what you are*
> *Up above the world so high*
> *Like a diamond in the sky*

> *Twinkle, twinkle, little star*
> *How I wonder what you are."*

They all held their breath in wonder, for it was Jerry Phails. Singing. Simply. Sonorously. The way they had all imagined he once could sing. Jerry emerged, somewhat shyly, from behind a nearby sand dune. "I sang it for Luke," was all he said.

Maggie turned to Bren. "Now, have you learned anything?"

He gave her a knowing smile.

"Let's go."

• • •

"I can't let you all go in at once," said Dr. Day.

"Why not? They're both thriving. You just told us so." It was the fifteenth day of the month. Maggie and Callahan had come for their daily visit with Luke. Elinor and Florian had arrived simultaneously, with the older children in tow. Luke, they were told, had been moved into a semiprivate room with a woman named Arista Bellefleurs.

"They still tire easily," replied the surgeon. "I'll tell you what. I'll let Methuselah decide what's best for them. She's practically managing the entire hospital staff." Dr. Day signaled into the room and Methuselah came out, full of welcome and efficiency. She was clearly in her element. Dr. Day waved a hand cheerfully at the crowd of visitors and escaped down the hallway.

"Here you all is. I declare these chillun grow an inch a day."

"Can we go in?"

"Why not? You know Luke cain't hardly say boo yet, but Rista's full of beans."

"Who is this Arista person?" Callahan asked, looking troubled.

"She an ol' friend of Luke's. Not ol' like us. But she know him well enough. She be a good woman. Henry Chang he got them put in the same room together. Thinks they be gettin' better quicker this way."

"If this is Henry Chang's idea, they'll be lucky to survive the night. What do you think of this arrangement, Methuselah?"

"I got no complaint."

"Well, then, it's probably okay."

"I'm glad you come fo' visitin', Florian. She be wantin' to talk to you about yo brother."

"Charles? Why, my brother Charles is her analyst. I can't talk to her about him."

"No. She be wantin' to talk about Winston. He ain't been 'round much lately. She miss him."

Florian paled. "My brother Winston died when he . . . when we . . . were only three days old. He was the smallest of the triplets. How would she know about him?"

"Rista she be a knowin' woman. You best ast her."

They moved toward the doorway.

Methuselah put up an arm. "Somepin' you all better know." She looked serious.

"What is it?" asked Maggie, still fearing that Luke might take a turn for the worse.

"They be married."

"What!" They all exclaimed at once.

"This morning the preacher he come by. Seems they be schemin' and plannin' for a fortnight. Since they be in 'tensive care together. Notes flying back and forth. Sneaky visits in wheelychairs. No trouble for them. Blood test come here. Preacher come here. Witnesses, they come here, too.

I be one of the witnesses." She looked rather proudly at them. "Luke and Rista, they just lie there and smile like two cats full up with canaries."

"Maggie, did you know about this?"

"No, Jamie."

"You all right?"

"Just need a moment to catch my breath."

"Me too." They sat down for a moment, not talking. The others shuffled. Maggie and Callahan looked at the floor, looked at each other, and then burst out laughing. "Now, let's go in and see that horny old bastard and his blushing bride."

Luke and Arista were indeed blushing, radiant, holding hands across the space that separated their two hospital beds. The room was filled with flowers. Luke could only smile with half his face as the stroke had severely weakened the left side of his body. But half a smile was more than enough. They were clearly in the kind of love that leaves no room for doubt on anyone's part.

Christian Davies had seen such love three times during the past two weeks, and the vision had filled him with strong emotion on each occasion. He had never actually *had* Arista Bellefleurs, he mused, but he had had a chance. He may have lost that chance to Luke Sevensons, but what better man? And, in the process, she had brought Christian back to life. Marrying Arista and Luke had been painful and wonderful all at once. In the midst of the ceremony Arista had looked up at him, into his eyes, as she had done on the occasion of that first Communion. He had wavered. She had flashed him the Clincher.

". . . till death do you part," he had continued.

"I do," she had said.

I DO. Christian had heard. Clear as a bell.

He wondered if Arista and Luke would manage sex, once they were out of the hospital. Luke was badly debilitated. But Arista, well, she looked unstoppable.

Earlier in the week two youngsters, in the same state of exulted passion, had come to him for a marriage consultation. Seth Hackett was a Protestant boy; his Bridget, a Catholic. Bridget's Belfast childhood precluded any possibility of their taking the matter lightly, as modern American youngsters might do. It had been a poignant experience for Christian—to talk with them, to hear their story—bringing back his own rugged Ulster childhood and his own loving courtship of Grace.

Meeting their parents had been dazzling as well. Elinor O'Neill was planning a concurrent marriage to Florian Agincourt. They planned to live in Ohio, with the other O'Neill children. Luke had given them the farm. Ivy Sue Hackett planned to divorce Ted Hackett and leave Ohio to live in Saudi Arabia with a boy who appeared to be only slightly older than Seth. Christian thought, by the look of Ivy Sue, she would have a nervous breakdown first, which would be a blessing. Ted Hackett could not even remember Ohio, let alone his wife and children, but he seemed to be a dutiful and well-meaning man in spite of his recent amnesia and more recent homosexual union. He planned to stay in Greenwich Village with a sculptor and a raven in order to study classical music. Christian hadn't the least idea what advice to give the young couple, except to cleave to one another.

The week had also held the baptism of wee Walker Wells, a gloriously happy infant. Amas and Illuminada Wells had come to Christian radiant from a recent religious conversion. They seemed convinced that Amas had experienced a miracle after his spine was cracked in an automobile accident. He had been told he would never walk

again, but to look at him now you would never know it.
They planned to move, with Amas's father, to South Car-
olina, where Amas had secured a position in the sanitation
department. But they wanted the baby christened here in
the city so Katelyn could be present. She had stood amid
her family crying with happiness. Christian thought it was
only a matter of time before she and her husband would
reunite. There was something about the way she moved
around him.

He had managed these last two exceedingly busy weeks
at Old Gray Presbyterian without the help of trusty Alice
May Patoon. Alice May, it seemed, had run off with a married man. Oh, not *any* married man for Alice May, Christian thought, chuckling in a most unchristian fashion, but
a homeless married man who had kidnapped both his sons
as part of the elopement. There was an all-states alert out
on the fugitive couple, though when Christian had heard
the whole story, he hadn't blamed the man. How could a
woman tell her husband that his children were dead when
they weren't? It was the most evil lie he had ever heard.
People could be so bad. He had prayed for the soul of
Mrs. Little and for the soul of the potter she now lived
with. And he hoped, fervently hoped, that the full-bodied,
large-hearted Alice May Patoon and the odd, little Nelson
Little would manage to make a life for themselves. He had
a hunch they were hiding in San Francisco. In Rabbi
Barkowitz's apartment. But he wasn't about to spread rumors, especially to the police.

Perhaps the most curious event of the past fortnight
was, however, the arrival in his life of one Deerfinder. The
Indian man had come to Christian hoping to convert to
Christianity.

"What would the Great Spirit say?" Christian had asked
him.

"Great Spirit is Jesus," Deerfinder replied.

Almost immediately the two men had recognized each other as friends; almost, thought Christian, as if they had known each other in another lifetime. Companions in longing, they often sat together and smoked their pipes and patted their dogs and talked long into the night about everything that mattered to them most: God and Grace and Maggie, it turned out, on most nights. Someday, they speculated, they would each find a new woman to love, if they didn't die first (or in Deerfinder's case, if Jamie Callahan didn't die first). In the meantime they had God and Fatpaws and Caleb and their respective unavailable women. And now, each other.

Until his friendship with Deerfinder had taken its form, Christian had not realized just how lonely he had been. He slept well now, knowing whatever troubles the next day would bring, he would have his conversation with Deerfinder at the end of it. And the book they were writing together was coming along nicely, too. It was to be a novel, set in Tibet at the turn of the century. In it, a Buddhist monk falls in love with a Christian missionary woman whose husband has been killed in an airplane crash. The novel would explore the grand themes of attachment and loss, and the differences between Eastern and Western thought.

At present he and Deerfinder were disputing the form the book would take. Christian preferred a straightforward narrative style with well-spaced chapters and indented paragraphs dividing characters and events—clear and precise, like an Order of Service. Deerfinder said this was a Western idea and proposed a free association of ideas—one consciousness flowing freely into another as if it didn't matter who was thinking, who was speaking.

"But each character *is* different, a unique individual, with his own immortal soul. Why confuse the reader?" Christian argued.

"No. No. This, most respectfully, an illusion," replied Deerfinder. "Consciousness is like a bucket of water. Pour the water through the sieve of birth, each little stream now thinks he is separate. But really all the same. Stream falls through the sieve, through the air to the earth. Different place. Different time. But then is in the same old puddle again. All together. Stream of consciousness doesn't matter. Only water matters."

"But what about responsibility? What about each man's choice as to how he will live?"

"Each man responsible for his own fall, I think."

And they were off into the evening's discussion. Deerfinder was a blessing. An unexpected blessing.

Most blessings are unexpected, thought Arista. Of course she had loved him for years, through all the years when he had helped her, but not like she loved him now. Now she could help Luke, and that juxtaposition in their relationship had released a wellspring of feeling she had not known she possessed. Not that Luke would ever stop helping others. Why, look at those drawings on the wall next to his hospital bed. They were Oakley Klapper's drawings—and they improved with each visit.

She felt like laughing, but laughing hurt her stomach, so she *thought* about laughing. Life was different since the surgery. There had been that black time. Not even black. Black was a metaphor. That *nonexistent* time between the anesthesia and the coming to. Twice. The first time, they told her, she had been, for all intents and purposes, dead. They had brought her around, fought her infection, put her out again, performed more surgery. And in the midst of it all there was the experience of nonbeing. She had seen no bright lights, floated through no tunnels, heard no celestial music. She had simply ceased to exist. Yet she had emerged from these experiences, from her anesthetic hallucinations, and her angel dreams convinced of another *kind* of existence. She had been somewhere, though somewhere was nowhere. She couldn't explain it. It was harder than reason.

Luke understood without explanation. Luke had died (just as he said he would) and been revived, too.

Why did you bring me back? he had asked.

WHAT CAN I TELL YOU?

Stroke of genius.

Perhaps she was further into faith than she knew, for every moment now seemed a gift. A gift received when she had stretched out the hand of her mind. Every moment was a moment more than she could expect to have had at all. For who *expects* life when it comes upon them?

She was eager to return to her apartment and prepare a home for Luke to come to. She would need to install ramps and railings, arrange books and utensils at wheelchair height, buy a hospital bed—a *double* hospital bed. The privacy would be wonderful, and the quiet.

She would have to arrange for Mariah the cat to be flown in. Raindrop and the puppies would stay on the farm with the Agincourts, the children, and Methuselah. She and Luke would soon have their own dog, for Greta Garbo was to come to them for a quiet retirement after Quentin and Buff passed on through Eve's hospice. And she must learn how to keep house properly. She must buy two tin washtubs.

Once Luke was well enough to come home, he would return to the hospital every day for physical therapy. He liked improving for her. That would give her the quiet time she needed to write.

Arista wanted to get back to her writing table. She had an idea for a new novel. It had come to her, like the angels, in a dream. She had thought her way through most of it. But how would it end?

WITH MAGGIE SILVERNAILS, THE MODERN AMERICAN INDIAN WOMAN, THE PAINTER, ALL ALONE WITH HER LOVER, JAMIE CALLAHAN, IN HIS STUDIO, FOR THE FIRST TIME IN FORTY YEARS.

Right. That would be

THE END.

Grace note: You should know that I'm not entirely satisfied with the outcome of the romance between Christian and Arista, but I can ~~live with it die with it fly with it~~

MAYBE I SHOULD HAVE THE LAST WORD.

ABOUT THE AUTHOR

ARDYTHE ASHLEY is a novelist and screenwriter who lives and works in Manhattan. She maintains a private practice in psychoanalysis, specializing in work with writers and artists. Her hobbies include watercolor painting and making major motion pictures. A film of her first novel, *Practice to Deceive*, has been completed.